BEHIND THE MASK

BEHIND THE MASK

IT'S NOT ALWAYS OUR ENEMIES
WHO BETRAY US.

DANA RIDENOUR

Ridenour

Print ISBN 13: 978-1-63489-903-1
e-book ISBN 13: 978-1-63489-902-4

Library of Congress Catalog Number: 2015960614

Printed in the United States of America
First Printing: 2016

20   19   18   17   16   5   4   3   2   1

Cover and interior design by James Monroe Design, LLC.

Wise Ink, Inc.
837 Glenwood Avenue,
Minneapolis, Minnesota 55405

wiseinkpub.com
To order, visit itascabooks.com or call 1-800-901-3480.
Reseller discounts available.

Visit: DanaRidenour.net

To Mom,
Who gave me my first book.

To Dad,
Who gave me my strength.

To Bill,
Who gave me my wings.

PROLOGUE

Savannah shivered in the frigid interrogation room of the Los Angeles FBI Field Office. A cold metal handcuff dug sharply into her left wrist. The door opened, and a man and a woman, both wearing dark suits and FBI tags dangling from lanyards, entered. They sat across from Savannah with somber expressions on their faces.

"Savannah, I'm Special Agent Adam Harper, and this is my partner, Katherine Summers."

Savannah nodded.

"Before I read you your rights, you need to listen closely to what I'm about to tell you. You have two choices right now. You are facing a lifetime behind bars in a federal penitentiary, and this will be your only opportunity to save yourself."

Savannah shifted in her seat.

Agent Harper continued, "The federal justice system is like a fast-moving locomotive. You can either get on the train, or you can get run over. Agent Summers and I have discussed your situation at length, and we both believe that you're a nice girl from South Carolina who got involved with events that spiraled out of your control."

Agent Summers made eye contact with Agent Harper and crossed her arms but remained silent.

Savannah tried desperately to control her breathing.

"We want to help you, but for us to do that, you have to help yourself. You have to be willing to talk to us and be completely honest. If you agree to talk to us, we'll let the United States attorney who is prosecuting this case know that you're cooperating with law enforcement. If you choose not to talk to us, we will transport you to the federal courthouse, turn you over to the US Marshals Service for processing, and place you in a federal prison. I can't emphasize enough how important it is that you make the correct choice. You're facing extremely serious charges, and you could potentially spend the rest of your life in prison."

Hot tears rolled down Savannah's cheeks.

Agent Harper leaned forward. "You're charged with conspiracy to violate the Animal Enterprise Terrorism Act, conspiracy to commit arson, and felony murder."

The room started to spin. Savannah choked down the bile in the back of her throat.

Agent Harper continued, "This is what's going to happen, Savannah. I'm going to read you your rights. If you choose to talk to us, I'll get you a cup of coffee and you can tell us your side of the story from the beginning. But remember, you do *not* want to get run over by this train."

He began to read Savannah her rights. She listened to the words without comprehending their meaning. Then

Agent Harper asked her a question she never thought she would be asked: "Savannah Riley, do you understand your rights as they have been read to you, and are you willing to talk to us now without a lawyer being present?"

CHAPTER ONE

Alexis

FBI Special Agent Alexis Montgomery—or Lexie, as she preferred to be called—strutted down the hall with new-found confidence; she had just completed an arduous two-week undercover certification course in Virginia. Built like a runner, the petite twenty-nine-year-old had come into work to tie up a few loose ends before leaving for her temporary undercover assignment in Los Angeles.

Lexie's squad supervisor, Mark Clarkson, a former undercover agent himself, supported her decision to join the undercover program. Mark was a rarity in the FBI: a supervisor who encouraged and cared about the agents under his command.

Lexie lightly rapped on the doorframe. "Hey there, boss."

Mark looked up and smiled. "Congratulations, Lexie! Come, have a seat. I heard you did great."

"I don't know about great, but I survived."

"Well, you should be proud of yourself. Undercover

training is grueling. You passed and made the SAC look good, too."

Lexie laughed. "I still have a few bruises to show for it."

Mark looked sheepish. "I know. I wish I could've prepared you a little more for it. Once you go through the school, you're prohibited from talking about it."

Lexie nodded. "I understand. I'm glad that I did it and survived it, but I *never* want to do it again."

"I'm proud of you, Lex. How many people washed out?"

"About half."

He nodded. "We lost about half when I went through the school ten years ago. Nice to see it hasn't changed. It takes a tough person to make it through, and you did."

"You know what's funny about undercover school?" Lexie said. "As an agent you spend years learning how to *be* an FBI agent. Learning how to walk the walk and talk the talk. Undercover school has to deprogram all those behaviors and mannerisms out of the agent since most streetwise criminals can spot a cop a mile away."

"Sometimes the simple things can blow your cover," Mark said. "You know, like always backing into parking spots or refusing to sit with your back to a door."

Lexie nodded. "By the way, thanks for going to bat for me with the front office. I know the SAC didn't want to give up a person for this assignment. I appreciate you fighting for me."

"I think you're going to be a great undercover agent." Mark smirked. "You've got a bit of a hippie streak. You'll fit right in with those crazy vegans. Just don't fit in too much and go over to the dark side. Promise me you'll sneak away and eat a cheeseburger occasionally."

Lexie laughed. "I'm only vegan for the case. I promise that when I return, you and I will go out and eat the biggest burger in New Orleans."

Mark's expression turned somber. "Just be careful. These extremist cells are paranoid and suspicious of everyone. If your gut tells you something is amiss, trust your instincts."

"I'll be careful. I've been doing research on the Animal Liberation Front. They have a super strict security culture. Members never discuss their actions with anyone who doesn't have a need to know, and they never discuss anything of a criminal nature over the telephone or on the Internet. I'm gonna have my work cut out for me."

"It'll be a challenge, but you're up for it. Can I offer you a piece of advice?"

"Of course."

"Make sure the case agent assigns you a good contact agent. You need someone that you feel comfortable with and who will dedicate himself or herself to your safety."

"I'll make sure."

"I know they taught you about contact agents in the school, but speaking from personal experience, a good contact agent can save your life or, at a minimum, your sanity. The contact agent is your lifeline, Lexie. He or she is your tether to the real world. Understand?"

"I understand."

"Is there anything you need me to handle for you while you're gone?" Mark asked.

"Thanks, but I think I'm all set. The first two weeks are

some sort of meet-and-greet trip. When I get back, I'll take care of any loose ends with my apartment or casework. My apartment lease is ending at the end of this month, so I'm moving everything into storage until this case ends. Figured I might as well save a little money on rent."

"You might fall in love with LA and decide to stay out there and take up surfing," Mark joked.

"Oh, I doubt it. You know me. I love the South. I'm not sure I could survive that far away from my peeps. Plus, I couldn't give up this good Cajun food."

"Let me know if you need anything from back here. I've reassigned your cases and informants to Matt. He probably won't give them back to you when you return."

Lexie laughed. "No worries; there are plenty more cases where those came from." She stood. "I'm going to attempt to conquer my e-mail. Wanna grab lunch later? I could use all the undercover advice you care to impart on me."

Mark smiled. "Sure. Now that you're an official member of the undercover inner circle, I'll give up some trade secrets."

* * * * *

LOS ANGELES, CALIFORNIA

The plane bounced down the runway after landing at LAX. Lexie gathered her overstuffed backpack and purse from the overhead bin. The case agent, Adam Harper, was scheduled to meet her at the baggage claim. Even though

Lexie had never met Adam, she figured she could pick him out of a crowd. He would probably be wearing those stupid 5.11 tactical pants that every male FBI agent liked to strut around in. Lexie despised them. The durable cotton pants had numerous pockets and reinforced knees, which the male agents loved. On Lexie's small frame, the overly baggy knees gave her a clownish appearance, so she refused to wear them for anything other than firearms.

Lexie had packed enough clothes to stay for two weeks. She planned to familiarize herself with the area and finalize any further backstopping that might be necessary for her alias. Backstopping was the term the FBI used to ensure that an undercover's alias passed muster if a subject researched it.

Special Agent Adam Harper patiently waited at the baggage claim, wearing 5.11 tactical pants and a black T-shirt just as Lexie expected.

"Alexis?" Adam asked.

"Yes," Lexie responded.

"I'm Adam Harper. Here, let me take your backpack for you."

Lexie handed it to him. "Thanks. I go by Lexie. How'd you recognize me?"

"I am a trained investigator," he said with a smile. "There's also a photo of you in the case file."

Lexie laughed.

They walked over to the luggage carousel to retrieve Lexie's suitcase. Lexie noticed Adam's receding hairline and guessed him to be in his mid to late thirties. He was in reasonably good condition, but Lexie found it annoying that he was wearing his sunglasses on the back of his head like so many of the young guys.

"How was your trip?" Adam asked.

"Uneventful."

"That's all you can ask for," Adam said. "Are you hungry?"

"Starving," Lexie answered.

"You like pizza?"

"Love it."

"Great. I know a fantastic pizza joint not far from here."

It took thirty minutes in traffic to drive the short distance to the pizza parlor. The hostess seated them at a quiet corner table. The smell of garlic and freshly baked bread filled the air.

"What kind of pizza do you like?" Adam asked.

"I've never met a pizza I didn't like."

"Since you won't be getting any meat or cheese for awhile, how about a meat lovers'?"

"Sounds perfect."

The server brought their drinks and took the dinner order.

"How long have you been in the FBI?" Adam asked with a slight smile. "You don't look old enough to be an agent."

Lexie chuckled. "I get that all the time. I've been an agent for five years. I was lucky enough to get in the door when I was twenty-four."

Adam looked surprised. "Wow, that's young. I think the average age in my academy class was twenty-nine."

"My class too," Lexie said. "I was the youngest and the smallest person in my class."

"How did you get in so young? Sorry, I don't mean to be such an inquisitor. One of the pitfalls of being an agent."

Lexie laughed. "I did an honors internship the summer before my senior year in college. That helped to get me in the door quicker. I already had top secret clearance."

The server brought the pizza and refilled their drink glasses.

"This pizza looks delicious," Lexie acknowledged.

"The pizza here never disappoints. What made you want to become an undercover agent?"

Lexie took a bite of hot pizza and immediately reached for her water glass.

"Damnit, I hate when I burn the roof of my mouth," she said after she washed down the hot bite. "Why did I become an undercover? I guess because my supervisor was an undercover agent, and listening to his stories made me want to get into the program. What about you? Any desire to do any undercover work?"

"No. I'm a relief supervisor for the squad, and I'm hoping to get a supervisor position in the next few years."

"So, you're on the management track," Lexie said.

"Yes. What about you? Any aspirations of being a supervisor?"

Lexie groaned. "Ugh, no way. I'm not ready for a desk job."

"So why did you join the FBI?" Adam asked between bites.

"You'll laugh if I tell you."

"No, I won't. Tell me."

"When I was in high school, we took a band trip to

Washington, DC. We toured FBI headquarters, and I knew that I wanted to become an agent. I guess you could say that tour changed the course of my life. I was fifteen years old."

Adam snickered. "You were in band?"

"Oh, shut up. I knew you'd laugh. What about you?"

"My dad was an agent. He retired as a special agent in charge two years ago."

Adam took a drink of his soda and continued, "Anyway, enough personal stuff. We have a ton of things to cover in the next two weeks. We wanted to hit the ground running, so we had an older undercover agent in the division pose as your uncle and rent an apartment for you. I think you're going to like the location. It's within walking distance of the beach."

"Seriously? That's fucking awesome!"

"It's in Venice Beach, which is a weird hippie eclectic area. Venice is perfect, since so many of the targets either live or hang out in that area."

They finished dinner, and Adam drove Lexie to the apartment.

"By the way, this is an undercover vehicle. You don't have to worry about the tag coming back to the bureau. Once you get settled and working, I won't come to your apartment. Your contact agent will stop by periodically, but you won't see much of me. Your contact agent was selected because she has undercover experience and looks nothing like a cop. She won't have any problem blending in.

"So my contact agent is a woman?"

"Yes. You'll meet her tomorrow."

"Great. I can't wait to get started," Lexie stated.

"I'm glad you're excited." Adam pulled up in front of a small apartment complex. Nothing fancy, but it looked safe.

"Ready to see your new pad?"

"Of course I am."

They stopped in front of apartment three zero one and Adam used the key to open the door.

"After you," he said.

The sparsely furnished one-bedroom apartment contained a bed, dresser, couch, and TV. It was stocked with all the necessities: pots, pans, towels, and sheets. Luckily, the agent who furnished the apartment remembered toilet paper. The kitchen cabinets were old and chipped, but the appliances worked. The carpet was worn thin and frayed around the front entrance.

Lexie nodded. "It'll work."

"We didn't want to get too fancy, but we wanted it comfortable for you. There's a small workout room around the corner."

"It's perfect."

"Let me show you the secret squirrel stuff," Adam said. He led Lexie to the bedroom closet. "There's a false wall in the back of this closet. I'll show you how it works." They entered the closet. Adam pushed the corner of the back wall, which opened to reveal a hidden safe.

"Nice," Lexie said.

"You can keep your laptop, gun, and badge in the safe. It's also stocked with several kinds of body recorders for you to use. Ready for the combination?" Lexie nodded and instantly memorized the combination he repeated.

Adam shook her hand. "I'll let you get some rest. You have to be exhausted after traveling all day." He handed her the keys to the apartment. "The mailbox key is on this ring too."

"Okay, thanks."

"I'll pick you up about nine in the morning. We'll chip away at our to-do list."

After he left, Lexie, exhausted and battling jet lag, immediately fell asleep.

* * * * *

Because of the different time zone, Lexie awoke at the crack of dawn. She showered, dressed, and killed time watching the morning news. Her phone chimed.

On my way. Pick you up in thirty minutes.

Adam wasn't alone when he arrived. A woman with jet-black hair was with him. "Morning, Lexie," Adam said. "Did you have everything you needed last night?"

"I did. Thanks for furnishing the apartment for me."

Adam motioned to the woman. "This is Detective Katherine Summers, our task force agent from LAPD. She's working this case with us."

"Call me Kate," she said as she reached out to shake hands.

Lexie shook hands with Kate. "Nice to meet you."

"I'm your contact agent," Kate said. "You and I will be spending a great deal of time together."

Kate was slender and looked to be in her late thirties.

"What'd I tell you," Adam said. "Kate looks nothing like an agent. She'll blend in well in your world."

Adam had a natural confidence that bordered on arrogance.

"Are you ready for a whirlwind tour of LA?" he asked.

"Absolutely. This is my first time to California."

"You're going to love it," Kate said. "Year-round perfect weather, beautiful beaches, and great food. I might be a little prejudiced, since I'm a California native, but I can't think of anyplace better to live."

Both Adam and Kate pointed out landmarks as they drove around the enormous city. The conversation flowed easily. Lexie discovered that she and Kate had many things in common.

Around lunch, Adam abruptly asked, "Anyone want waffles?"

Lexie and Kate simultaneously answered in the affirmative.

"Good, because my favorite waffle spot is down the street."

Soon, they pulled up to a restaurant named The Waffle.

"That's original," Lexie said sarcastically.

"You're going to love this place," Adam said.

The peak lunch rush resulted in a packed restaurant. The trio of agents waited ten minutes for a table to become available. The hostess seated them at a table on the patio.

Lexie studied the menu as the waiter approached the table. She looked up from the menu and for a moment found herself tongue-tied. The waiter's work T-shirt clung to his chiseled body. What really stood out were his sky-blue eyes.

"Hello. My name is Brandon. I'll be taking care of you. Do you know what you want to drink?"

Kate ordered water with lemon, while Adam and Lexie both ordered coffee.

"Wow! That waiter is hot," Lexie said a little louder than she intended. "The waiters don't look like that in New Orleans."Kate and Adam both laughed.

"Is New Orleans your first FBI office, Lexie?" Kate asked.

"Yes, I've been there a little over five years now."

"How do you like it?"

"I love New Orleans. It's such a magnificent city—great culture, great restaurants. I'm originally from Alabama, so it's nice to be close to home. I'm able to visit my family and friends pretty regularly."

"I thought I detected a Southern accent."

Kate laughed. "My accent gets worse when I get around my family. Have you always lived in LA?"

"Yep, born and raised. I joined the police department when I was twenty-two years old."

"What made you want to be a police officer?"

"My best friend and I applied together. She never followed through, but I decided to give it a shot. Ended up loving the job, and fifteen years later, here I am."

"Are you married?" Lexie asked.

"Divorced. I have one son who starts high school in the fall. What about you?"

Lexie shrugged. "I'm single with no prospects. I've found that some men are intimidated by a woman who carries a gun."

"I'm intimidated by you both," Adam joked.

"What about you, Adam?" Lexie asked.

"I'm married, and we have two perfect children. My daughter is five, and my son is two."

Brandon brought the food to the table. The side of hash browns that Lexie ordered filled a dinner-size plate.

"I hope you two plan to help me eat this platter of hash browns," Lexie announced.

"We should've warned you that the servings were large," Adam replied. "I'm sure I can help you out," he added with a grin.

Lexie dug into her waffle. "This is the best waffle I've ever had in my life," Lexie said with a mouthful of food. "We have to come back here again."

"You don't have to talk me into it. I love this place," Adam agreed.

After lunch, Adam and Kate continued their tour. They hit the west side and showed Lexie Brentwood and Santa Monica.

"Tomorrow we'll go to the JTTF office and introduce you to the investigative team," Adam said. "Even though the office is a covert site, we'll still need to be careful. We don't want you to be seen going into the office, so Kate and I will sneak you in through the garage entrance. This might be the only time we take you to the office, but it's important that you have the opportunity to meet your support team."

"I agree. What time should I be ready to go?"

"We'll pick you up around nine. We can grab some coffee and then head to the Valley."

Adam pulled up in front of Lexie's apartment. "See you tomorrow," Adam said.

"Bye, guys. Nice meeting you, Kate."

"Nice to meet you, too," Kate said. "I'm excited about working this case together. We're going to have a good time."

"I think so, too."

* * * * *

The next morning, Adam and Kate pulled up right at nine. After a few pleasantries, the case brief began. As they crept along in five lanes of wall-to-wall traffic from Venice to the San Fernando Valley, Adam inundated Lexie with names of targets, victims, and groups.

"See that white building over there?" Kate said as she pointed to a building just off of the 405 freeway. "That's the main FBI office. Whatever you do, *never* step foot in that building. The animal rights and environmental extremists sometimes surveil the FBI office, taking photographs of agents coming and going from the building."

"That's pretty damn dedicated. Do you guys ever work out of the main office?" Lexie asked.

"I go to the main office occasionally for meetings," Adam answered. "Since Kate works mostly covert matters, she never goes there."

"I'm assigned full-time to the Joint Terrorism Task Force, so I work out of JTTF on a daily basis," Kate said. "Have you ever worked at a covert offsite?"

"No. I've just worked out of the FBI and DEA offices in New Orleans."

"Most of the rules won't affect you, since you're working

undercover, but there are a few rules that go with a covert location you'll still need to know. First, never wear anything that says FBI or identifies you as law enforcement."

Lexie laughed, and then she realized that Kate was serious.

"I tell you this because, believe it or not, we have had our share of bureau morons who strut up to the front door wearing a badge, gun, and FBI shirt."

Lexie shook her head. "I can't believe we have people working for the FBI who don't understand what the word *covert* means."

"We've had agents park their bureau vehicles out front with police lights visible. One guy even had his ballistic vest and raid jacket lying in the passenger seat of his car, visible to anybody walking by. I could tell you idiot agent stories all day long."

"We're getting close to the office," Adam announced. "Lie down in the backseat, Lexie."

Adam pulled the car to the back of the building and entered the attached garage.

"The door is down; you can get up now. We'll give you the grand tour."

Housed at a covert site in the San Fernando Valley, the Joint Terrorism Task Force office looked like a regular business. The secure front entrance opened to a tiny, unassuming reception area. But behind the reception desk wall was an entire squad area equipped with twenty-five desks and computers.

Lexie was introduced to the investigative team, which consisted of an FBI analyst, another LAPD detective, a

UCLA police officer, the squad supervisor, and an FBI accountant. A couple of other agents were used periodically when needed for surveillance purposes.

Lexie spent the next several hours reviewing case files and looking at photographs. When Adam dropped her off at her apartment that evening, she thought her brain might explode from information overload. Before he left, he handed her an envelope with her new undercover driver's license, credit card, and social security number.

Starving, she decided to walk over to a small Mexican restaurant down the street. She ordered a bean burrito—only vegan entrees from now on. As she handed over her credit card, she caught a glimpse of her new name and felt a thrill of excitement.

She was leaving Alexis Montgomery behind and becoming Alexis Marie Taylor, vegan animal rights extremist. Tomorrow, she'd take one more trip back to New Orleans to make the final preparations for her assignment in Los Angeles, and then she'd be ready to embark on Operation Blind Fury.

CHAPTER TWO

Savannah

AUGUST 2010 - LOS ANGELES, CALIFORNIA

Savannah Riley had just finished putting the last of her clothes away when a frenzied female burst through the door.

"You must be my roommate," the girl said as she plopped down on Savannah's bed. "I'm Haley."

"Hey," Savannah said, startled.

Haley was a tiny girl with huge brown eyes and mahogany hair. She had bright pink streaks in her hair and piercings in her eyebrow, ears, and nose. Tattoos of all sizes and colors were inked on various parts of her anatomy, and she wore oversized clothes on her five-foot frame.

"I went ahead and took this side of the room. Is that okay with you?" Savannah asked.

"Oh sure. I'm not picky. I love your accent. You can't be from California."

"Pawley's Island, South Carolina," Savannah stated. "Where are you from?"

"Everywhere and nowhere, really."

Savannah thought the answer strange, but she was

fascinated with Haley and eager to learn all about her. She offered to help her bring in her boxes from the hallway.

"You didn't bring much stuff," Savannah commented.

"I don't need very much."

Trying to keep the conversation flowing, Savannah asked the question that every college student dreads: "What's your major?"

"I'm undeclared, but leaning toward environmental science."

Haley picked up the framed family photo sitting on Savannah's nightstand. "Is this your family?" Haley asked.

"Yep, that's my mother, father, and twin brother, Hunter. My brother is a freshman at The Citadel."

Haley raised an eyebrow. "What's The Citadel?"

"It's a military college in Charleston, South Carolina. My grandfather and father are Citadel graduates, so Hunter is following in their footsteps."

"You didn't want to go there?" Haley asked.

"No way! That place is too strict and rigid for my tastes."

"What's it like having a twin? You guys don't look that much alike," Haley said as she put the photo down.

"It's fine, I guess. Hunter is five and a half minutes older than me, but he treats me like I'm his baby sister."

"You guys aren't close?"

"No, not really. Hunter's the favorite." Savannah sighed. "He's the perfect son. Does everything that he's supposed to do and now he's going to the mighty Citadel."

"That sucks. Why did you choose SoCal?"

"Film school," Savannah answered. "I figured if I want a career in the film industry, I needed to move to California.

What's your story?"

"I don't have a story. I'm here for school . . . no story."

"Well, you're definitely not from the South," Savannah said.

Haley narrowed her eyes. "How do you know that?"

"Because you don't share. Most Southerners are pretty open. We tend to talk too much and share everything."

"I'll keep that in mind when it comes to telling you information."

"Oh, I didn't mean that I would tell your business. I just meant . . . well, I don't really know what I meant. Ignore me. I'm rambling."

Haley smirked. "You do tend to ramble."

Savannah hung her head.

Haley play-punched her. "Oh come on, I'm messing with you, girl. You can ramble all you want." She picked up a smaller frame with a photo of Savannah hugging a blond girl, both sporting huge smiles.

"Is this your sister?"

"No, that's my friend Nora. We've been best friends since grade school."

"She's pretty," Haley commented.

"She's dating my brother. If he has it his way, she'll become my sister-in-law after he graduates from college." Savannah snorted. "I'm sure they'll produce perfect, fair-headed children and have the perfect, quintessential Southern life."

"Wow, that sounded a little bitter," Haley said.

Savannah sat down on her bed. "Well, when you walk in on your twin brother boning your best friend and you find out their secret relationship has lasted longer than any relationship that you've ever had, bitter seems like a perfectly fine response."

"That's harsh. You seriously caught them in the act?"

"Yep. I'm over it now."

Haley rolled eyes. "I can tell."

Savannah giggled.

"Where did you say you were from?" Haley asked.

"Pawley's Island. It's a small island in South Carolina, north of Charleston."

"Los Angeles is a long way from South Carolina."

"Exactly why I'm here. I grew up on this tiny island where the tides dictate life. Island children run around shoeless and carefree. I could cast a net for shrimp and trap crabs for dinner when I was ten. Nothing exciting ever happened on the island. It was a great childhood, but I want more from life. I want mystery and exhilaration instead of the same old, dull routine."

Haley placed a variety of seeds and nuts on the shelf above her desk. "That's understandable." She motioned toward the snacks. "Help yourself."

"Thanks. What's with all the squirrel food?"

Haley laughed. "It's not squirrel food. I'm a strict vegan."

"Is that like a vegetarian?" Savannah asked.

"Vegans don't consume any animal products or anything derived from an animal, including dairy. If it has a face, I don't eat it or its products, and I don't wear it."

"I've never met a vegan, so I'm curious. Why no dairy? The cows aren't hurt for their milk."

"Are you kidding? The dairy industry is barbaric.

Think about it, Savannah; cows produce milk for the same reason humans do—to nourish their young. Cows are artificially impregnated to force them to produce milk. Calves are taken from their mothers within a day of being born; the males are either sent to veal crates or feed lots, and the females are kept to become dairy cows like their mothers."

Savannah, who had been folding a shirt, stopped and gave her full attention to Haley. "What are veal crates?"

"Come, sit down." Haley motioned toward her bed.

Savannah moved a pile of clothes to make room. She sat cross-legged across from Haley.

"Calves are kept immobilized in tiny, dark crates to keep their flesh tender. The calves are kept in these crates for a few months, fed a diet low in iron to keep their flesh white, and then slaughtered and sold as veal."

"That's horrible!"

"It's shocking what goes on behind the walls of a factory farm," Haley added.

"What do you drink, if not milk?" Savannah asked.

"I prefer soy milk, but I also use almond milk and rice milk. I can give you a DVD to watch if you want to know more about being a vegan."

"Sounds interesting. I'd like to learn more. I'm ashamed to admit that I don't know anything about veganism. Why are you a vegan? Is it for health reasons or because of the animal cruelty?" Savannah inquired.

"I'm an animal rights activist. Everything I do is to save poor, defenseless animals. Animals shouldn't give their lives so we can eat their flesh or wear their skins."

Savannah looked down at her newly purchased leather

boots. "What do you do about purses and shoes?"

Haley leaned over and grabbed her tattered backpack from the foot of the bed. "This backpack is made from hemp. See how strong it is? I have purses and shoes made out of hemp, canvas, and other man-made materials. I don't use products or wear cosmetics that were tested on animals either. I'd be happy to teach you more. I have a whole collection of animal activist DVDs. You can learn about factory farming, animal testing, and laboratory vivisection. After you learn the truth, you'll *never* eat meat again."

Savannah shuddered. "I'm afraid to ask, but what's vivisection?"

Haley tucked a stray strand of hair behind her ear and continued. "Vivisectionists are monsters. They cut up innocent, *live* animals in laboratory experiments and call it research."

"I thought researchers used computer simulations in place of live animals."

"That's what they want you to believe, but what goes on behind laboratory doors is horrific." Haley stood up, walked over to her closet, and pulled out a shabby box. She rummaged through the box and removed several DVDs, pamphlets, and books. "This should get you started." She handed the items to Savannah.

❋   ❋   ❋   ❋   ❋

Savannah loitered outside of a noisy house on Thirtieth Street, waiting for her newfound friends to arrive. She had reluctantly accepted an invitation for a girls' night out with several of the women in her English class. The plan was to go to a party at a house that was known for having good booze and hiring great bands. Savannah had elected to meet them at the house because she had dinner plans with Haley. She tried to get Haley to go to the party, but Haley bailed when she found out who Savannah was meeting. She described Savannah's friends as *soulless bitches.*

Savannah heard the trio of girls coming before she saw them. Julie's high-pitched laugh was distinctive and a bit annoying.

"Hey, girl!" Julie bellowed from halfway down the block.

"Hey, Jules," Savannah responded.

The other two girls, Beth and Cindy, were nearly carrying Julie.

"You look like you've already had a few," Savannah said.

"That would be an understatement," Beth, the smallest of the trio, said. "We tried to talk her into going back to the dorm, but she insisted on coming to the party."

"Let's go inside, bitches!" Julie yelled.

"You heard the lady," Savannah said.

The door was wide open, so the four friends staggered in. A crowd of people was gathered around a makeshift bar set up in the corner. Two men were making colorful drink concoctions for partygoers. There was a keg of beer just inside the door, and a skinny, pale young man handed each of the girls a plastic cup filled to the brim with foamy beer. The deafening noise coming from the adjoining room made talking almost impossible.

"Let's check out the band," Julie yelled.

With beers in hand, the four pushed their way into the room where angsty music was playing at high decibels. As soon as Savannah set eyes on the lead guitar player, the rest of the world vanished. Sweat dripped from his coal-black hair, and his muscles flexed under the tight, wet, T-shirt. A wave of desire swept over her, and she felt unbelievably alive. Amid the chaos, their eyes locked and they held the gaze for what seemed like forever. Savannah felt her face flush.

"They're good," Cindy yelled, bringing Savannah back to reality.

Savannah broke eye contact with the handsome guitar player and tried to casually look around the room. Every female in the room was posed in some sort of seductive manner, desperately trying to draw the attention of the guitar god.

Savannah glanced back at the guitar player, who was still staring at *her*. She looked around to see if there was another woman near her. When she did this, his face softened into a grin.

Savannah jumped when Beth screamed in her ear, "Julie isn't looking so great. Let's get her home before she blows chunks."

Beth grabbed Julie by the arm and tugged her to the other room. Julie stumbled, and Savannah caught her around the waist.

"Are you kidding me?" Cindy shouted. "We *just* got here."

"I love you girls," Julie slurred.

"Can you help us get her back to the dorm?" Beth asked.

Savannah glanced back at the room with a tinge of regret and sighed. "Of course."

CHAPTER THREE

Alexis

Lexie unpacked the last of her belongings and settled into her tiny one-bedroom apartment in Venice Beach. Before she plugged in her phone to charge, she deleted her messages from Kate. She had to remember to delete any conversations that she wouldn't want prying eyes to see.

The next morning, Kate picked up Lexie in a nondescript Hyundai Elantra. The car would blend in without drawing suspicion. Lexie was relieved to see Kate already had two cups of coffee in the cup holders.

"I took the liberty of grabbing a cup for you too," Kate said, motioning toward the coffee.

"I might actually kiss you," Lexie said, laughing.

"Well, let's not get too carried away; it's just coffee with a little cream and sugar. I didn't spring for a latte. You have to earn latte status," Kate joked.

Lexie took a sip from the steaming cup. "Thank you. My apartment doesn't have a coffeemaker, and I'm a coffee addict."

"Remind me, and we'll buy you a coffee maker on the

way home from work," Kate said.

They drove north on the Pacific Coast Highway.

"Where are we going?" Lexie asked.

"We're meeting Adam near the Malibu pier. He has a surprise for you."

"What kind of surprise?"

"If I tell you, then it wouldn't be a surprise."

Lexie smiled. "This is a beautiful drive."

"I enjoy driving the PCH. It relaxes me."

"I can see why," Lexie said. "The seashore is spectacular."

Lexie peacefully watched the morning sun glisten off the water.

"Are you a detective with LAPD?"

"Yeah. I made detective three years ago. My agency assigned me to the JTTF a year ago."

"All that alpha male testosterone. You sick of the swinging dick routine yet?" Lexie asked.

Kate smirked. "Early in my career it was a little difficult-—the constant dirty jokes, the raunchy bravado, the subtle digs—but it's not bad now. Or maybe I just got used to it and can tune it out. What about you?"

"Some of the guys in my office didn't think I'd survive the undercover school because I'm so small."

"Guess you showed them."

"Yeah. Seems like I work twice as hard to get half the respect."

"Do you think that you put extra pressure on yourself to always be the best?" Kate asked.

"Maybe, but it's still a good ol' boy network."

They drove a half hour up the coast. Kate pulled into a

large parking lot near the pier. Lexie spotted Adam sitting alone on a bench.

Adam smiled when Kate and Lexie walked up. "What do you think of your new digs?"

"Outstanding," replied Lexie. "Venice Beach rocks."

"Yeah, well, you'll get over that soon enough. The freaks will wear on you after a while."

"Lexie, what do you think of your new wheels?" asked a voice from behind her. It was Mike Gregory, the squad supervisor Lexie had only briefly met on her previous familiarization trip.

"Damn, Mike. You're like a bull in a china shop. Lexie, do you remember my supervisor Mike?"

"Of course. Hello, Mike," Lexie said, shaking Mike's hand. "What wheels are we talking about?" "Oops, guess I spoke a little too soon." Mike laughed. "That's your next big surprise."

"Thanks, Mike," Adam said as he feigned annoyance.

"Okay, now I have to know," Lexie chimed in. "Spill it, Adam!"

"It's waiting in the parking lot for you. You didn't think we were going to chauffeur you all over the place, did you?"

"Okay, guys, I have to see it. Take me to my chariot!"

Lexie followed Adam to the corner of the parking lot where a slightly beaten-up Volkswagen bug was waiting for her.

"It's perfect!" Lexie squealed. "I love it, and it fits in perfectly with the crappy apartment in Venice."

"Hey, hey, hey, the apartment is not crappy; it's vintage," Adam stated as he pretended to be hurt.

Lexie laughed. "I wanted a VW bug when I was a teenager, but my parents wouldn't buy me one."

"I just made your dreams come true," Adam joked.

Lexie liked the fact that Adam had a sense of humor, which was rare in the bureau. Most agents took the job way too seriously. "I will cherish my bug and my vintage apartment too."

During the meeting, Adam showed Lexie photographs of Phillip and Jeannette Jordan. Several targets of the investigation were known to stay at their house from time to time. The fact that Lexie's apartment was within walking distance of the Jordan home was no accident.

After the meeting, Adam, who had driven the VW to the parking lot, left with Mike. Lexie opened the door to her car but then paused, turning back to Kate. "I'm a little nervous about attempting a cold bump."

"You'll be fine, Lexie. Look for a friendly face and be natural."

"I hope so. I've done so much research on the North American Animal Liberation Press Office website, but reading about the movement and infiltrating it are two different things. What if I sound like an idiot when I try to talk to people?"

"You don't have to be an expert. Let them teach you."

"I want to do a good job. My reputation as an undercover agent is riding on this case."

"I haven't known you long, but I have confidence in you, Lexie. Call me if you need anything or if you want to talk," Kate said.

"Will do," Lexie replied, and she was off to Venice.

After arriving home, Lexie walked over to the Boardwalk and grabbed a soy latte. She was getting used to soy milk, but it didn't taste as good as dairy. She sat at an outside table at a small organic coffee shop and surfed the Internet while she sipped her latte. Her Apple laptop was registered in her undercover name and was strictly for undercover use. Adam told her their subjects would take any opportunity they got to search through her stuff, including the laptop. Lexie knew, if given the opportunity, they would not only search the laptop, but they would also install spyware to keep track of what she was doing online.

While online, Lexie found websites for numerous animal activist groups in the area. Her strategy was to volunteer with the aboveground activities and eventually find out who had knowledge of the underground activities. The ultimate goal was to get recruited to participate in underground, illegal direct action with members of a domestic terrorist cell. The FBI had no interest in the people just trying to save feral cats. The underground cells were the ones committing the felonies that Lexie and her team were targeting. This task wasn't going to be as easy as she originally thought.

Lexie walked past Phillip and Jeannette's house on her way home. She figured if she made a habit of walking past the house on her way to and from the Boardwalk, she might see people coming and going from the house. Several old junk cars were parked out front that probably belonged to people crashing at the house. Lexie chuckled. *There have to be more old VW buses in Venice than the rest of the United States combined*, she thought. It seemed like every hippie in

Venice drove a VW bus. She casually strolled by the house and returned home.

CHAPTER FOUR

Savannah

A month into the school term, Haley came back to the dorm to find Savannah crying. "What happened, Savannah? Did somebody die?"

Savannah's eyes were swollen. Wet discarded tissues were crumpled up beside her.

Haley sat down next to Savannah and put her arm around her. "Tell me what's wrong."

Savannah wiped the tears from her face and blew her nose. "I watched the *Earthlings* DVD you gave me."

Haley hugged Savannah. "That's a tough one to watch."

"It was horrible! So much torture and murder. I'm sick to my stomach."

"You're a good person, Savannah. That's why the movie bothered you so much."

Savannah shrugged off Haley's arm from around her shoulder. "I'm not a good person. You've taught me so much about veganism, and I still want to eat things that I shouldn't. I'm a horrible person."

"Savannah, becoming a vegan is not an easy thing. It

takes commitment. Most people become vegetarians first and then take the next step to living a vegan lifestyle. You jumped right into veganism, so you can't expect to be perfect. Don't be so hard on yourself."

"I've slipped twice in one week. I needed a snack between classes yesterday, so I grabbed a Snickers bar. The day before that, I put honey in my tea without even thinking."

"You put bee puke in your tea?" Haley laughed.

"It's not funny. I forget that bees have faces too."

"I'm sorry I laughed. Everyone slips in the beginning. I'm proud of how far you've come in only a month."

"I've lived such a sheltered life. I never thought about all the animal cruelty in the world. The hidden camera footage in the DVD was utterly sickening. Haley, I promise I will *never* eat meat, drink milk, or wear leather again. I'm serious. Nothing with a face, ever again."

"That's my girl," Haley said. "Hey, I bet I can cheer you up."

"How?"

"Want to go to a demonstration?"

"Sure! I've never been to a demonstration. Where?"

"Dr. Albert Middleton's home. He's a vivisectionist at UCLA. He's a fucking barbarian, and tonight we're going to let his neighbors know they live next to an animal torturer."

"I'm in," Savannah responded.

"Are you sure?"

"I've never been so sure of anything in my life. I don't want to just be a vegan. I want to be an activist like you."

Haley smiled a small smile at first, but as it grew her

eyes sparkled. She threw her arm back around Savannah's shoulder. "Let's go change the world."

* * * * *

The group of demonstrators at Dr. Middleton's house carried huge signs depicting chimpanzees being tortured in laboratory experiments. Savannah wore one of Haley's antivivisection T-shirts. One of the demonstrators, a guy dressed in black, his nose and mouth covered with a bandana, handed Haley a bullhorn.

"You ready for this, Savannah?" Haley asked.

"I am!"

"Carlos, take half the group to the other side of the street," Haley ordered. "I want demonstrators on both sides of the street so they can't avoid seeing our signs. Let's put the loudest of the group in this asshole's driveway."

"Will do."

"If anyone comes walking by, remember to hand them a leaflet."

Haley put the bullhorn to her mouth. "One, two, three, four, open up the cage door! Five, six, seven, eight, smash the locks and liberate! Nine, ten, eleven, twelve, vivisectors go to hell!"

The chanting became deafening when the crowd joined in. Savannah was a little hesitant at first, not knowing what to do. She carried a sign and watched the other protestors. Before long, she joined in and was marching and chanting with the rest of the group.

A woman wearing designer workout clothes and pushing a baby in a stroller saw the demonstrators and quickly turned the other way. Savannah ran up to her with a leaflet.

"Hello. Please take one of our leaflets that will show you your neighbor, Albert Middleton, tortures and kills innocent animals."

The woman started walking faster. "I don't want any trouble. Leave me alone."

Savannah returned to the group. "She seemed scared of us," Savannah told one of her fellow demonstrators.

"They're either scared of us, or they get confrontational."

"She wouldn't even take the leaflet," Savannah said.

"She's an ignorant, rich bitch. She wants to live in her wealthy neighborhood and ignore what's happening all around her."

"This is my first protest. I thought more people would talk to us."

"It depends on the place. People are more engaging on college campuses. In private neighborhoods, they usually ignore us and call the police."

A few minutes later, the UCLA police arrived. Two officers, one not much older than Savannah, approached the group.

The older officer, whose uniform was stretched a little tight across his midsection, addressed the demonstrators. "Ladies and gentlemen, you need to move away from this residence. You're required to stay at least three hundred feet from the house."

The guy with the bandana covering much of his face approached the officers. "We have a right to be here. You can't make us leave. It's freedom of speech."

The officer took two steps forward, nose to nose with the bandana guy. "If you don't move farther away from the house, we will arrest you. It's your choice."

Savannah, Haley, and the other demonstrators begrudgingly moved down the street. Bandana guy, who Savannah learned was named Jesse Rudolph, continued to challenge the two officers. Moments later, he was cuffed and thrown into the back of the UCLA police car and carted off to jail.

Adrenaline pumped through Savannah's body. Her heart raced, and her palms were sweating. The situation was terrifying but exciting and liberating at the same time. Eventually the police made the demonstrators leave the neighborhood, citing violations of noise ordinances.

As they traveled back to their dorm, Savannah chattered on incessantly. "That was amazing! Half the neighborhood now knows about this douche bag."

"Most of them already knew," Haley said. "This wasn't the first time we've been to his home."

"How can he do it? What kind of person can chop up and kill an innocent animal with no remorse?"

"He's an evil bastard, Savannah. That's why we fight. Sometimes we have to pick them off one at a time. If we show up in his neighborhood enough times, then the neighbors will get tired of having him around. Not that they give a shit about our cause, but they don't want to be inconvenienced. Eventually they'll pressure him to leave their nice, expensive community."

"Then what happens?"

"We find out where he moves to and do the same thing

there. If we keep up the pressure, he or his wife will become weary of the moves and he'll find another line of work."

"Does it always work?"

"Nope. Sometimes we have to step up our game."

"What does that entail?"

"You're not ready for that yet." Haley grinned. "But soon."

* * * * *

Months later, on a beautiful December afternoon, Savannah and Haley, who had become nearly inseparable, chatted effortlessly as they strolled down the Venice Beach Boardwalk.

"Hey, thanks for inviting me to the New World Militia meeting," Savannah said.

Haley glanced over her shoulder. "Just call it NWM. Do you know the difference between an abolitionist group and a welfarist group?"

"Not really."

"Abolitionist groups are involved in more direct action campaigns. The members tend to be more radical and believe that no risk is too great to save an innocent animal. They use tactics such as vandalism, arson, and animal liberations to get the attention of animal abusers. Animal welfarist groups usually don't believe in committing illegal acts. These groups believe that changes in legislation are the means to abolishing cruelty to animals."

"What kind of group is New—I mean—NWM?"

"Make no mistake, Savannah, NWM is an abolitionist

group. You seem ready to step up your game, but I need to know for sure."

"I am . . . I definitely am."

Savannah's phone rang. She looked at the caller ID and ignored the call.

"Who was that?"

"Nora." Savannah sighed. "I'm still pissed off that she didn't have the decency to tell me she was fucking my brother. Plus, she's so derogatory about my choices. We've been best friends for so many years; I thought she would be more understanding."

Haley shook her head. "People outside our movement never are."

"I'm finding that out. My parents haven't been understanding either. My father told me that humans have killed and eaten animals since the beginning of time. They all act like I have two heads simply because I'm vegan."

"You haven't told Nora or anyone else about the NWM meeting, have you?"

"Oh hell no."

"Good. There are a few things we need to discuss before we go to the meeting. First of all, are you sure you want to get involved at this level?"

"Yes. Of course. I'm one hundred percent in, Haley."

"Let's walk out on the beach so no one can overhear us. And turn off that damn cell phone. I don't trust those things."

Savannah shut down her phone and tossed it in her purse.

Haley continued, "NWM meets at Jeannette and

Phillip's house, which is just a few blocks from here. You're going to love them. They're an older couple who supports our cause both spiritually and monetarily, if you know what I mean."

"I do."

"The two of them love animals, and they've been involved in activism for years. Activists even stay at their house and pay whatever rent they can afford. But there are some security rules you need to know before you attend the meeting."

Savannah nodded.

"The first rule of Fight Club is you do not talk about Fight Club. We *never* talk about past illegal acts. Blabbing is the quickest way to have the FBI on your doorstep asking a bunch of questions. When an activist is arrested at a demonstration or on some trumped-up, bullshit charge, our motto is, 'No one talks, everyone walks.' As Phillip says, no one can physically force words to come out of your mouth."

"I understand. Keep my mouth shut and don't ask a bunch of questions."

Haley continued, "Phillip is kind of a hero in the animal rights community. He was arrested one time while trying to stop the seal clubbing in Canada. Phillip was held in custody and interrogated for ten hours. The Canadian authorities actually brought in foreign linguists to try to interview him because when they questioned him, he just sat and looked at them. He was so nonresponsive that they thought he didn't understand English."

"So, he didn't say anything?" Savannah asked.

"Not a word. Just sat and stared."

"I can't wait to meet Phillip."

"This group is really serious about security. Keep your cell phone off during the meeting. If you have any questions, ask me later when we're alone."

"What's the big deal about the phones?"

"If your phone is on, then the FBI can track you. They might be able to listen in, so it's better to keep it turned off. Or better yet, don't bring it."

"Good to know. I'll keep it turned off and in my purse."

"You're lucky I'm your roommate. Who else would teach you this stuff? Hey, let's go back over to the Boardwalk and get a medical marijuana card for you."

"Now?" Savannah asked.

"Sure. Why not?"

"I've never smoked marijuana."

Haley abruptly stopped and stared at Savannah. "Never?"

"No, never."

"It's no big deal." Haley grabbed Savannah by the arm and pulled her to a nearby marijuana collective. "Look, they even post symptoms on the sign, so you know what to say to the doctor. Tell the doctor you have severe menstrual cramps."

"A doctor will prescribe marijuana for cramps?"

"Sure. Once you see the doctor and get your prescription card, you can go to any collective and get your prescription filled. If you prefer not to smoke, you can get baked goods instead."

"Let me think about it."

"Okay. We can come back tomorrow. Let's get to the

meeting before we're late."

Savannah and Haley walked into Phillip and Jeannette's house for the meeting. A small wirehaired terrier mix greeted guests as they arrived. The house reeked of stale beer and marijuana. The hardwood floors were scratched, and dog hair collected in the corners.

While the others were enjoying snacks, Savannah followed the sound of a sad, haunting melody coming from the corner. She gasped when she saw who was playing the guitar. *Could it really be him?* She looked around for the rest of the band, but he was alone with an old, beat-up, acoustic guitar. Both handsome and intimidating, he radiated confidence. Guitar guy's coal-black, tousled hair hung partly over one eye. He was thin, but not too thin, and covered with tattoos. He had ear gauges the size of quarters. Savannah thought having earlobe holes would be gross, but she found the edgy look surprisingly sexy. She knew, of course, her father would hate him, her brother would want to kill him, and Nora would want to have him arrested, which made him all the more appealing. This dark, dangerous man would not fit into her old Southern life, but then again, he didn't need to. She had a new life, and this guy would fit in nicely.

Haley smiled at Savannah. "Maybe before you two walk down the aisle in your imagination, I should introduce you."

Savannah had forgotten there were other people in the room. Haley grabbed Savannah's hand and dragged her to the attractive, mysterious guitar player. "Nick, Savannah. Savannah, Nick. There, I introduced you. If you get married one day, you can blame me."

Haley strolled off, leaving Savannah standing awkwardly in front of Nick.

After a few seconds of uncomfortable silence, Nick finally asked, "Didn't I see you at that row house party the other night?"

Savannah managed a nod.

There was an uncomfortable silence, and then Nick spoke.

"Do you play guitar?"

Savannah stared into his chocolate-brown eyes and simply whispered, "No."

That was it, just no. Her brain was Jell-O, and she couldn't speak.

After several more uncomfortable seconds passed, he asked, "Do you want to learn?"

Savannah's skin tingled, and her heart beat uncontrollably. She uttered one word. "Yes."

CHAPTER FIVE

Savannah

It had been three weeks since she met Nick at Phillip and Jeannette's house, and she had spent nearly every day with him since. Now that she was back in South Carolina for the holidays, Savannah knew she should be more excited to be back home with her family, but she missed Nick so much that her chest ached. Most of her newly acquired friends in the animal rights movement were atheists, so celebrating Christmas was not a priority for them. Savannah made a mental note to ask Nick about his spiritual beliefs. Other than the fact that Nick played lead guitar in a rock band, Savannah knew hardly anything about him or his past— he was always more interested in hearing about her life than talking about his own. What she *did* know was that when she was with him, her world was complete. Savannah was ecstatic and terrified at the same time. In a mere three weeks, she had given her heart, soul, and body to a man who was virtually a stranger. When it came to Nick, she threw caution to the wind. She hoped her grades hadn't suffered because she put studying on the back burner after she met Nick.

Savannah was stretched out in the demonstration hammock at the Pawley's Island Hammock Shop. She was meeting Nora for lunch and some much-needed girl time, but she felt a little nervous about seeing her best friend. Their relationship had become strained since Savannah left for college. Nora was jealous of her relationship with Haley and never had anything positive to say about Nick.

As she swayed in the hammock, waiting for Nora to arrive, Savannah's thoughts drifted back to a special day on the beach in Malibu. A few days before Savannah was to fly home for Christmas, Nick asked her to spend the day with him. He instructed Savannah to wear comfortable clothes and hiking boots. Nick picked her up in his old, beat-up Honda. When she climbed into his car, she noticed the cooler and blanket in the back seat. The two talked and listened to music as Nick drove Savannah to Point Dume State Park in Malibu. They arrived at the hiking area, and Nick parked the car near the trailhead. The picturesque, dome-shape cliff jutted into the Pacific Ocean. The point was surrounded by white sand beaches and sparkling blue water.

Nick retrieved his backpack, blanket, and cooler from the back seat. "Ready to see a beautiful beach?" Nick asked.

"More beautiful than the one we're standing on?" Savannah inquired.

"You haven't seen anything yet. Follow me!"

Savannah followed Nick to the trailhead, and they hiked up the cliffside. She was impressed with Nick's gracefulness as he effortlessly hiked up the cliff. She, on the other hand, was a little on the clumsy side. Good thing Nick was carrying the pack and the cooler.

At the top of the cliff, they stopped to admire the view. From the top, Savannah could see the entire Santa Monica Bay, north Malibu Coast, inland Santa Monica Mountains, and even a very distant Catalina Island.

"This is a great location to spot gray whales," Nick said.

"Nick, this view is breath-taking."

"I thought you might enjoy it."

Savannah, an amateur photographer, paused to take a few photos. The pair made their way down the other side of the cliff, which led to a secluded beach. The golden rays from the sun reflected off the intense white sand. The only noises were the gentle sounds of the waves breaking on the shore and an occasional caw from a seagull.

"So nice of you to reserve the beach for us," Savannah said.

"Only the best for you."

They strolled to the end of the deserted beach, and Nick unpacked his backpack. He set up a small, one-person tent and unrolled a blanket for them.

"What's the tent for?" Savannah grinned.

"Well, I thought you might need a little protection from the sun."

Savannah laughed. "It's December; I don't think I have to worry about a sunburn." She breathed in the salty air. Having grown up at the beach, she loved the ocean. "I'm amazed how different the beaches are out here."

"I've never been to the East Coast. How are the beaches

different?"

"The water temperature for one thing. It's way too cold for me to swim out here. The ocean gets as warm as bath water in the summer in South Carolina."

Nick spread out the blanket and unpacked the cooler, which contained a six-pack of chilled Corona and salsa for the tortilla chips. He laid out the spread on the blanket and opened a beer for each of them. Nick handed one to Savannah. "To saving the animals," Nick said as he touched his bottle to Savannah's.

"To us," Savannah added. "Thank you for bringing me here. It's lovely."

As they drank their beer, Savannah told Nick about growing up on Pawley's Island. She told him all about her family and her best friend, Nora. After a while she realized she was monopolizing the conversation. She asked Nick about his family.

Instead of answering, he reached over and took Savannah's hand. With his other hand, he lightly touched her cheek. Savannah shivered. "I have something in mind that's much better than talking," Nick said. He leaned over Savannah and lightly kissed her lips. He pulled her close to him, pressing his body against hers. Savannah's heart raced. She wondered if Nick could feel how fast her heart was beating. Savannah wanted this man more than she had ever wanted anything in her life.

"Should we move inside the tent?" Nick asked.

Savannah smiled and nodded.

Nick spread out the blanket inside the small tent and pulled Savannah down on top of him. Their soft kissing became more aggressive. Savannah's skin tingled.

"Nick, there's something I need to tell you."

"What is it?" Nick asked as he continued with the kissing.

"I'm a virgin."

Nick hesitated and tipped his head to the side.

"Do you think I'm weird?"

"Of course not. I'm just surprised."

"It's not that I don't want to, because I do. I wanted you to know before we went any further."

"Are you sure you're ready for this?"

"Yes. I'm ready, and I want my first time to be with you."

Nick removed Savannah's shirt, and, while softly kissing her shoulder, he released her bra using one hand.

"Tell me if you want me to stop."

"I will."

Nick sat up and stripped off his shirt to reveal his flawless skin and perfect six-pack abs. He laid Savannah down flat and pressed himself against her. She could feel him growing inside his tight jeans. She reached down and unbuttoned his jeans. Nick peered into Savannah's blue eyes as he pushed down his jeans and boxer briefs, freeing himself from the confines of the denim. He unbuttoned Savannah's jeans and slid them off to reveal her matching black bra and panty set.

While softly kissing Savannah's flat stomach, Nick removed her panties. He reached over and pulled out a foil pack from the front pocket of his backpack and placed it beside them. Savannah's eyes roamed up and down Nick's body. His broad shoulders and muscular chest made

Savannah shudder. Nick was perfect.

"Are you sure you want this to happen?" Nick asked softly.

"More than I have ever wanted anything in my life," Savannah replied, her voice cracking.

Nick kissed Savannah's neck. She had never felt such ecstasy or anticipation. He grabbed the packet, quickly opened the foil pack, and slid on the condom. He looked at her, asking permission with his eyes. He gently rolled on top of her—

"Savannah!" Nora yelled as she jogged over.

Savannah was ripped out of the memory, which she'd been replaying in her head every spare moment she was alone. In her attempt to quickly roll out of the hammock, Savannah fell and tumbled out onto the ground. Giggling ensued, and Savannah suddenly felt very foolish about her irrational fear of seeing Nora. After dusting off the dirt from her clothes, the two strolled over to Roz's Rice Mill Café for soup and sandwiches. Savannah had missed the home-made soups and the key lime pie from Roz's. Savannah and Nora sipped their sweet teas and perused the menu. Nearly everything included some kind of meat, seafood, or dairy product. It was easy to be vegan in Los Angeles, but not so much in Pawley's Island, South Carolina.

The waitress, order pad in hand, approached the table. "Afternoon, ladies. Do you know what you'd like to order?"

"I'll have a cup of clam chowder and the grilled grouper sandwich," Nora said.

The waitress jotted down the order and turned to Savannah. "What about you, sweetie?"

"I'll have the grilled portobello mushroom salad, but please hold the goat cheese."

"Why that's the best part, honey," the waitress told her.

"I know, but I'm vegan, so I don't eat any animal products."

Nora just looked at the waitress and shrugged as a way to show she agreed with her.

"Sure thing, hon. I'll have 'em hold the good stuff." The waitress scurried away with a dumbfounded expression.

Savannah could feel Nora staring at her.

"Why on earth did you order a portobello salad?" Nora asked.

Savannah rolled her eyes. "I told you I gave up meat."

"Well, giving up meat is one thing, but how can you give up seafood?" Nora demanded.

"I don't eat anything that has a face."

"You were raised on seafood, and now, after living in the land of fruits and nuts for a mere four months, you're telling me you can survive on bean sprouts?"

Savannah's expression hardened.

Nora quickly added, "I bet you cave when you see the key lime pie come out. Besides, shrimp and crabs are ugly enough to eat." She gave Savannah at tentative smile.

Savannah relaxed when she saw Nora was trying to lighten the mood. "Tell me about your classes," Savannah said.

Nora lived at home and was attending Coastal Carolina.

"They're good. I'm knocking out all my prerequisite courses."

"How are you and Hunter?" Savannah asked.

Nora blushed. "I wanted to talk to you about that. I hate that you found out about us the way you did. I'm sorry. I wanted to tell you, but it was never the right time."

"I thought we could tell each other anything."

"We could . . . we can," Nora said. "I just didn't know how to tell you that I was in love with your brother."

"Are you and Hunter really in love?"

Nora shifted awkwardly in her chair. "I don't know. I think so. He treats me really well. Are you okay with me dating your brother?"

"Hunter and I have never seen eye to eye on anything, so it's hard for me to see you two together."

"He's different with me, Savannah. He's loving and protective."

"He's an ass to me most of the time, so excuse me for being skeptical. And, for the record, I'm still mad at you for not telling me."

Nora looked down. "I understand. But can we try to have a nice time?"

For the rest of lunch, Savannah carefully avoided the topics of animal rights, Haley, and Nick. One uncomfortable topic was all she could handle.

* * * * *

Savannah woke up early on her last day in South Carolina. Previous attempts throughout the week to get her family to understand her devotion to the cause had proved futile. Armed with her activist DVDs, she approached her family at the breakfast table. "Good morning," she said.

Her mother, father, and brother were each in different stages of eating breakfast. Her brother had started his second plate of bacon, eggs, and toast.

"Want some Wilber?" Hunter taunted as he waved a piece of bacon in the air. The children's book, *Charlotte's Web*, had been Savannah's favorite story growing up. She loved the small pig in the book named Wilber.

Savannah made an effort to not behave like so many of the angry radical vegans she had met in the animal rights movement. It was getting increasingly difficult to remain civil when Hunter was antagonizing her daily.

Savannah ignored Hunter and smiled at her parents. "Anyone up for watching some DVDs with me today?" She tried showing the DVDs to Nora earlier in the week, but Nora had refused to watch.

Through a mouthful of food, Hunter said, "I'll watch them with you if I can have snacks. How about some pork rinds or chicken wings?"

"Screw you, Hunter."

"Savannah! That's enough," her mother scolded.

"Tell him to leave me alone."

"Hunter, show your sister some respect," her father added.

"Thank you, Dad," Savannah said.

Savannah's father put down his coffee mug and faced his daughter. "Savannah, while we respect your decision not to eat meat, you need to respect our choices as well."

"If you and Mother would watch my DVDs, you would both understand why I'm so passionate about the movement."

"Your mother and I both understand what happens at slaughter houses. We choose to eat meat products, and I am sorry if that upsets you, but neither one of us want to watch your DVDs. Those damn DVDs are one-sided propaganda. You're too young and naïve to understand that your new *friends* are taking advantage of your innocence."

Savannah pushed away from table, her chair scraping the floor.

"Don't you want some breakfast?" her mother asked.

"I'm not hungry." Savannah stormed off. She went to her room and ripped her cell phone from the charger. She dialed Nick's number. He hardly ever answered his phone, but miraculously he answered on the second ring.

"Hello," Nick said.

"Thank goodness you answered. I needed to hear a friendly voice."

"Guess your visit isn't going well."

"I'm ready to be back in LA. My family is getting on my nerves. Especially my asshole brother."

"You'll be back tomorrow. Just ignore your brother until you leave."

Savannah flopped on her bed. Tears streamed down her face. "I miss you."

"I miss you too, babe."

"My parents aren't supportive."

"Did you expect them to be?"

"I don't know what I expected, Nick. I didn't expect them to be so closed-minded. I'm glad that Haley and I are looking for an apartment for this summer. I don't want to move back here over summer break. I can't stand the thought of living with these people ever again."

"Have you mentioned staying in LA to your parents?"

"Hell no. I have to either find an internship or a job before I can broach the subject with them or they'll freak."

"Probably better to have that conversation over the phone once you get your shit together," Nick offered. "What do you have planned for your last night?"

"Mother is fixing a special dinner tonight. Nora is coming over too. It should be nice unless I kill my brother. He's such a shit."

"Hang in there. Tomorrow you'll be home and I'll take you out for a nice vegan dinner."

"Good, because I'm starving here. Nick, when I get home, I want to have a discussion about becoming more involved."

"Involved in what?" Nick asked.

"The movement. I want to be more involved in the movement. I'm ready."

"Let's not discuss this over the phone. We'll talk about it when you get home."

"Promise?"

"Of course. Enjoy your last night with your family. Try not to kill your brother."

"I'll try. Thanks for listening to me vent."

"Anytime."

Savannah waited to hear the click of Nick's phone.

* * * * *

Hunter arrived with Nora a couple of hours before dinner. Savannah had made some snacks, and the trio was sitting in the Carolina room eating hummus and tortilla chips when she noticed the uncomfortable glances being exchanged between her brother and Nora. Savannah's mother and father joined the group and made polite chit-chat. The tension grew, and finally Savannah couldn't stand it any longer. "What?" she asked. "Just say what's on your minds."

Her mother started the conversation. "Savannah, we're worried about you. You've changed so much in such a short period of time, and we're all concerned."

"Oh my God, is this an intervention of some kind?" Savannah asked. "You've got to be kidding. I'm a vegan, not a drug addict, for God's sake."

"It's not just the vegan thing," Hunter bluntly stated. "It's a combination of your strange new friends, the animal rights bullshit, and the weird dude you're dating."

Savannah took a deep breath and tried to control her anger. "Look, Hunter, I appreciate the protective brother routine, but you don't know Nick."

"How well do you know him, Savannah?" Hunter asked.

"Mind your own damn business!"

"That's not fair," Nora said. "Your brother loves you and is concerned about you. We all are."

Savannah turned her anger toward her parents. "So this nice little family get-together was merely a ploy to schedule an intervention. Thanks a lot. Well, I don't need an intervention, and I don't need any of you. I'm doing fine on my own."

"Sure you are," Hunter said. "You're doing fine spending Mom and Dad's hard-earned money to traipse all over LA with a bunch of weird hippies, eating sprouts and trying to save the world one pig at a time. Then you come here spouting your rhetoric and trying to get everyone to watch your propaganda DVDs. Do you have any idea how crazy you sound?"

Savannah felt her cheeks flush. She clenched her fists. Tears welled up in her eyes. *Do not cry*, she told herself. She wanted her family to see her as strong and confident, not weak and emotional.

"Enough, Hunter!" Savannah's father turned to face her, his only daughter. "This is not how we wanted to approach this topic with you, Savannah. We all love you very much, but you're not using good sense. You accept what these crazy people tell you hook, line, and sinker, and you don't take the time to think for yourself. You need to give up all this animal rights crap and concentrate on your studies. I'm paying a ton of money for you to attend that liberal school, so you can at least bring home decent grades."

Savannah's mother interrupted and tried to de-escalate the situation. "Savannah, your father and I are extremely proud of you. You've grown into a beautiful, confident young lady, but we worry that some of your new friends don't share your beliefs and values. You're trying so hard to—"

"*You* didn't let me finish, Rebecca." Savannah's father seethed at the slight to his authority. He took a breath before continuing, "Savannah, we do love you, and we'll support you no matter what you choose in life, but be careful with these people. Don't let them talk you into doing anything you don't want to do."

"These people?" Savannah yelled. "These people are my friends and my family now. They watch over me and care about me. They support me and don't judge me like you all are doing."

"Oh, come on," screamed Hunter. "They support you only if you eat what they tell you to eat, believe what they believe, and do exactly what they tell you to do. Where is the freethinker who left here four months ago?"

Savannah's mother sat alone on the love seat trembling; tears rolled down her cheeks.

"Shut the fuck up, Hunter!" Savannah screamed. "You don't have any idea what you're talking about. Besides, you're one to talk. Why don't you just go back to the brainwash center you call The Citadel. You have no room to talk about freethinking, Mister Regulation Uniform and Perfect Hospital Bed Corners. You live in a world where everybody looks the same, dresses the same, acts the same, thinks the same. You probably all share one brain behind those stone walls; so don't ever talk to me about being a freethinker. I'm the only person in this family who's not afraid to think outside of Southern ways. I want to thank all four of you for one thing. You've made my future clear. I now know where I want to be and who I want to be with. So thank you for that. I can't wait to get on that plane tomorrow."

Savannah ran out of the room before her tears could betray her. Her last words still lingered in the air, even after she slammed her bedroom door.

CHAPTER SIX

Alexis

After almost nine months in LA, Lexie finally managed to make a few friends in the animal rights community. She volunteered at the animal shelter and handed out pamphlets about factory farming in front of the local grocery stores. Facebook was a great source for finding out about protests and other events in the area. She enrolled in a class at Santa Monica College to give validity to her alias. The security culture of the underground movement caused paranoia among its members, so Lexie had to know her alias background as well as she knew her real background.

Lexie called Kate en route to a demonstration. Kate answered in a chipper tone.

"You're in a good mood," Lexie said.

"It's a beautiful Saturday morning, and I don't have to work. Oh no, Lexie, are you working this morning? Do I need to come to work?"

"Relax, I'm going to a demonstration. No big deal."

"Where's the demonstration?" Kate asked.

"It's downtown. I found it online. Have you ever heard about the mass slaughter of dolphins that takes place each year at the Taiji Cove in Japan?" Lexie didn't give Kate a chance to answer. "It's a government-sanctioned, barbaric slaughter. I can't believe this goes on, and I can't believe that I never knew about it. It's horrific."

"You got yourself all worked up," Kate said.

"It's hard not to be worked up. Each year, between September and March, some 20,000 dolphins, porpoises, and small whales are killed in this bloody cove. The Japanese government claims that the slaughter is part of a cultural tradition, but according to investigators, the whole massacre is commercially driven. Many of the dolphins are sold to amusement parks. So, the poor creatures end up in captivity, on the food market, or simply left injured to die. The practice is fucking unbelievable!"

"Whoa, girl. Take a breath," Kate said.

"I was up most of the night doing research."

Kate laughed. "It sounds like you've had a few too many cups of coffee this morning."

"Yeah, I might have surpassed recommended caffeine levels," Lexie said.

"You think?" Kate quipped.

"I'm hoping to meet some new people. I'll call you when I get home."

"Be careful, and call me if you need anything."

Lexie deleted the call from her call log and went over her backstory in her head. She started thinking about the training she received in the FBI's undercover school. The FBI was the best in the world when it came to undercover certification. As part of the training, prospective under-cover agents received classroom instruction during the daylight hours. In order to make the training more realistic, experienced FBI undercover agents were brought in from the field to portray criminals during evening training sce-narios. Instructors selected different students each evening to operate as undercover agents. Students in the group not selected as undercover agents were tasked with secondary roles: surveillance or backup.

Lexie had learned the importance of supporting an undercover operation as well as participating as the under-cover agent. The instructor running the scenario gave the team a quick rundown of the scenario and who the under-cover was supposed to meet. Inevitably, the instructor left out important details, in an added effort to simulate real-life situations and add to the stress level of the undercover. Sce-narios ranged from conducting a drug deal in a motorcycle gang clubhouse to attending a formal cocktail party to gain counter-terrorism intelligence. It was the responsibil-ity of the team and the undercover to know the elements of the crime and come up with a logical backstory for the undercover. The backstory was referred to as a legend. It included the undercover's alias, date of birth, address, employer, and most importantly, how the undercover knew the other players in the scenario. Students were thrust into various scenarios with only their made-up backstory and their ability to talk. Needless to say, things often went south. Training ran into the early morning hours. Sleep deprivation techniques were used to make the training scenarios seem more real. Students were purposely kept awake following the late-night scenarios to socialize with instructors and experienced undercover agents. Lexie figured out early that she and the other students were not only being judged by their performances, but also by how well they worked a room during social interactions. Undercover work predominantly involved talking to people and building relationships.

Lost in thought, Lexie nearly missed her turn. She took a breath, parked the car, and located the other demonstrators.

Lexie remembered Kate's advice to find a friendly face and talk to that person. Savannah Riley not only had a friendly face, but she also had a Southern accent. Lexie, being from the South herself, used that commonality to approach Savannah.

"Where are you from?" Lexie asked.

Savannah smiled. "South Carolina, and you?"

"Alabama, originally, but now I live in Venice Beach. I had to ask, because I haven't met many Southerners since I've moved here," Lexie added.

"Me either," Savannah said.

"I'm Lexie." She extended her hand to Savannah.

"Oh hi. I'm Savannah." Shaking Lexie's hand, she continued, "That's my roommate over there with the bullhorn. Her name is Haley."

Bingo, Lexie thought. She recognized Haley from one of the photos the FBI analyst showed her. "Nice to meet you, Savannah."

The two chatted off and on during the course of the demonstration. LAPD arrived as expected and dispersed the crowd. Lexie was surprised when Savannah approached her after the demonstration.

"Hey, Lexie, do you wanna go with me and Haley to the Veggie Grill for a snack?"

"That sounds like fun. I'd love to go."

"Great," said Savannah. "Do you know where it is?"

"The one in Santa Monica?" Lexie asked.

"Yeah, that's the one. If you don't know where it is, you can follow us."

En route to the restaurant, Lexie called Kate, putting the call on speakerphone. Kate answered on the first ring.

"Hello, Lexie."

"Wow, you're quick answering your phone."

"Only when you're gallivanting about. How was the demonstration?"

"Great. I can't really talk, because I'm following a couple of girls over to the Veggie Grill in Santa Monica. I don't want them to see me talking on the phone."

"Nice."

"Can you write down a license plate number for me?"

Lexie could hear Kate shuffling around on the other end.

"I'm ready to copy."

"They're driving a newer-model, red Toyota Prius, South Carolina plate number delta yankee sierra one two seven."

"I got it."

"Oh, and Kate, the passenger in the car is that Haley girl from the photograph I saw in the office."

"Even better. Do you want me to come out to cover you?"

"No, I'm fine. We're just going to hang out at the grill. I'll call you when I'm clear."

"Sounds good. And Lexie, be yourself. You'll do great."

When Lexie arrived at the restaurant, she quickly claimed the seat next to Savannah at a long table. As they sat, more people from the demonstration joined them but casually ignored her. When a group of men with tough-looking animal rights and anarchist tattoos walked in, Haley left the table and raced over to their leader—or who Lexie assumed was their leader. He looked the most hard-core. Lexie could feel him staring at her while he whispered to Haley. When Lexie looked up from the table, the men had been seated at a table on the other side of the restaurant, and Haley was walking towards her. "Where are you from, Lexie?" Haley asked.

"Alabama."

"What part?"

"Mobile. Have you ever been there?"

"No," replied Haley. "What are you doing in California?"

Lexie could see where the questions were going. Haley was drilling her on her background. *Good*, Lexie thought. *Bring it on.*

"Just hanging out and going to school."

"Where do you go to school?" Haley continued.

"Santa Monica College. What about you?"

Before Haley could answer, Savannah chimed in.

"Haley and I both go to USC."

Haley gave Savannah a sour look, but Savannah was oblivious. Lexie definitely caught the suspicious vibe.

"So Lexie, how did you find out about the demonstration today?" Haley wasn't finished with the inquisition.

"I found it on Facebook."

Lexie hoped the words coming out of her mouth were making sense, because it was obvious Haley was on a fishing expedition. Haley eventually relaxed but still shared nothing while Savannah and Lexie continued getting to know each other.

"How long have you been a vegan?" Lexie asked Savannah.

"Only since I started college," Savannah replied. "I didn't know anything about animal rights or veganism until I met Haley. What about you?"

"I'm a pretty new vegan too," Lexie responded. "I became a vegetarian first. I've only been a vegan about a year or so."

Savannah leaned forward. "Can I ask you something, Lexie?"

"Sure, anything."

"How did your family react when you told them you were a vegan?"

Lexie chuckled. "Not exactly favorably. How about yours?"

"They treated me like a drug addict in need of rehab. They actually arranged an intervention for me while I was home for the holidays."

"Are you serious?"

"Completely! I had a huge fight with my parents, brother, and best friend the night before I returned to school. It was horrible. That's why I asked. I'm not sure how to fix things with my family, and I thought you might have some advice, since you're from the South too."

"That's a tough one," Lexie said. "I think it helped that

I eased my family into my lifestyle one stage at a time. I became a vegetarian first, so later when I switched to completely vegan, it wasn't that big of an adjustment for them. I still have to remind them not to buy me anything leather and to avoid cosmetics unless they're from cruelty-free companies. But we don't discuss my activist activities."

"That's probably a wise decision," Savannah said.

"So it was really bad?" Lexie asked. "With your family, I mean."

"Oh God, it was terrible! I wish I had handled things differently."

"Well, if you ever need someone to talk to, I'm around," Lexie told Savannah.

"Thanks, I might just do that."

After they finished eating, Lexie, Haley, and Savannah walked to the parking lot together.

"Thanks for inviting me along," Lexie told Savannah and Haley.

"No problem; it was fun," Savannah stated. "Do you want to get together tomorrow and grab some coffee?"

This is too good to be true, Lexie thought. "Sure, that would be great. Where and when?"

"Well, since you live in Venice, how about Groundwork Coffee on the Boardwalk? Do you know the place?"

"I know it well. I go there all the time," Lexie said. "What time?"

"Two o'clock work for you?"

They exchanged cell phone numbers and said goodbye. Lexie finally had something of significance to put in an FD-302. Lexie was expected to type up one of the FBI's investigative reports each time she gathered any information that could be evidentiary in nature.

Lexie returned to her apartment and called Kate.

"How did things go?" Kate asked.

"About as well as can be expected. Haley was quite the inquisitor."

"Do you think she was suspicious of anything?"

"No, I think she was just being a typical paranoid activist. She grilled me on where I was from and so forth. Nothing I couldn't handle. Savannah and I exchanged cell phone numbers."

"That's great," Kate said. "I'll check subscriber information on her account and subpoena her number. It'll be interesting to see who she's communicating with."

"I'm meeting Savannah for coffee tomorrow at two o'clock. Maybe she'll bring Haley."

* * * * *

The next morning, Lexie got up and went for a long run on the beach. The California shoreline was absolutely breathtaking. Lexie couldn't get enough of the white sand beaches that seemed to go for miles. After her run, she took a shower and had a quick lunch. It was nearly time to leave for her coffee date with Savannah. She quickly refreshed herself on her legend, reminded herself to not act like a cop, and headed to the Boardwalk.

Lexie walked past the activist flophouse on her way to the coffee shop. She noticed that the trim was rotten in places and that the chipped paint revealed an olive green color under the dirty tan topcoat. The same old cars were parked in front of the house and on the street. Lexie arrived at the coffee shop a few minutes early, so she waited out front. She observed a host of Venice Beach characters, from a wino singing "Jingle Bells" to an old man on roller skates who skated up and down the Boardwalk playing a guitar. A few minutes later, she saw Savannah come around the corner. The women ordered soy lattes and sat at an outside table.

"Do you live close by?" Savannah asked.

"Yeah, just a few blocks from here."

"That's awesome."

"Where do you live?" Lexie asked.

"Haley and I live on campus at USC."

"D'you have a boyfriend?" Lexie asked.

Savannah's cheeks flushed.

"I have a Nick. He's pretty incredible."

"Looks like somebody's in love."

"I dunno, maybe. Though I wish I knew what the hell he was thinking half the time."

"Why don't you ask him?"

"Nick's not a conversationalist. He doesn't talk about himself. He thinks it's tacky."

"Wow, sounds super healthy," Lexie said.

"Yup," Savannah laughed in reply.

The two women chatted about growing up in the South. Lexie liked Savannah, and it was apparent Savannah was comfortable with her. The women decided to get together over the weekend for dinner and a chick flick.

Lexie walked home following her usual path. A couple of guys were hanging out on the front porch of the flophouse when she strolled by. A strong odor of marijuana wafted from the house. Lexie had a new goal: to get inside that house.

* * * * *

Lexie's mouth watered as she smelled the spicy entrees that were being carried from the kitchen to the tables. She heard the sizzle of fajitas being served as she, Kate, and Adam followed the hostess to a table.

"So," Adam started, "Kate tells me that you're kicking ass and taking names."

"I wouldn't go that far, but I do think I'm finally making a little progress."

The server delivered their drinks and took their food orders. Lexie couldn't pass up the veggie fajitas.

"You know you can order a meat dish out here if you want," Adam stated.

"Meat actually makes me sick to my stomach when I try to eat it now," replied Lexie. "Besides, I feel much healthier not eating meat."

"Oh my, they've brainwashed you already," Adam said jokingly.

"Not yet, but they sure are trying."

Lexie gave Adam a thumb drive. "This is the report from my meeting with Savannah."

"Wow! You're quick."

"I like to write my reports when they're fresh on my mind."

The waitress brought their entrees. Lexie loaded her fajitas with fresh salsa and hot sauce. By the end of the meal, she had worked up a sweat from the spice.

"I took your advice, Kate. I found a friendly face and started chatting with her at the demonstration. Once I heard her Southern accent, I knew I was home free. Savannah and I are going to dinner and a movie over the weekend, and with any luck she'll bring her roommate."

"That's great, Lexie," Adam interjected. "We wanted to talk to you about Haley. We don't have any intelligence on Savannah, but Haley is a suspect in a series of vandalisms at several UCLA faculty members' homes."

"No wonder Haley was so close-lipped when it came to sharing her information. I'll have to see if I can get her to warm up to me the next time we hang out together."

"Just be careful," Adam advised. "Haley has participated in the animal rights movement a long time. Don't let her find any cracks in your story. Believe me, she'll be looking for reasons not to trust you. Never turn your back on her, and never trust her."

"I'll be careful, boss," Lexie told Adam. "Savannah has a boyfriend named Nick, but I don't know his last name yet."

"I'll have the analyst put together a list of all the activists in the area who go by Nick," Adam said.

"Once I meet him, I'll be able to identify him from a photograph. I better hit the road so I can beat the traffic."

CHAPTER SEVEN

Savannah

Los Angeles, California

Savannah and Nick were sitting outside in the courtyard near her dormitory.

"How are things with your parents?" Nick asked.

Savannah sighed. "About the same. I've only talked to them a handful of times since the Christmas break debacle. I told them I wanted to stay out here over spring break."

"Bet that didn't go over well."

"No, not really. They offered to come out here to visit me, so I told them I'd think about it."

Nick ran his hands through his thick, tangled hair. "What about Nora and Hunter?"

"Well, Nora and I talk about once a week, but I haven't spoken to Hunter since Christmas break. I have nothing to say to him. Even when I talk to Nora, it feels strange."

"Strange how?" Nick asked.

Savannah shifted around so she could look Nick in the eyes. "I feel like I'm always walking on eggshells with Nora. Our relationship is so fragile right now, maybe even superficial. I can't trust her anymore, not after she sided with my parents and Hunter. I know she's in love with my brother, but I feel so betrayed. She and I have been best friends our whole lives, and now she sides with them."

Nick scooted closer to Savannah and put a protective arm around her. She breathed in the smell of his cologne.

"I'm sorry that happened to you, Savannah, but I'm not surprised. People outside our movement don't understand. I haven't spoken to my parents in almost three years. They don't even know where I'm living these days. It's hard, but it's not the end of the world. It does get easier as you become more involved and you see the good that you're doing."

"Speaking of that, when are you going to teach me more about the movement?"

Nick smiled. "How about now?"

"Really? That would be great!"

"Savannah, I know this culture is far different from how you were raised. But if you truly devote yourself to the movement, you'll understand why we do what we do."

"I want to," Savannah said. "I want to understand everything. I want to save animals and to feel like I'm making a difference in the world."

Nick pushed a stray strand of his inky-black hair out of his eyes and stared at Savannah. "Are you willing to put your freedom on the line to save animals and to protect the people in our movement? This is a serious commitment and not a hobby. There are people in the movement who put their freedom and lives on the line to save innocent creatures. It is our duty to protect those people so they are free to save animals and are not suffering at the hands of an intolerant government. You have to decide if this is the life you want to live."

"That's all I've thought about since I got back here. The life I had in South Carolina isn't mine anymore. I want a life out here with you. I love you, Nick, and I want to stand beside you and help you." The words came tumbling out of her mouth before she could stop them. A tear trickled down her cheek, and she bit her bottom lip.

The seconds ticked by at a snail's pace. Nick broke the awkward silence when he reached over and grabbed Savannah behind the neck and pulled her close to him. His tongue found its way into her mouth as he kissed her feverishly. When they finished kissing, he rested his forehead on hers. "I love you too, Savannah. I tried not to fall in love with you, because love complicates things. I wanted to keep things casual and uncomplicated between us, but somewhere along the line I fell in love. But despite that, you have to commit to the movement for yourself, not for me. No matter what you feel for me, you have to want this for you."

Savannah exhaled. She couldn't believe he'd said those three words back to her. She threw her arms around Nick's neck and kissed him again. She nuzzled her face into his neck.

"I understand, Nick, and I *am* making this decision for me. I want to do everything I can to save innocent animals from torture and death. I'm doing this for the right reasons."

Nick grinned, and Savannah's heart raced.

"Well, okay then. Get ready for ALF 101."

Savannah already knew that ALF stood for the Animal

Liberation Front. The Animal Liberation Front carried out direct actions against animal abusers by rescuing or freeing caged animals and causing large financial losses to companies who supported the exploitation of animals. Their actions involved damage and destruction of property belonging to animal abusers. Savannah had previously learned, by making a fool out of herself, to pronounce each letter in A-L-F. Once, she referred to the group as Alf in front of Haley's friends. Haley told her that the group was referred to as A-L-F, and that Alf was a small, furry alien from an old television sitcom. Savannah wouldn't make that mistake again.

Nick turned to face Savannah. "ALF members take precautions not to harm any animals or humans, but sometimes their campaigns involve danger and almost always involve breaking the law. The goal of the ALF is to liberate animals from places of abuse such as laboratories, factory farms, and fur farms and place them in good homes where they will be free from suffering. Another goal of the ALF is to reveal to the public the horrible conditions and atrocities that occur to innocent animals behind locked doors."

Savannah nodded.

Nick's demeanor completely changed as he took both of Savannah's hands in his and stared into her blue eyes. "We have to talk about the security culture of our movement. Savannah, you *must* make security your number-one priority. The alternative to not adhering to a strict security culture is spending years of your life in prison. First rule: do not trust anyone completely."

Savannah couldn't believe what she was hearing. "Nick,

I trust you completely."

"Well, you shouldn't. You have to understand that every person has a breaking point. When faced with numerous years in prison, most people will break. The police and FBI will do anything and say anything to gain your trust and get you to turn on the other members of your group. That's the way they operate. That's why the smart people in our movement who are involved in any kind of illegal direct action operate on a strict need-to-know basis. *Never* discuss any kind of direct action. Don't trust your best friend, your parents, your boyfriend, or other activists. Even if the person you tell is trustworthy, he or she may end up being tricked by the police. It's never okay to discuss your involvement or someone else's involvement in illegal activities."

Savannah removed her hands from Nick's and crossed her arms.

Nick continued, his voice growing more and more insistent. "If you do have to discuss direct action, do so only with those who have an absolute need to know and only have the discussion face to face. Always discuss direct action outside, away from people who may overhear you, and don't have any cell phones or other electronic devices with you when you have those discussions. The FBI has ways of eavesdropping on activists in houses and vehicles, so never discuss any sort of plans or actions inside someone's house or in a vehicle. Never discuss direct action over snail mail, e-mail, or phone. This includes instant messages and texts, Savannah. I know how you love to text, so just don't do it."

Savannah was starting to feel annoyed by Nick's patronizing tone.

"I'm going to install PGP on your laptop. Do you know how to use it?"

"No. What does PGP mean?" Savannah asked.

"Pretty Good Privacy. It's a data encryption and decryption program that's impossible to decode. I use PGP for all e-mails, and I have a whole partition on my computer encrypted. I'll teach you how to use it."

"Why do we need to go to this much trouble? You and I aren't breaking any laws."

"The police and FBI constantly target animal rights activists. It's better to be safe, even if you and I aren't involved in criminal activities. 'Keep the FBI guessing' is the best philosophy."

"Look, Nick, I've read the guidebook and studied the ALF website. I know the dos and don'ts. I'm not an idiot."

"I'm sorry, Savannah. I'm not trying to treat you like an idiot, but this stuff is so fucking important. People tend to get in trouble when they forget about security. You're new to this way of life, and I want you to completely understand what you're getting yourself into."

"I do, but it's not like I'm going to build a fucking bomb, so do I really need to be so concerned about security?"

"You might not be assembling any bombs, but you might have knowledge of someone doing something illegal, and you have to know how to protect yourself and others."

Savannah groaned. "Okay, you're right. I'm listening."

"The FBI and police go to great lengths to infiltrate our movement. Government agents come in the form of undercover agents and snitches. These government agents will pretend to be activists in order to befriend you. Be extremely careful about who you get involved with in the movement. Once you participate in an illegal action, never discuss it again. Don't discuss it even with the people who participated in the action with you. I've had friends convicted of crimes who were caught because they discussed old actions with people they thought they could trust but who became government informants. Cops will actually pay people to wear a wire and try to get information from people who were once their close friends. You never know when a former friend will fall on hard times financially or get arrested for a crime completely unrelated and cooperate with law enforcement to get the charges thrown out. I know this sounds very cloak-and-dagger, but believe me, it's all necessary." Nick relaxed a bit. He squeezed Savannah's shoulders. "Okay, that's all the training for today, young Skywalker."

Savannah laughed. Nick was the last person you would ever suspect to be a *Star Wars* fan. She loved the fact there were many layers to Nick, and she wanted to explore all the layers, starting with the one under the tight-fitting, black T-shirt he was wearing.

"All this training has made me hungry," she told Nick as she leaned over and kissed his earlobe.

"Hungry for what, Miss Savannah?" he asked in his best Southern drawl.

"I think you know what I want from the menu," she whispered into his ear as she continued to nibble on his earlobe.

"Well, who am I to say no to that request?" He stood up and pulled Savannah to her feet.

"Where to, my young Jedi?" Nick asked.

"How about my dorm room? Haley is at the library and should be there for a couple more hours, so we have the place to ourselves."

Nick smiled his renegade smile.

"Lead the way, girl!"

Savannah opened the door to her dorm room. "After you," she said, motioning for Nick to enter. She locked the door behind them.

Nick pulled a condom out of his wallet and placed it on the nightstand. Laughing, they yanked off their shoes and socks. As soon as Nick touched her, Savannah could feel herself responding. How was it possible that this guy could cause her body to have such an instant reaction? With one hand, Nick removed the lightweight sweater Savannah was wearing, and with the other hand, he reached behind Savannah and unhooked her bra. She giggled and wondered how long it had taken him to master that skill.

"Everyone needs a special talent," Nick told her, as if he had read her mind.

Savannah reached down and removed Nick's snug-fitting T-shirt from his perfectly chiseled body. Removing his shirt was her favorite part of the undressing ritual. She loved the feel of his muscles under her hands. She breathed in his earthy scent and kissed his gorgeous chest. When she looked up, she saw Nick staring at her with his dark and dangerous eyes. How was it possible she knew so very little about this man, but she could love him so much?

As they lay in bed, snuggled up tight, Savannah asked,

"Where did you grow up?"

"In a small town just outside of Portland. Why?"

"You never talk about where you grew up or your family, and I was curious."

"Well don't be, because it wasn't anything too exciting," he responded as he moved to get up from the bed.

Savannah's eyes and mouth must have displayed disappointment, because he laid back down. "I'm sorry. I don't like talking about my family. It has nothing to do with the way I feel about you."

Savannah stared at the ceiling.

"Pouting isn't going to work." She kept pouting.

"Okay," he said in an exasperated voice. "I have a younger brother named Randy, and I don't get along with him or anyone in my family."

Savannah wanted more, but she was unsure whether to push for more information or just let it go for now. She decided to push just a little more. "What happened? Why don't you get along with your family?"

Nick let out a loud sigh. "It's like what happened when you went back to South Carolina. My family doesn't understand me. And worse, they don't even try to understand me, so after a while, I gave up on them."

"Is that what's going to happen between me and my family?" Savannah asked.

"I hope not. I sincerely hope not. It depends on how closed-minded your family members are about your life choices. My family refused to accept my lifestyle, and every time I visited them, it was constant conflict. After a while, it wasn't worth it to me to try anymore. I gave up and never looked back."

Savannah reached over and squeezed Nick's hand. "I'm here for you, Nick, anytime you need me. I will always be here for you."

Nick leaned toward Savannah and brushed his lips across hers. "Thank you."

Someone knocked on the door.

"Haley's home," Savannah said. "One minute, roomy," she hollered.

"Do you need me to come back?"

"Nope, just need one minute," Savannah yelled.

Nick quickly threw on his clothes. Savannah put on her pink bathrobe—a gift from her mother. She opened the door, and in strolled a grinning Haley.

"So what kind of dirty deeds were going on inside my dorm room while I was dutifully studying at the library all by my lonesome?" Haley asked.

"Nick was helping me study," Savannah replied with a faked innocence.

"What was he helping you study? Anatomy?" teased Haley.

They laughed, and Haley strolled over to the mini refrigerator and dug out three bottles of beer. "I could use a drink. What about you two?"

"I'll take a beer," Nick replied.

"I bet you worked up quite a thirst, young man," Haley continued to tease.

"That I did," Nick responded.

There was an easiness among the three of them that Savannah enjoyed. She was happy.

* * * * *

The next day, Savannah met Lexie on the Santa Monica Promenade for dinner and a movie. There was a crowd at the Real Food Daily, and they ended up waiting twenty minutes to get a table. Luckily they had plenty of time before the movie started. They walked next door to a little shop that carried crystals, candles, and other kinds of Zen ware.

"Are you religious?" Savannah asked Lexie. "If that's too personal, you don't have to answer. You can tell me to mind my own business." "I don't mind answering," Lexie stated. "I grew up in a religious family, but I've ventured away from organized religion over the years. I guess I would describe myself as more of a Buddhist. What about you?"

"I was raised Presbyterian. I never gave much thought to other religions until I came to school out here and made friends with so many people from other religions and people who don't believe in God at all. The girl who sits next to me in my History class is Hindu. She and I have lunch together some, and she's told me all about her religion. I didn't know the first thing about Hinduism until I met her."

"What about your roommate?" Lexie asked.

"Haley and Nick are both atheists. I wasn't sure how I felt about that at first, but now I'm okay with it."

"What about your family? Did they stroke out when you told them that Nick didn't believe in God?"

Savannah looked down at a candle she was contemplating buying. "I haven't told them much about Nick. They're so closed-minded about my life out here. They haven't shown an interest in anything I'm doing, so I don't feel I owe them any information about my relationship with Nick."

"I'm sorry, Savannah. I didn't mean to be so nosy."

"That's okay. You aren't being nosy. Besides, I started this conversation by asking you first. It doesn't bother me to talk about it."

"Okay, good, as long as I didn't upset you. I don't want to ruin our evening by bringing up a bad topic."

"Not at all. It actually helps to talk about it. You understand the Southern culture. Haley and Nick are nonchalant about blowing off family, but I have trouble closing the door on my family. Up until I came here, they had always been loving and supportive of me, and I can't simply turn that off overnight. I think, given enough time, they'll come around and understand my lifestyle choices. At least I hope they will."

"I'm sure they will. It might take them a little time to get used to everything, but I'm sure they'll come around. They love you, and that hasn't changed."

Savannah smiled. "Lexie, you're the best! You always make me feel so much better."

"Can I ask you something?" Lexie asked.

"Of course."

"What's it like having a twin? I always thought it would be cool to have a twin."

Savannah sighed. "Hunter and I don't get along like most twins. When we were small, we were inseparable, but somewhere around middle school, he started acting like a jerk. I don't know if it was his hormones or what. He started treating me like I'm younger than him, and it's obvious that he's Dad's favorite.

"That surprises me," Lexie said. "I always thought twins stayed close their whole lives."

"I think most do. Hunter and I have completely different personalities."

Lexie looked at her watch. "Guess we better get back to the restaurant."

After dinner and a mediocre chick flick, they stopped for a dairy-free sorbet. The two finalized plans for a shopping excursion the next day.

"See ya tomorrow," Savannah yelled as they parted ways, going toward their respective cars.

"I'll pick you up tomorrow at your place. Feel free to invite Haley."

"Okay, I will."

CHAPTER EIGHT

Alexis

"Okay ladies, I'm going to show you two newbies how to shop vintage style," Haley announced. The three women were going on a shopping excursion.

"What's that mean?" Savannah asked.

"We're hitting the secondhand stores on Melrose Avenue," Haley said. "Great clothing at rock-bottom prices."

"Sounds good to me," Lexie said.

"I've never been in a thrift store," Savannah confessed.

"Vintage store," Haley corrected.

"Okay, I've never been in a vintage store."

"I bought my prom dress in a second-hand store," Lexie said. "My father lost his job my junior year, and I wanted to go to the prom. I saved up my money and found a pretty dress in the thrift store—sorry, *vintage* store. I was so proud of that dress."

Lexie had made up the prom dress story. She had learned in UC school that good anecdotes made the legend, and therefore the person, more believable. She was careful not to make up stories very often, though, because each was a new lie to remember.

After a couple of hours of shopping, they decided to take a lunch break. Finding a vegan restaurant in LA was never a problem. If you threw a rock in any direction, you would hit a vegan restaurant. They sat down. Savannah looked through her backpack, admiring all of her newly acquired treasures.

"This is so much fun," she squealed. "I love vintage shopping."

"Me too," Lexie added. "And thanks for showing us all of these great places, Haley."

"No problem, girls; it was my pleasure. By the way, thanks for driving, Lexie."

Lexie looked at Haley, then at Savannah. "You know, it's been a long time since I've made any real friends," Lexie said. "It's nice to finally make some friends I can trust and be myself around."

"Why do you say that?" Haley asked.

Before speaking, Lexie reminded herself to be careful and not come across as too pushy when gathering information from Haley. She and Savannah had a natural chemistry, but Haley was far more paranoid than Savannah. "It seems like nobody has ever understood me, and now I finally found people I can be friends with who don't judge me." Lexie swallowed hard.

Haley narrowed her eyes at first but then smiled. "Well, I guess that's what we're all searching for," she said.

"How long have you been an activist, Haley?" Lexie asked.

Haley briefly hesitated, as if trying to decide whether

to discuss the subject with Lexie. "Since I was fourteen years old."

"Really? Wow! That's awesome. How'd you get involved?" Lexie pressed.

"An older boy in my high school was an anarchist, and I followed him around like a lost puppy. I though he was so cool, so I hung out with him and some of his friends. They were all involved in various kinds of activism, mostly environmental. The guy's girlfriend was an animal rights activist, so she took me under her wing and taught me all about the movement and how to become vegan. The rest is history, I guess."

"That's so cool," Lexie told her. "Growing up in Alabama, I didn't get a lot of encouragement from my family or friends. I wish I would have had like-minded people to hang out with and to learn from when I was younger. It's nice that you're helping Savannah."

Haley smiled. "If you ever need anything from me, just ask," she told Lexie.

"Thanks. That's nice of you."

Lexie decided not to push the issue further. Her strides in winning over Haley today had been enough.

The three new friends continued shopping until they were exhausted. Lexie dropped off Savannah and Haley and went home to her small apartment. She grabbed a diet soda and sat down to type her report. She stared at the computer screen. Usually words came easily, but tonight she felt out of sorts. She dialed Kate.

"How'd the day go?" Kate asked.

"We had a fantastic day. Haley came with us. We had

coffee, shopped, stopped for lunch, and shopped again. Total girls day."

"Was Haley suspicious of you?"

"No. She seemed more relaxed around me this time. We actually had a great time."

"Did you learn anything new?" Kate asked.

"About what?"

"Uh . . . about the case."

"No. Nothing worthy of a 302," Lexie said.

"All day and you didn't come up with anything?"

Lexie was startled. She had worked so hard that day. "Damn it, Kate. I was building rapport. Not everything has to be about gathering evidence."

"Okay, what's wrong?"

"Nothing's wrong. Why?"

"You sound strange, so spill it."

Lexie took a deep breath and exhaled loudly. "Kate, I don't have any real friends."

"What are you talking about?" Kate asked.

"I have closer friends in my undercover life than I do in my real life."

"I'm sure that's not true. You're lonely. That's a side effect of working undercover."

"I'm serious. At lunch, we were talking about friendship and accepting people, and I realized that in the real world I have very few friends. I have plenty of acquaintances through work, but I don't have anyone in New Orleans that I would actually call a close friend. And I definitely don't have anything that would qualify as a romantic relationship."

"Listen to me," Kate said. "You're a deeply embedded undercover agent. The emotions you're experiencing are normal. You're relating to your subjects on a personal level, which is good, but that doesn't mean your real life is shit."

"I didn't say my real life was shit. I said I didn't have any close personal friends in my real life. I've spent the last five years building my career, and I don't have anything to show for it. No friends, no love life; hell, I don't even have a dog."

Kate laughed.

"It's not funny," Lexie said.

"I'm not laughing at you, Lexie. You're having identity conflict, and you can't see how far you've come and how great you are. It's normal."

"I guess all this sounds pretty pathetic."

"No," Kate said. "Not at all. It's something that we can deal with. Let's talk about what you learned on your shopping extravaganza so we can decide what to put in your 302. You know how the brass likes to see paperwork."

CHAPTER NINE

Savannah

In the car on the way to Phillip and Jeanette's house for a New World Militia meeting, Savannah decided it was time to ask Nick and Haley about inviting Lexie to join their group.

"I have something to ask you two," Savannah started nervously.

"What's that?" Nick asked.

Savannah bit her lip. "Can we ask Lexie to come with us to the next NWM meeting? I know we haven't known her for very long, but she's really cool, and I think she would be a great addition to the group."

Nick, who was driving, sighed and glanced into the rearview mirror at Haley. "Savannah, you don't know anything about the girl."

"Lexie and I have been spending quite a bit of time together, and I trust her."

Nick seemed irritated. "You trust her, huh? Do you trust her with your freedom? What about with my freedom or Haley's freedom? Because that's what you're doing if you bring her into our core group. Do you know her well enough to be able to say she wouldn't give us up if she were ever questioned by the police or by the FBI? Can you honestly say you trust her to that level this soon after meeting her?"

Savannah rolled her eyes. "Jesus! I don't know, Nick. How long does it take before you trust someone to that level? Haley, you've spent time with her. What do you think?"

Haley took a deep breath before answering. "Well, she seems okay so far, but I think she needs more vetting before we invite her to a meeting. I'm not saying she won't pass muster, but I think we need to do a little more digging into her background before we ask her to join us."

"How do we do that?" Savannah inquired.

"We start by running her information through a few databases on the Internet to make sure she's telling us the truth. If there are no red flags with her background, then maybe we'll think about inviting her to a meeting. Is she on social media?"

"She has a Facebook account. Why?"

"I have a friend who has a good facial recognition program. I'll have him run her photo through his database to see if she pops up as a cop or a police informant."

Savannah laughed.

"What's so funny?" Haley asked.

"Lexie's no informant."

"Just what do you think an informant looks like, Savannah?"

"I dunno know exactly. But I know Lexie's not an informant."

"Do you happen to know her birth date?" Nick asked

Savannah.

"No, but I can find out."

"Start with getting her date of birth, and we'll go from there."

"But be cool when you do it; don't act suspicious," Haley added.

"I can do this, guys. I'm not stupid. Besides, I was the star of my high school drama club. I do have some acting abilities." Savannah pressed the back of her hand to her forehead, pretending to faint.

"Oh boy!" Nick replied. "This ought to be good."

Nick parked the car, and the three approached the front door. Before Nick could knock, the door slung open and Jeannette greeted them. Jeannette always dressed like she had recently returned from Woodstock. Peace sign earrings dangled from her ears, and faded ink revealed that she got her tattoos long before they were mainstream. "Come in, come in, friends. How are you three doing this fine evening?"

Nick hugged Jeannette. "Doing great, lovely lady, and how are you?"

"Doing fantastic, and thank you for asking."

"How many folks are we expecting tonight?" Nick asked.

"We should have about ten, counting you three."

"Any news from Badger?"

"I heard from him yesterday," Jeannette replied. "He sent me a PGP message letting me know that he might be here tonight."

"Great!" Nick said. "I've missed that lunatic."

Jeannette chuckled. "He might be a lunatic, but he's a

brilliant lunatic."

A few minutes after the meeting began, there was a knock at the back door. Phillip went to answer it and returned with a young, shaggy-haired man. Nick jumped up and embraced the newcomer.

"Badger, how the hell are you, brother?" Nick asked.

"I'm great, Nick. How about you? You still hanging out on campus, trying to bang college freshmen?"

Savannah was taken aback by the comment. The two slapped each other on the back and continued to laugh.

Savannah leaned over and asked Haley, "Who's that?"

"That's Badger," Haley responded. "He and Nick are old friends."

"Oh, he's never mentioned him," Savannah stated.

Haley gave Savannah a quizzical expression. "Has Nick ever mentioned any of his friends to you?"

"Point taken."

During the meeting, Savannah's attention kept straying to Badger. She wondered how long he and Nick had been friends. Badger was the opposite of Nick in almost every way. He was short and skeletal with long, straggly blond hair. His pale blue eyes were his best feature. On the whole, he looked unkempt, and Savannah wondered if he smelled as bad as he looked. She wondered if Nick would tell her more about this Badger guy later, when they were alone.

Amber, one of the girls at the meeting, had managed to befriend a girl who worked at the UCLA laboratory. She was working on getting information out of her about the security system at the lab. Another NWM member, Jeff, was working on getting a set of walkie-talkies they could use on their next animal liberation mission. Two other people were present at the meeting, a guy and a girl, but they never spoke. Savannah just knew their names were Ryan and Darla. She did not know anyone's last name other than Nick's and Haley's. In fact, she wasn't sure if the first names the other members used were even their real names.

Badger was working on obtaining information regarding a beef feedlot somewhere north of Los Angeles. He was careful not to divulge too much information about his potential plan for the feedlot. He passionately informed the group of the terrible conditions and treatment the feedlot cattle had to endure. Badger promised the group that when his research was complete, he would enlist several members to help him carry out his plan.

The meeting adjourned, and Savannah saw Nick and Badger go out to the backyard together. She stayed inside, chatting with Amber and Jeannette while munching on vegetables and Jeannette's delicious red pepper hummus. A half hour later, Nick came back into the house alone. He hung out with Jeff for a few minutes and then made his rounds, visiting with the rest of the group. He walked up behind Savannah and encircled her in his arms. "You and Haley about ready to leave?" he asked.

"Whenever you are."

"Let's thank Phillip and Jeannette and take off."

The ride home was quiet. Nick dropped Savannah and Haley at their dorm room around eleven. They washed their faces, brushed their teeth, and collapsed to watch a little TV before bed.

"Haley, can I ask you something?"

"Oh no, here comes the inquisition," Haley joked.

Savannah smiled. "I know we don't normally discuss other people's pasts, but how do Nick and Badger know one another?"

"Savannah, why can't you just leave it alone? I'm sure Nick will tell you what he wants you to know when he wants you to know it."

"It's not like I want to know if they burned down a fur farm together, I just want to know more about Nick, and he's so damn tight-lipped. It drives me crazy not knowing anything about him. Please just give me something. I won't tell him you told me."

Haley muted the television and took a moment to consider the request. "You're going to get me in serious trouble with Nick."

"No, I won't. I promise. I'll never tell him you told me anything. I'll take it to my grave. Please just give me something."

"Ugh, you're so frustrating. Why can't you be content knowing Nick loves you and is trying to protect you?"

"What is he protecting me from?"

"Jeez, you are exasperating! Okay, but you can *never* tell Nick that we talked about any of this stuff. Promise me, Savannah."

"I promise. I promise."

Haley rolled over on her side so she could face Savannah. "Nick has lived all over the Pacific Northwest. He's been heavily involved with anarchist groups in most of the areas where he's lived. While he was living in the Bay Area, he met Badger. Nobody knows for sure how many direct action campaigns the two of them waged over the years, because the only two people who know for sure are Nick and Badger, and they'll never talk. I do know that the two of them spent a period of time living off the grid—no IDs, no permanent residences. And I do know there were some pretty serious direct actions that took place in and around the Bay Area when they were both living there."

Savannah sat completely silent, listening intently to every word that came out of Haley's mouth.

"The FBI hauled them both in for questioning, but neither one of them talked, which meant they both walked. The FBI will make up shit to try to get you to give them information. When they don't have any evidence, they start grasping at straws to put together the pieces. Their main interview tactic is to try to pit people in the movement against one another by saying that someone in your group is providing information. The feds really suck. They call us terrorists, when all we're trying to do is free innocent animals from the real terrorists."

"So," Savannah asked, "do you think Nick and Badger are planning a direct action of some kind in this area?"

"I don't know. Probably. You'll know if and when you need to know. You know the rule: only tell people about the action who have a need to know. If you're going to be involved in the plan and have a need to know, then Nick will tell you when the time is right. Now shut up! We never had this conversation, understand?"

"Yes, I understand," replied Savannah. "And Haley?"

"*What*?"

"Thank you."

Haley unmuted the television and started flipping through the channels.

"You're welcome."

CHAPTER TEN

Alexis

Lexie was bursting with excitement. Savannah had called and invited her to go to dinner later that day with her and Haley. Lexie was meeting with Kate and Adam to form a game plan and to pick up a fresh body recorder. She wasn't sure if anything of a criminal nature would be discussed, but she wanted to be prepared, just in case.

Lexie arrived at the deserted meet location a little before ten o'clock. Kate and Adam were waiting for her in the corner of the parking lot. Adam smiled as Lexie rolled up.

"Hey, girl. How are you doing this fine morning?" Adam asked.

"Great! And you?"

"Oh, you know, just fighting the good fight. Of course I never know if I spend more time fighting the bad guys or fighting our management."

Lexie laughed. The FBI bureaucracy had to be the worst of all federal agencies. Cutting through the red tape took more time than the actual investigation.

"So what's the plan?" Kate asked.

"I'm meeting Savannah and Haley at the Veggie Grill at six o'clock for dinner. I'm not sure if anyone else is coming."

"Who called you about the meeting?" Adam asked.

"Savannah called me, but I could hear Haley in the background. She didn't call to chitchat either. She asked if I could meet them for dinner and told me where and when."

"That sounds positive," Adam stated. "We have a source who's been attending the New World Militia meetings. He reported to his handler they're having a meeting this evening and that Haley and Savannah usually attend the meetings. If we're lucky, maybe they'll invite you to go. The source obviously doesn't know about you, but you need to know about him."

Adam pulled out a file from his backpack and showed Lexie a photograph of a nice-looking, clean-cut man in his early twenties. "His name is Ryan, and he's a student at UCLA. We recruited him about a year ago. So far his involvement has been limited to aboveground activities such as protests and demonstrations. He started attending NWM meetings a few months ago. Try not to spend time talking to him unless you need to make things look natural."

"Got it," replied Lexie.

"Our surveillance team also identified Savannah's boyfriend. His name is Nick Harris, and he has a lengthy criminal history."

"What kind of criminal history?"

"Mostly property damage and vandalisms, but he does have an assault and battery conviction from a year ago. I've requested the police report and should have it in a few days."

"It surprises me that Savannah would be with someone who has a violent criminal past. I wonder if she knows."

"I don't know, but you be careful dealing with him, Lexie."

Adam gave Lexie a new body recorder and a camera hidden in a button that Lexie could sew onto a shirt or jacket.

"Does the white button work for you?" Adam asked. "If not, we can request one in black."

"White works fine. I'll sew it on when I get back to the apartment."

"Do you think anyone will search you?" Kate asked.

"I don't think so, but I did notice these people tend to hug one another, so I'll be careful where I run the wires."

"Do you need any help getting ready?" Kate asked.

"No, I can handle it, but thanks."

Adam ran over the plan. "If you get invited to the NWM meeting, shoot Kate a text if possible. If you do go, call or text her once you're clear and can talk,"

* * * * *

Lexie spotted Savannah's Prius in the parking lot. Before getting out of the car, she texted Kate and then quickly adjusted her sports bra. She was also wearing a hoodie, which would help keep someone from feeling the equipment under the bra. The button was sewn into the collar of her shirt, peaking out from beneath her hoodie. She parked next to the Prius and went inside to meet the girls. She was surprised to see a guy sitting at the table with Savannah and Haley.

"Hey, guys," Lexie said as she approached the table.

Savannah jumped up and ran around the table to hug her. "Lexie, this is my boyfriend, Nick."

Lexie smiled. "Hi, Nick."

Nick stood and reached out his hand. "Hi, Lexie. I've heard a lot about you."

"Have you guys ordered yet?" Lexie asked.

"No, we were waiting for you," Savannah replied.

"Great, I'm starving."

They ordered their food, and while they waited for their order to arrive, Nick questioned Lexie. "Where're you from, Lexie?"

"Mobile, Alabama," Lexie responded.

"What on earth brought you to LA from Alabama?"

"School, mostly, but I've always wanted to live in California. I grew up seeing California in all the movies, and I wanted to see if it was as wonderful as it looked on the big screen."

"And what do you think?" Nick asked.

"Are you kidding? I love it, and I never plan to leave. The weather is perfect and there's so much to do."

The server brought their food to the table, and everyone dug in. Lexie had ordered the imitation chicken sandwich. She was surprised how much she enjoyed the food at many of the vegan restaurants.

"Have you ever lived anywhere else other than Mobile?" Nick asked.

Lexie's undercover credit history included a couple of

places where she had supposedly lived, so she figured she had better mention those places. "Well, I lived in Louisville, Kentucky, for a short while, and also in Nashville when I was younger."

"Why did you live in those states?" Nick asked.

"My dad lost his job, and we bounced around while he worked odd jobs."

Lexie hoped Nick's interrogation of her was a good sign. She decided to ask him a couple of questions, to make the conversation seem a little more realistic. "Are you from California?"

She thought he wasn't going to respond, but after he took a sip of his soda, he answered. "I grew up in Oregon, but I've lived in California for the past few years."

"Do you go to USC with Savannah and Haley?" Lexie asked.

"I go to USC part time."

"That's cool," Lexie said.

Haley jumped into the conversation. "What are you studying, Lexie?"

"Right now, photography, but I'm worried about the job market. I love photography, but I don't want to end up working at some Sears studio taking photos of screaming toddlers."

"Ugh, I can understand why you wouldn't want to do that," Haley agreed. "Sticky, mad two-year-olds all day doesn't sound like a load of fun."

They were finishing up their dinners when Lexie saw Nick nod to Savannah, who was devouring her carrot cake. The moment Lexie had been waiting for had occurred.

"What are you doing this evening, Lexie?" Savannah asked.

"I don't have any plans."

"Do you want to go to an Animal Rights meeting with us? The meeting is in Venice, not far from your apartment."

Lexie was doing cartwheels on the inside, but she didn't want to appear too excited. "Sure, sounds good to me."

"Great," Savannah added. "Just follow us when we leave here."

The foursome left the Veggie Grill, and Lexie followed them to the flophouse in Venice. On the way over, she put her phone on speaker and called Kate.

"Hey, girl."

"Hi, Kate. I'm driving to the activists' house in Venice. I got an invite to the meeting, and I'm following Savannah, Haley, and Nick over."

"Fantastic job, Lexie."

Lexie was pleased to hear how excited Kate sounded. It was difficult to get a reaction out of Kate, so Lexie knew this meeting was a big deal. "I'll call you tonight when I get home."

Lexie quickly deleted the outgoing call from the log on her cell phone. She parked her car behind Savannah's Prius. The four walked up to the front door together. Jeannette welcomed Lexie and showed her around the house, offering her refreshments. Since they had just come from dinner, Lexie passed on the food, but did accept a cup of hot tea when it was offered.

"How many of these meetings have you been to?" Lexie quietly asked Savannah.

"I think this is my fifth one," Savannah said. "Most of the people are super nice once they get a chance to know you."

A few more people arrived for the meeting, and Savannah introduced Lexie to the people she knew. When a straggly haired guy arrived, he immediately grabbed Nick. They walked out to the backyard to talk in private.

"Who was that?" Lexie asked Savannah.

"Oh, that's Nick's buddy, Badger. He was at the last meeting. I don't really know him, so Nick will have to introduce you to him."

"No problem. Just curious."

"Well don't be too curious around here," Savannah said. "These people don't like curiosity."

"Good to know. I don't want to alienate people before they have a chance to get to know me."

There were eleven people at the meeting. Lexie wondered if this was the regular group. She didn't want to press Savannah on too many details at the first meeting. Her body wire was set to record for four hours, give or take a few minutes either way.

The meeting was low-key. The group discussed some upcoming protests in the area. One girl reported on the security at the UCLA lab that housed primates for experimentation. The security system seemed extreme, and Lexie wondered if these people were sophisticated enough to bypass that level of security. The Badger guy didn't say anything throughout the whole meeting. Nick didn't discuss much during the meeting either but told the group that he was working on a few things and might need some help in a week or so.

Lexie mingled with the group following the meeting and sipped another cup of hot tea, trying to memorize all the names and faces at the meeting. At the conclusion of the evening, Savannah walked Lexie to her car. "I hope you weren't weirded out by anything you heard tonight," she said.

"Not at all. Thank you for inviting me. Do you think it would be okay if I attend the next meeting with you?"

"Sure," Savannah said. "That would be great."

Lexie arrived home and immediately found a yellow legal pad. She furiously scribbled notes from the events of the evening. She wrote so fast her handwriting was barely legible. She wanted to get as many details down on paper as quickly as possible. Names, faces, topics discussed, and the Badger/Nick relationship were just a few of the notes scratched out on the legal pad. When she was satisfied with her notes, she called Kate.

CHAPTER ELEVEN

Savannah

Three weeks had passed since Nick allowed Savannah to invite Lexie to the NWM meeting. One afternoon, Savannah and Lexie were recruited by Haley to help make signs for an upcoming demonstration. The three were in the campus courtyard painting the signs when a stylishly dressed group of sorority girls cheerfully strolled by. One of the sorority girls noticed Savannah and whispered something to the other girls, who looked at Savannah and laughed. Savannah's heart sank when she realized who the girls were: her former friends Cindy, Beth, and Julie.

"Go to hell, bitches," Haley yelled.

The sorority girls laughed and marched away.

"I hate those sorority bitches," Haley said.

"Me too," Lexie added.

Savannah stared at the ground.

"What's the matter, Savannah?" Lexie asked.

"Those girls . . . those girls used to be my friends. I was with them at the frat party when I first saw Nick. They were in my English class last semester."

"They were bitches then, and they're bitches now," Haley said. "Those sorority types are all the same. Just looking for a doctor husband so they can pop out a bunch of bratty kids who look and act like them."

"Tell us how you really feel," Lexie joked.

Haley laughed.

"I gave serious thought to rushing a sorority," Savannah said.

"You're not like them, Savannah," Lexie said. "You're an individualist."

"You don't have to always be friends with people who look like you," Haley said. "Take our friendship for example. You never would have been friends with me in high school because I look different."

Savannah looked at her paint covered hands. "You're right. I wouldn't have given you the time of day in high school. And that would've been wrong."

"Goes to show you that not everything is as it appears," Haley said.

"That's deep," Lexie said, chuckling.

"Shut up, smartass," Haley said. "If it weren't for me, Savannah, you might have ended up like one of those brainless sorority tramps. I saved you from that awful fate."

"You certainly did," Savannah acknowledged.

The three women laughed.

Savannah watched a group of yuppie students, all wearing Greek symbols, congregate across the courtyard. "In all seriousness, Haley, you did save me from that fate," Savannah said, pointing at the group. "My mom was a Tri Delta, so she wanted me to rush. I thought that college life was all parties and sorority functions, but then I met you. I realize now that there are bigger issues in the world besides what sorority to rush or which fraternity party to attend. I've changed for the better since being in college."

Haley put down her paintbrush and hugged Savannah.

Lexie cleared her throat and said, "You two want to be alone?"

"Are you jealous?" Savannah joked.

The three women went back to painting their demonstration signs.

"How come you didn't recruit Nick to help with the signs?" Lexie asked.

Savannah answered, "I haven't seen much of Nick since the last NWM meeting. He and Badger have been busy."

Savannah knew that Nick had been spending time with Badger. She figured that the two of them were planning something and wondered if they were going to involve her eventually. Savannah wasn't sure if she really wanted to be included, but she knew she would never refuse Nick if he asked for her help. Nick would involve her if and when he needed her. It was one of those need-to-know situations, and she would just have to be patient.

"What's Badger's story?" Lexie asked. "Does he have a girlfriend?"

Lexie knew that she had to make her questions not sound like an interrogation.

"Are you crushing on Badger?" Haley asked.

Lexie blushed.

"You are! You want Badger," Haley said.

"He's kind of cute in a scruffy way," Lexie said. "I'm

not crushing on him. I was just wondering if he had a girlfriend."

"Badger is an interesting dude," Haley said. "You might not be able to tell from his appearance, but he's brilliant. He graduated from Stanford on a full-ride."

"Wow, that's impressive," Lexie said.

"He's some kind of computer genius," Haley continued.

"I'd like the chance to get to know him," Savannah said. "I hope Nick brings him around more."

"He's shy, but maybe we can hook him up with Lexie," Haley said, throwing her arms around Lexie. "You two would make a cute couple."

"I didn't say I wanted to go out with Badger. I just asked if he had a girlfriend."

"Same thing," Savannah said.

"You two are killing me," Lexie said, faking exasperation.

The three finished making their signs, and Lexie returned home.

The next morning, Nick was waiting outside of Savannah's classroom after her last class of the day. She burst into smiles when she spotted his ratty Honda parked out front. Nick folded Savannah in his arms and squeezed.

"Hi ya, gorgeous," he whispered in her ear.

"It's good to see you. I've missed you so much."

"Wanna go for a ride?" Nick asked.

"Sure!"

They drove to the coast and took a walk along a stretch of deserted beach. The powdery sand stretched as far as Savannah could see.

Nick turned to Savannah, his expression more dark

and serious than usual. "Savannah, are you ready to take the next step with your activism?" he asked. "Before you answer, think about it carefully. Make sure you're truly ready before we have this next discussion. It's okay if you're not ready, but I need to know before I involve you any further."

Savannah felt a knot form in her stomach. Was she ready? She didn't want Nick to see how utterly terrified she felt. As if she had no control, she felt her head bobbing up and down in the affirmative. Her heart was answering for her without getting permission from her head.

"I need to hear you say it," Nick told her.

Her voice croaked a little as if she hadn't used it in a while. "Yes, Nick I'm ready. I'm more than ready."

"Okay," Nick continued. "What I'm about to tell you has to stay between you and me. You can't discuss it with anyone."

"I understand," Savannah agreed.

Nick nervously ran his hands through his hair. "Tomorrow night we're going to make those fuckers at UCLA pay for what they've done to those innocent animals in the lab. This is what I need you to do. I'll pick you up tomorrow night about ten. Pack a small backpack with plain black clothing. If you don't have a plain black shirt, take one of your black T-shirts and turn it inside out. Don't bring anything with your identity on it. Badger and I will provide everything else you'll need. Dress normally when you leave your dorm room and bring the backpack with you. Haley will be involved as well, but do not discuss anything with her. Someone may overhear your conversation, so avoid the urge to talk about it. Under no circumstances should you or Haley bring a cell phone; the feds can track those. Leave it turned on and in your dorm room."

"What about my driver's license or my student ID?" Savannah asked.

"You won't need them. Just stick about twenty dollars in your pocket and nothing else. Badger and I will go through everything with you tomorrow night. You still want to do this?"

"Yes. Absolutely. I won't let you down."

Nick smiled and threw his arm around Savannah's shoulders. They strolled along the beach, watching the sun fall from the sky. As the sun set and the sky turned the color of pink cotton candy, Savannah knew she would never love anyone as much as she loved Nick Harris.

Nick dropped Savannah off at her dorm. Haley was in their room stretched out on her bed with a bowl of popcorn and her history book.

"Hey, girl," Haley said as Savannah entered the room.

"Hi, Haley."

"Been with Nick?" Haley asked.

"Yep, we went for a walk on the beach."

Haley looked up from her book and made eye contact with Savannah, and they shared their secret with merely a stare. An entire unspoken conversation took place between them. Savannah always wanted a sister, and now she had one.

* * * * *

The next evening, Savannah and Haley, dressed in dark jeans, left their dorm room and were picked up down the street by Nick. They had their black, long-sleeved shirts in Haley's small backpack.

"You ladies look like you're ready to fuck somebody up," Nick commented as they crawled into his Honda.

"You'd better believe it, Nicholas darling," Haley commented.

Nick leaned over and gave Savannah a quick peck on the lips. "Hi, babe," he said as he gave her his "I want to fuck you now" expression.

"Hey, handsome," she responded.

"Is everybody clean?" he asked.

"Yep," Savannah responded. "No cell phones or IDs. Only a twenty-dollar bill in my pocket and the key to our dorm room."

"Good girl."

Nick drove to Phillip and Jeannette's house. "This is our alibi, girls. We were here playing Sequence and watching movies with Jeannette. Have you both seen *Men in Black*?"

"I have," Savannah stated.

"Me too," Haley added.

"Okay, then we watched *Men in Black*. I rented it earlier from Redbox, just in case anyone actually checks."

"Good thinking," Haley commented.

"When we get to the house, I'll go over the game plan. Badger will pick us up out back at exactly one o'clock. We have to be ready to roll out as he pulls up."

Nick parked his car in front of the house and had the movie in his hand as they went in the front door.

Jeannette greeted them with hugs and kisses. She had a platter of sandwiches, fruit, and veggies waiting for them on the counter. "Help yourselves to some food, troops."

"Thanks, Jeannette," Nick replied. "You're the best."

"What movie are we watching tonight?" she asked.

"*Men in Black*," Nick responded.

"Sounds good. I wouldn't mind watching it again," Jeannette stated. She took the movie from Nick.

"Where's Phillip?" Nick asked.

"He's at the store picking up some chips and beer."

"This is the story, ladies. We arrived, had some food, played Sequence, watched a movie, and had a little too much to drink, so we stayed a few extra hours to sober up before driving back to campus. That should buy us six or seven hours. Everyone got it?"

Savannah, Haley, and Jeannette all nodded in unison.

CHAPTER TWELVE

Savannah

Savannah, Haley, and Nick went to the back bedroom to prepare for the operation. Phillip returned home with chips and beer. He and Jeannette settled in the living room and watched the movie. They were careful not to disturb the mission preparation.

Nick unpacked a black bag that had been hidden under the bed. Inside were his black clothing, black ski masks, a pair of night vision binoculars, bolt cutters, three large hammers, four cans of red spray paint, and six handheld walkie-talkies. "Badger will have the rest of the supplies we need for tonight in the car," he told them.

Savannah and Haley changed into their solid black shirts. Savannah turned her long-sleeved Kings of Leon shirt inside out so the emblem didn't show. Nick pulled out a roll of duct tape. He taped up his boots and then taped both Savannah and Haley's tennis shoes.

"This is so we don't have to throw our shoes away at the end of the night. We don't want to leave shoe prints anywhere. Plus, the tape will hide the shoe insignias from any surveillance cameras."

Nick tossed each of them a pair of black gloves. "Try these on and see how they fit."

Savannah was impressed. Nick had thought of everything. He even managed to get her a small pair of gloves to fit her tiny hands. She wondered how many operations Nick had been part of. It gave her a sense of security to know Nick was so competent and organized.

"Are you okay, Savannah?" Nick asked.

Savannah tried to put on her most confident expression. "Sure, I'm fine. Just a little excited is all."

"Good." Nick smiled. "You'll be fine."

Nick spent the next hour giving Savannah a lesson on how to operate all the equipment. It was no surprise to Savannah that Haley already knew how to use everything.

"Savannah, you're the lookout. You'll stay outside the lab and watch for campus security. This is your walkie-talkie, but you must maintain radio silence unless someone approaches the lab. Understand?"

"Got it. Radio silence unless someone approaches the lab."

"Haley, you're part of the destruction team with me and Badger. We will destroy as many computers and as much laboratory equipment as we can in the allotted time. Anything we see that looks expensive, we'll destroy. The more money we cost these bastards, the more likely they are to shut down."

Haley nodded.

"Badger has arranged for another group to join us. We'll rally with them at the back of the lab and enter together.

They'll be responsible for liberating as many animals as possible. They'll bring crates and other equipment to remove the animals and take responsibility for the rescued animals."

"What happens to the animals after they're removed?" Savannah asked.

"The underground teams who liberate animals have a whole network of people who assist them with the animals, including veterinarians, animal sanctuaries, and private citizens. They handle the liberated animals with great care, especially if there are primates involved. Primates require special attention. If you think it's hard to find a home for a bunny, try finding a home for a chimpanzee."

"I guess I never gave a lot of thought about what happens to all the animals after they're liberated," Savannah said.

"It's not like we can take them home to our tiny dorm," Haley joked.

"The liberation group will arrive at the back of the lab simultaneously with us. They'll be in a large panel van. If all goes well, a girl who works at the lab will be waiting to give us access to the premises. Her boyfriend is some kind of computer genius with a background in security systems. He'll disable the security cameras at the back entrance where the vehicles will be parked. Everyone will be wearing ski masks and dark clothing, so we don't really give two shits about the cameras inside the lab. In fact, we want those fucking puppy killers to witness the destruction of their precious equipment. Any questions so far?"

Both Savannah and Haley shook their heads, so Nick continued with the plan. "Savannah, this is the important part. If the police show up, you warn us on the radio and then get the hell out of there. Take off on foot and don't come near the vehicles. Run as fast as you can, and dispose of the walkie-talkie as soon as possible. Use the twenty dollars in your pocket to get home."

Nick wrote a telephone number on a piece of scratch paper. "This is the telephone number for Daniel Thornton. He's a lawyer who handles cases for animal rights activists. Memorize the phone number or write it on your arm. If for any reason you get arrested, ask for your attorney and do not say anything to anybody. The police may even bring in the FBI, but don't let that scare you. Just remain silent and speak to no one but the attorney."

Savannah picked up a permanent marker and wrote the telephone number on her forearm. After the ink dried, she pulled her sleeve down to cover it.

Nick looked at the clock on the nightstand. It was nearly time to meet Badger. He had Savannah and Haley repeat their roles in the operation.

"Everyone ready?" he asked.

"Ready," Savannah replied.

"Let's roll," Haley added.

The three nodded to Jeannette and Phillip as they headed to the back door.

"Good luck, gang!" Jeannette hollered.

"Thanks," replied Nick. "See you soon."

Like clockwork, Badger rolled up in a nondescript car and picked the three up in the alley behind the house. Savannah and Haley hopped into the back seat while Nick jumped in the front passenger seat. The car reeked of gasoline.

"Are we ready to burn this bitch to the ground?" Badger asked.

Savannah's heart skipped a beat. She wondered if he was serious. After all, she barely knew Badger.

"Shut up, Badger," Nick said.

Badger seemed a little too comfortable driving over to UCLA. Using the rearview mirror, he smiled at Savannah. Two large black duffle bags sat in the back seat with Savannah and Haley. Savannah wanted to look in them but decided against it.

Nick turned around so he could face Savannah and Haley. "Savannah, we're going to drop you at your post first. There's a dark corner across from the lab where you'll be able to keep an eye out for security. Remember to maintain radio silence unless you need to warn us of an approaching threat. Both teams should be in and out of the lab in a little less than forty-five minutes. Don't forget, if this goes south and the police end up here, you run like hell."

"I will."

Badger was staring at Savannah in the rearview mirror. He had an ominous look as he told the group, "If any of us get arrested, remember: *no one talks, we all walk*. Not a word to the police or the fucking FBI!"

Something sinister was in his voice. Savannah had a bad feeling in the pit of her stomach.

"Once we drop you, do one quick radio check when you're in position."

"Got it," Savannah acknowledged.

"Haley, you grab one of the bags in the backseat and

toss me the other one when we get out."

"Okay," Haley confirmed.

"When we finish, we'll give the all clear signal on the radio. That's your cue, Savannah, to move across the street. We'll swing by and pick you up and clear out of here."

As they neared the corner where Savannah would be posted, Nick looked back and smiled at her. "You ready?"

"Definitely."

"Okay, get ready to jump out."

Savannah took one last look at her friends. "Good luck, guys."

Badger slowed down, and Savannah was out of the car in a flash. She found her spot just as Nick had described it.

Savannah pushed the button on the walkie-talkie and announced, "Red Team in position and needs a radio check."

She listened for confirmation.

"Blue Team reads Red Team loud and clear," she heard Nick's voice respond.

"Green Team is less than two minutes out and reads everyone loud and clear," an unknown male voice responded.

Nick's voice responded, "Ten-four. Begin radio silence."

Savannah thought she heard something, but realized it was her own thunderous heartbeat. *Calm down, Savannah.* She didn't know if she was scared or excited. *I wonder if this is what it feels like to be a Navy SEAL.* She could picture her twin doing this sort of stuff, but never herself. She looked at her watch; it was one forty-five. *With any luck, we'll be out of here in less than an hour. Just keep breathing.*

At her post, Savannah patiently watched for security.

She jumped at every noise. The minutes passed at a snail's pace. About forty minutes into the operation, Savannah's heart stopped when she heard the shrill, ear-piercing noise of a fire alarm. Her hands shook, and she pushed the button on the walkie-talkie. Her voice was an octave higher and cracking when she tried to reach Nick on the radio.

"Red Team to Blue Team."

Nothing.

"Red Team to Green Team."

Nothing. She tried again.

"Red Team to anyone."

She finally heard Nick's voice on the other end.

"Red Team, get out of here! Now! Go now!"

Savannah wanted to run, but her feet were frozen to the ground. Off in the distance, she heard the high-pitched sirens of fire trucks. She could see the glow of a fire coming from the lab. She willed herself to move, and move she did. She ran faster and harder than she had ever run in her life. She ran until her lungs betrayed her and she succumbed to the stitch in her side. She was clear of the UCLA campus, but wasn't actually sure where she was.

Savannah knew the first course of action was to get rid of the walkie-talkie and her gloves. She took off down an alley in search of a safe spot to toss the evidence. She smashed the walkie-talkie on the pavement and tossed the mangled mess in a large dumpster behind a dry cleaner. She removed her gloves and tossed them into the dumpster, too. It was almost two thirty in the morning, and she needed to figure out how to get back to her dorm.

Horrible thoughts were running through her head.

She wondered if Nick and Haley made it out. Were they trying to find their way home? Were they in jail? Were they injured or dead? She wanted more than anything to be safe and warm in her own bed. Pent-up emotions surfaced, and she burst into tears. She tried to stop, but it was as if a dam broke and a flood of emotions rushed out. She found a taxi parked near a section of neighborhood bars. She had to get through the night. The next day would be better. She was sure of it. Nick would straighten everything out.

CHAPTER THIRTEEN

Alexis

Lexie awoke to the blaring noise of her cell phone. She scrambled out of bed and grabbed her phone from her dresser.

"Hello," she croaked.

"Lexie, this is Adam. Have you heard what happened at UCLA?"

Lexie shook herself awake. "No, what happened?"

"There was an ALF direct action early this morning. A group of masked intruders broke into the lab, destroyed the computers and laboratory equipment, and set fire to the whole lab."

"Shit! How did they get past the security system?" Lexie asked.

"That's still unknown at this time. Lexie, someone was killed in the action."

"What? Holy shit! Who?"

"A security guard who was on duty in another part of the lab. He may have been responding to the commotion when he became trapped and couldn't get out of the building. We were told he was thirty-six years old and had three children, including a brand-new baby."

"Oh my God! That's terrible."

"Lexie, do you think this attack was perpetrated by your targets?"

"I don't know. I haven't heard talk of any plans for actions over at UCLA, but then again, you know how much my people hate UCLA. They wouldn't have mentioned it to me unless they planned to use me in the attack. Has it been on the news yet?"

"It's on right now. They have a news helicopter filming the firefighters on the scene."

Lexie was already in front of her TV flipping through the channels. Sure enough, the story was breaking on all the local stations. The news was going back and forth between what was happening in real time and clips shot earlier that morning with flames shooting out of the building.

"Since this is all over the morning news, you need to reach out to *your* people and see what kind of response you get."

"I can do that. Normally none of those people will talk much over the phone, but Savannah might be new enough to the movement to talk. I'll try to get her to meet me for coffee, and we can talk in person."

"Just remember to record everything," Adam warned. "This might be our only shot to get these people if they are involved in some way. They're going to be over-the-top paranoid."

"Yeah, I know. I'll reach out to Savannah and see what happens. Let me know whatever else you find out on your end. I'll call you as soon as I make contact."

"This happened on your watch, Lexie, so we need to get to the bottom of this."

A surge of anger hit Lexie.

"Why are you so sure that my people were involved in this crime?"

"It stinks of NWM, that's why."

"I'll let you know what I find out," Lexie seethed.

CHAPTER FOURTEEN

Savannah

Savannah made it back to her dorm room shortly after three in the morning. Haley wasn't there. She checked her cell phone, but there were no messages. She wanted to call Nick but knew she shouldn't. She looked down and realized she had forgotten to remove the duct tape from her running shoes. She ripped off the tape, placed it in a plastic bag, and threw it in the bathroom garbage. The cleaning service would be by in a couple of hours, and they removed the trash from the bathrooms daily. She checked herself to ensure she had disposed of all possible evidence that could be used against her. *Please call me, Nick. I need to hear your voice and know you're safe.*

Savannah washed her face and crawled into bed, but sleep eluded her. She replayed the events of the night in her head. She was convulsing from the cold; or was it fear? What had she done? What had Nick and Haley done? Since there was no possible way she could sleep, she turned on the TV and flipped through the channels. She stopped on the NBC channel showing late breaking news with the caption: "Fire At UCLA Lab. One Confirmed Dead." Savannah's throat seized shut; she was unable to breathe. Her heart thumped like a bass drum. *Holy fuck! Someone's dead.* Her first thought was Nick. *Was it Nick?* She then remembered it was Nick's voice on the radio. *No, it couldn't be Nick. Haley? Could it be Haley? No, Nick would take care of Haley. Jesus! Who was dead?* Then she saw it, the ambulance parked near the fire engine. She saw the gurney holding a body bag being loaded into the ambulance. Without any notice, she vomited on the floor in front of the TV. She grabbed a nearby trashcan and heaved again into the can. Her stomach seized, and she continued to vomit until she had nothing left in her stomach. Bile burned the back of her throat. The reality of what had happened set in, and her body convulsed. She stared at her cell phone. *Please ring. Please ring. Please ring!* She needed to talk to Nick. *He will call*, she told herself. *He will call soon.*

Savannah grabbed a towel and some cleaner. After she cleaned up the floor, she rinsed out the trashcan in the bathroom shower. She checked her cell phone again to make sure the ringer was turned up. *Please call, Nick. Oh, please call!* She checked the news again, but they were only showing the earlier footage. There was still no news regarding who died in the fire. Savannah crawled into her bed and then she did something she hadn't done in a long time. She folded her hands together and prayed.

CHAPTER FIFTEEN

Alexis

It was almost eight in the morning, so Lexie figured it was late enough to try to contact Savannah. She pulled out the digital recorder she used to record telephone conversations. Lexie turned on the device and recorded her preamble, stating her undercover employee number instead of her real name. She added the date, time, and who she was calling. Lexie placed the call to Savannah, but she didn't answer. Lexie left a short message.

"Hey girl, it's Lexie. Just saw some crazy shit on the news. Want to meet for coffee or lunch? I don't feel like going to class today."

She hung up her phone and wondered what her next course of action should be. She decided to grab a body recorder, in case she ran into one of her targets, and go for a walk over on the Boardwalk.

On her way to the Boardwalk, Kate called her.

"Hey, Lexie, how are you doing with all of this?"

"Still trying to wrap my brain around it." Lexie chewed on her fingernail. "I'm confused because ALF actions are usually nonviolent. They claim to take all precautions not to harm any animals, human or otherwise. Why the sudden violence?"

"I wish I knew," Kate said. "It does seem to deviate from their MO."

"Do we have any more information about the fire?" Lexie asked.

"Yeah, it looks likes a security camera picked up two vehicles involved in the action, an older model, dark-colored Toyota Camry and a gray panel van. We're working with the UCLA police to enhance the surveillance video to try to get the license plates. The video is pretty grainy, but it looks like three people arrived in the Toyota and five people arrived in the van. The people in the van carried in crates, probably to rescue the lab animals before they destroyed all the lab equipment. We're working with UCLA and LAPD to develop leads. I'll keep you in the loop."

"Thanks, I appreciate it. Hey, Kate, do you really think my people are involved in this?"

"I don't know, Lexie, but if I had to guess, I would say yes."

"Adam blames me for the fire."

"What? Why do you say that?" Kate asked.

"He told me this all happened on my watch."

"That's ridiculous, Lexie. Adam is a jackass. The fire isn't your fault, and he had no right to say that to you."

"It did happen on my watch," Lexie said.

"We aren't even sure that the fire was set by our targets," Kate said. "It might be a whole different terrorist cell. Keep your eyes and ears open. Let me know before you do any face-to-face meets with any of the targets."

"I will," Lexie promised.

"I'll call you later today, or earlier, if I learn anything further."

Lexie wandered past Phillip and Jeannette's house on her way to the Boardwalk. She noticed Nick's car was parked in front of the house. It seemed odd his car would be there so early in the morning. She decided it warranted a call to Kate, who answered on the first ring.

"Hey, Kate, I just walked past the activists' house, and Nick Harris's car is parked in front of the house. It seems a little weird that his car would be there this early in the morning."

"Hmm, that does seem strange. I'll make a note of it. In fact, I'm not far away from the area, so I might swing by and take a quick photo and document it for the case file. You never know when something like that could be import-ant. Good thinking to do the walk-by."

CHAPTER SIXTEEN

Savannah

Savannah jumped out of her skin when her phone rang. She had fallen asleep with the phone in her hand. She almost answered it before noticing Lexie's name on the screen. She badly wanted to talk to someone, anyone, but decided she had better not answer it until she spoke with Nick. She let the call go to voice mail. The phone chimed to indicate that she had a voice message. She listened to the message from Lexie. It was comforting to hear her friend's voice. She desperately wanted to call her back, but she was scared she might say something she shouldn't.

Savannah decided she should act as normal as possible, so she showered and put on fresh clothes. She had a ten o'clock chemistry class she couldn't afford to miss. Maybe chemistry class would help pass the time until she heard from either Nick or Haley. On the way to class, she texted Lexie. *Heading to chemistry. Maybe we can meet for lunch.* A few minutes later, her phone chimed. She read the text from Lexie. *Cool. Text me after your class.*

Savannah sat in the last row with her phone on vibrate

in her lap. She was prepared to grab it and run out the door as soon as it rang. She must have checked her watch a hundred times during the ninety-minute class. The class finally ended, and Savannah was the first one out the door. She couldn't wait one more minute. She had to see a friendly face. She picked up her phone and texted Lexie. *Lunch. Real Food Daily at one?* A few moments later Lexie texted back, *See you there.*

CHAPTER SEVENTEEN

Alexis

Lexie arrived at Real Food Daily a few minutes before one o'clock and was seated at a corner table. The savory smells emanating from the kitchen made her mouth water. She ordered an acai berry tea and quickly went to the restroom, where she activated her body recorder. Lexie returned to the table and saw Savannah enter the front door. She jumped up and gave Savannah a big hug.

"Hey, girl, how are you?" Lexie asked.

"I'm fine. How are you?"

Lexie smiled. "I'm good. I'm really glad you texted me. This is my favorite restaurant, and I've been dying for a wet burrito."

"Is that an acai berry iced tea?" Savannah asked in a reedy voice.

"Yeah. I'm addicted to the tea here."

The waitress came over and took their order. Lexie initially kept the conversation casual, but after a few minutes, she lowered her voice and asked, "Have you seen the news?"

The color in Savannah's face drained, and her body

became rigid. "I saw the fire on the news this morning before I left for class," Savannah said. "Have they said who was killed in the fire?"

"I don't think the police have said." Lexie had to remember she had inside information that had not been released. If she forgot and talked about what she knew, her cover would be blown.

Savannah fiddled with the zipper on her hoodie.

"Are you okay?" Lexie asked.

"Yeah, I'm fine, why do you ask?"

"You seem a little off-kilter."

"I'm fine. I just had a rough time in my chemistry class. I'm still trying to shake off a bad grade. Plus this fire at the lab is terrible. I hope none of the animals were injured or killed. It upsets me to think of all those poor animals in the lab during the fire. They had to be terrified."

"I know. The news hasn't mentioned the animals in the lab, and they probably won't ever mention them. Any idea how the fire started?" Lexie asked.

Savannah fidgeted in her chair. She tugged at the sleeves of her hoodie, hiking them up her forearms. "I haven't heard anything," she replied.

Lexie noticed what looked like numbers written on Savannah's forearm.

"Did you get a tattoo?" Lexie asked.

"What?"

"Your arm." Lexie pointed at the numbers.

Savannah quickly pulled down her sleeves. "That's nothing. It's ah . . . It's notes. I sort of cheated on a quiz."

"Are you sure you're all right, Savannah?"

"I'll be okay. I'm not feeling well today. I think I might need to go lie down. I'm sorry to ruin our lunch date, but I think I need to cut lunch short and go back to the dorm and rest."

"Do you need me to drive you home?" Lexie asked.

"No, I can drive myself home, but thanks for asking."

"I don't mind," Lexie added.

"I know you don't. And thank you, but I'll be fine. I just need to get home and get a little rest."

Savannah asked for her food order to go. The waitress brought her order in a paper bag. Savannah was digging in her backpack for money when Lexie intervened.

"I've got this one. Don't worry about it; you go home and get some rest."

"You don't have to do that," Savannah said. "My wallet is in here somewhere."

"No worries," Lexie said. "It's my treat."

"That's sweet. Thank you."

"No problem. I hope you feel better soon. I'll call you if I find out any information on the fate of the lab animals," Lexie added.

"Thank you," Savannah said. "And I'll do the same if I hear anything."

Savannah slung her oversized backpack over one shoulder and took off out the door carrying her to-go bag. Lexie sat alone and ate her burrito and had a second acai berry tea. She paid the bill and stopped off at the restroom to turn off the body recorder.

* * * * *

Lexie called Kate on her way home. "Want to meet me at the apartment?" she asked.

"Sounds good. I'll give it a little time and then head over."

Kate waited about a half hour, and then she parked down the street from Lexie's apartment and walked over. Lexie was waiting for her and quickly opened the door.

"How'd it go?" Kate asked.

"I didn't get the smoking gun, but something is definitely not right with Savannah."

"What do you mean?"

"Well, she was visibly upset and looked like she hadn't slept in a week. She couldn't make it through lunch and had to get her food to go. She claimed she wasn't feeling well, but it looked like a case of the nerves to me."

"What did she say?"

"She said she got a bad grade in chemistry and was upset about it. Then she said she was worried about the animals in the lab. When I first brought up the fire, I thought she was going to pass out. I swear, Kate, the girl was white as a sheet."

"Really? That's interesting. What else?"

"She didn't seem like herself. She was nervous and jittery and had numbers written on her left forearm."

"What kind of numbers?" Kate asked.

"I don't know. It might have been a phone number, but I couldn't get a good look at it. When I brought it up, she said it was nothing and pulled her sleeve back down. I hate to say it, but I think she was either involved or knows something. I have my footage ready for you to download."

"I'll see if we can enhance the video and make out the numbers on her arm. I brought you a new recorder, just in case you have a meet before I get this one downloaded. You need to have a recorder with you whenever you are out and about. You never know when she may call you and want to talk. I think Savannah needs a friend right now, and hopefully she'll confide in you."

"Jesus, Kate, I think that poor girl really knows something."

"You may have stumbled onto our group of arsonists, and Savannah is definitely the weak link. I'm not sure if it's luck, or if you're the best damn undercover agent in the FBI."

"I'll go with the best damn undercover theory."

They both laughed as Kate packed up the body recorder and placed it in her purse. "Oh, I forgot to tell you something," Kate said. "LAPD has been checking all the video cameras within a two-mile radius of the arson. They found a video from an alley where a female tossed what looks like some kind of equipment in a dumpster. She also tossed a pair of gloves. The FBI Evidence Response Team was dispatched to the dumpster to gather the evidence."

"Wow! That's huge."

"I haven't seen the video yet. I've been told it's grainy, but you can definitely tell it's a female tossing the items. The lab was still on fire when the video was taken, so it has to be one of the perpetrators in the video."

Lexie ran her hands through her hair. She was shaken and surprised by the news.

"Stay by your phone, and I'll call you with any updates," Kate said.

"I will. I'll give Savannah a call later tonight to check on her."

"I'll get out of your hair and let you have some peace."

"Actually, if you aren't doing anything, would you like to stay for some tea?" Lexie asked. "I'm a little wound up, and it would be nice to have some company. That is, if you aren't in the middle of something else."

"Sure, I'd love to stay. As your contact agent, you're always my first priority, Lexie. Got any cookies to go with the tea?"

Lexie laughed. "Of course I do. Two kinds, in fact."

Lexie fixed a pot of tea, and the two women enjoyed tea and cookies together. Neither brought up work for the next hour.

* * * * *

Before going to bed, Lexie tried calling Savannah. The call went straight to voice mail. "Hey girl, it's Lexie. Hope you're feeling better. I'll check in on you tomorrow."

CHAPTER EIGHTEEN

Savannah

Savannah sat on the bed, her textbook open. She had read the same paragraph several times and had no idea what it said. She examined her ragged fingernails and decided to go to Phillip and Jeannette's house. She grabbed her purse and was nearly knocked over when Haley burst through the door. Savannah had never in her life been so glad to see another human being.

"Oh my God! Are you okay?" she squealed.

"Shhh, I'm fine," Haley reassured her.

"Where's Nick?" Savannah asked.

"He's okay. Still hiding, but he's fine. He'll come see you tonight."

"Are you sure you're okay? I was worried sick about you and the others. Tell me what happened."

"I shouldn't tell you anything. The less you know, the better."

"That's not fair, Haley. I'm just as involved as you and Nick. I was there too."

"You know the rules, Savannah. I can't talk about it."

"Fuck the rules!" Savannah said, grabbing Haley. "I was there. You can't cut me out of this. Not after what you've put me through. Tell me what happened."

"Okay. Okay. Lower your voice. Someone might hear us. We'll talk about this once and only once. Understand?"

"I do."

"Let's go outside. I don't want anyone to overhear us."

Haley looped her arm through Savannah's arm, and the two walked to the open courtyard and sat down. Haley looked around to ensure that there were no people to overhear their conversation. "Why do you need to know? You're better off not knowing the details."

"I need to know what happened after I left," Savannah said.

"Why? It's better for all of us if you forget about it."

"I can't forget about it, Haley. Someone died in the fire. I need to know what happened."

Haley took a deep breath and sighed loudly. "After we dropped you off at your lookout point, we met the other team at the rendezvous spot. Everything was going as planned. Our lab contact met us and got us into the lab. Once inside, the liberation team gathered the animals and placed them in containers. Nick, Badger, and I smashed the lab equipment and computers. I left to help the liberation team load up the animals. Nick was riled up, but Badger was calm as a cucumber. A little too calm, in my opinion. He and Nick were destroying the equipment in one of the other rooms when I heard someone yell, 'We're going to burn this bitch to the ground.' I thought it was someone goofing around, but suddenly I smelled smoke. Nick came running in and made the other team get out with whatever animals they had in their containers. We had to run to get out of there alive. The fire alarm and sprinkler system went off, but the fire was already raging when we hit the door to the alley where the car was parked. Nick threw Badger in the backseat and drove us out of the area. We ditched the car and hid out until it was safe to return to town. Nick decided it was best for everyone involved if Badger left and went into hiding."

Savannah's eyes were wide and she made several attempts to speak, but no words came out.

"Are you all right?" Haley asked.

Tears welled up in Savannah's blue eyes. She could no longer control the rush of emotion. Her body convulsed, and she cried uncontrollably.

"Holy shit, Savannah, everything is going to be fine." Haley grabbed Savannah and hugged her. "Take a breath girl; everything is going to be okay."

"I was so worried. The police haven't said who died in the fire. I was thinking all kinds of horrible thoughts."

"It's okay, Savannah. We're all okay. I'm okay, Nick is okay, you're okay. We just need to hold it together and stick to our stories. This will all blow over soon enough."

Savannah slowly caught her breath. Her mascara had run down her face, and she knew she probably looked like a raccoon. Haley dug a Kleenex out of her jacket pocket and wiped the mascara from Savannah's cheeks.

"I'm sorry. I don't know what came over me."

"That's okay. You've been sitting here all by yourself not knowing what happened. We should have figured out a way to get word to you sooner. I forgot this was your first mission."

"I'm so glad you and Nick weren't injured. What on earth was Badger thinking when he decided to burn the lab down? Did Nick know he was going to do that?" Savannah asked.

"*No!* Absolutely not. He was so mad at Badger. I don't think I've ever seen Nick that mad as long as I've known him."

"If all of the activists made it out alive, who was killed in the action?" Savannah asked.

"I don't know," Haley replied. "Nick has been trying to find out through some of his contacts but hasn't had any luck. Guess we'll have to find out from the TV news like everyone else."

* * * * *

Savannah studied while Haley took a much-needed nap. Savannah's cell rang. She quickly grabbed it, expecting to see Nick's name, but was saddened to see Lexie's name instead. She answered the phone and walked out of the dorm room so she wouldn't wake Haley.

"Hey, Lexie. How are you?"

"I'm fine, how are you?" Lexie asked.

"Oh, I'm doing much better."

"That's good. I wanted to check on you, because you seemed pretty overwhelmed at lunch today."

"Thank you. I'm doing much better. I've been in bed

most of the day, sipping soda and studying chemistry."

"Is there anything you need?" Lexie asked.

"Oh, that's nice of you, but I'm okay. I think I have a stomach bug. I'll be fine in a day or so."

"All right, well I just wanted to check on you. Promise me you'll call if you need anything at all."

"I will. I promise."

When Savannah re-entered the dorm room, Haley was standing in the middle of the room, her arms crossed, wearing an angry expression. "Who were you talking to?" she demanded.

Savannah was shocked at Haley's rudeness. "I was talking to Lexie. Why?"

"What the hell did you tell her?" Haley seemed barely able to control her fury.

"Nothing! Do you really think I would tell anyone about what happened?" Savannah was so angry that she felt the blood rush to her face. She did not want to cry and show any weakness to Haley.

"Why did you walk out of the room to talk to her?" Haley demanded.

"Because I was trying to be a good roommate and not wake you up. Why are you acting like such a bitch?"

Savannah pushed past Haley and stormed over to her desk. She slammed her palms down on the desk, and then turned to face Haley.

"While you and Nick were out playing hide-and-seek, I was stuck here trying to go about my everyday business, so as to not look suspicious. Part of my everyday business was going to class and chatting with friends. I couldn't just ignore Lexie when she called me, not without her wondering what was up with me, so before you go accusing me of telling the world our business, maybe you should take a fucking minute and remember we're in this together."

Haley uncrossed her arms, walked over to her bed, and took a seat. "I'm sorry, Savannah. I guess I'm a little on edge. Forgive me. It's so hard to trust anyone in this movement. For a moment there, I forgot I was talking to you. I really am sorry."

Savannah sat down next to Haley. She draped her arm around her shoulder and leaned her head against Haley's head. "It's okay. No worries."

Haley reached around and hugged Savannah. As they were hugging, Nick walked in the door.

"Are we going to have a sordid love triangle?" Nick joked.

Savannah sprung off the bed and nearly knocked Nick over as she leaped into his arms.

"Wow! Now that's a greeting," Nick exclaimed. "Maybe I should almost die every week."

He didn't have time to make any more jokes, because Savannah was frantically kissing him. He kissed her back, almost to the point of pain.

"Okay, enough!" Haley said. "I'm still in the room."

Nick and Savannah stopped kissing, and as if they read each other's minds, they both jumped on top of Haley.

"Threesome!" Nick yelled.

All three were laughing like little children at Christmas. It was the first time that they had laughed in a long time.

"How'd you get into our dorm?" Savannah asked.

"The security here is not exactly Fort Knox," Nick said,

smiling.

"Do you want something to eat or drink?" Haley asked, opening the tiny refrigerator.

"I'm starving! Let me take you ladies out for dinner," Nick said.

Nick had already picked up his car from Phillip and Jeannette's house, so he drove to the restaurant. They were careful not to discuss the fire or anything related to animal rights in public. Savannah barely touched her food because her stomach was in turmoil. She couldn't stop thinking about that person in the body bag. Someone was dead because of them. The three engaged in polite small talk. It all seemed ridiculous in light of what they had just been through, but it filled the silence, and if anyone was listening to their conversation, they wouldn't have heard anything suspicious.

CHAPTER NINETEEN

Alexis

Lexie's cell phone woke her bright and early. *Shit,* she thought. *Who would be calling me at this hour?* She picked up the phone and saw Kate's name. "Hello," Lexie croaked.

"Sorry to wake you, but the powers that be want to have a meeting this morning, and they want you present for it."

"They want me to come to the office? I thought that I was supposed to be limiting my time around FBI personnel."

"I know. They're having the meeting at the JTTF. You can leave your car someplace away from the office, and I'll swing by and pick you up. I'll bring you in through the garage like we did the first day."

"What time?" Lexie asked.

"Ten o'clock sharp. Don't be late, because I think the special agent in charge is going to be there."

"Oh, great," Lexie sighed. "Just what I need, some pompous ass putting his two cents into our investigation. Between the SAC being there and Adam blaming me for the fire, this should be a fun meeting."

"Wow, somebody got up on the wrong side of the bed."

Kate laughed.

"I know. I'm sorry. I don't mean to be taking it out on you. I'll be there with bells on."

"Let's do lunch after the meeting. Just the two of us," Kate added.

"Sounds good. I'll hit the shower then come your way."

"Okay, see you a little before ten."

Lexie deleted the call from her call log, tossed the cell phone down, and covered her head with her pillow. This meeting was going to suck.

* * * * *

Lexie parked her car at a nearby grocery store and jumped in the passenger seat of Kate's sedan. She reclined the seat so she was out of sight.

"I have the feeling this is going to be one giant circle jerk," Lexie said.

"You're probably correct with that assessment."

Kate parked the car in the garage, and the two entered the office from the back.

"Try to behave yourself, Lexie."

"I'll try, but I can't make any promises."

Lexie whispered in Kate's ear, "Someone needs to tell all these morons this is a covert offsite and they really shouldn't look like a bunch of FBI agents when they come here."

Lexie noticed an older man making his way in her direction.

"That's the SAC coming this way," Kate informed her.

"Glad you told me so I don't say anything stupid."

The SAC approached Lexie and extended his hand. "Hello, Alexis. We haven't had the pleasure of meeting yet. I'm Jeff Rhodes."

"Hello, sir," Lexie responded.

"I understand from Mike and Adam you're doing a wonderful job. I want to personally thank you for coming out here and giving us a hand with this case."

"It's my pleasure, sir. I appreciate the opportunity to work a full-time undercover operation. It's been a great experience so far."

"That's good to hear. Is there anything you need from me?"

"No, sir, I have everything I need right now."

The SAC walked off, and Kate made her way back to Lexie.

"You sure disappeared quickly," quipped Lexie.

"I make it my business to avoid the brass of any agency."

"Good policy."

"What did the SAC have to say?"

"Nothing much. Typical upper management . . . promise the world, but deliver nothing."

Everyone took their seats. The SAC took control of the meeting and thanked everyone for coming. After a quick introduction, he turned the meeting over to Mike.

"I think most of you know me, but in case we haven't met, I'm Supervisory Special Agent Mike Gregory. I supervise the domestic terrorism squad here at the JTTF. The FBI, UCLA police, and LAPD are jointly working to solve this horrible arson that claimed the life of an innocent party."

It was obvious that Mike was accustomed to giving case presentations. He showed photos of the UCLA lab arson in his Powerpoint presentation and gave the known facts. Mike explained the accelerant used for the fire was gasoline. He described the arsonist as unsophisticated. He showed a grainy surveillance video of the back door area of the lab. Two vehicles, a van and a car, arrived within a minute of each other. Masked individuals exited both vehicles but the quality of the video was so bad it was impossible to tell much about the people. Lexie couldn't tell if they were men or women in the video. The license plates on both vehicles were unreadable, but Lexie assumed they were probably stolen plates.

Mike showed a second video that LAPD had recovered from an alley surveillance camera a couple of miles away from the crime scene. The video showed what appeared to be a female smashing a piece of equipment and discarding it and her gloves in a dumpster. He told the group that the FBI Evidence Recovery Team recovered the items and sent them to the FBI laboratory for analysis.

"Based on the level of security at the lab, the FBI and the UCLA police are investigating the possibility this was an inside job," Mike explained. He showed photos of a badly charred body. "This is our victim: Brian Woods, a thirty-four-year-old father of three. Brian was working in the south side of the lab when the fire broke out. It appears he ran in the direction of the fire, probably to render assistance to anyone working late at the lab or possibly to try to save the animals. Woods became trapped and was unable to make his way out of the burning building.

Agents interviewed his wife and discovered he wasn't supposed to be working the night of the fire. He traded shifts with a coworker so that the coworker could go to his son's ball game. We have an agent checking into the coworker's background. We're also checking the backgrounds of all individuals who had access to the lab."

Mike showed a photograph of Brian Woods with his wife and children. A knot tightened in Lexie's stomach. The victim had a name and a face now. This innocent man would never return home to his three small children.

Following Mike's presentation, the group participated in an investigative strategy session. Lexie was stunned at the *suggestions* that people were offering. Trying not to show her annoyance, she smiled and nodded at most of the ideas. The only person who seemed to have a real understanding of the extremist security culture was the FBI intelligence analyst, Derrick Dorn. Derrick was a soft-spoken domestic terrorism subject matter expert. During the group discussion, Derrick made eye contact with Lexie and rolled his eyes, which made Lexie smile.

The meeting adjourned and Kate grabbed Lexie by the arm. "Let's get out of here."

"I'm two steps ahead of you," Lexie told her.

After they were away from the office, Lexie vented. "What a ridiculous dog and pony show. Everyone in that room seemed to have an opinion on how we should be running this investigation. What a bunch of jackasses."

Kate started laughing.

"What are you laughing at?" Lexie asked.

"You. Surely you've been in the bureau long enough to

realize most people in management are idiots. They didn't get to the top because they were outstanding investigators. They blue flamed to the top, and none of the people in that room, with the exception of Adam, has ever made a case in his career. To them, it's all about the title they hold, not the work. It's no different in my agency," Kate explained.

"I guess you're right, but it's annoying when people who don't have a clue what's going on try to tell me how to do my job. Did you hear the moron who suggested that I pretend to be a bomb expert? They act like they know more about these people than I do. They don't know the first fucking thing about them or their way of life." Lexie took a breath.

"Boy, you are wound up!" Kate laughed.

"I know! I had to sit in that stupid meeting with my mouth shut, listening to all those ridiculous ideas for so long, when what I wanted to do was stand up and tell each and every one of them they were all full of shit."

"Maybe we should get you a margarita instead of lunch."

Lexie laughed. "I guess I sound like a raving lunatic."

"Nope, you sound like a frustrated FBI agent just trying to do her job."

"Kate, sometimes I wonder if I made the right career decision."

"What do you mean?"

"I joined the FBI to make a difference. To help keep our nation safe."

"That's what you're doing, Lexie."

"Is it?" Lexie said. "The bureau is top-heavy with managers, and there's so much red tape involved in every decision."

"You're simply frustrated, and that's understandable."

"I don't think that's it. These animal activists that I've befriended seem so . . . I don't know, real. They have a mission in life, and they're passionate about that mission."

Kate gave Lexie a sideways look. "Their passion caused the death of an innocent person. You can't lose sight of that fact."

"I know. But what if that was a mistake? What if they didn't mean for that to happen?"

"We could *what if* this topic to death, but that fact is, Brian Woods, a father of three, is dead."

"It's not so black-and-white," Lexie said.

"It *is* black-and-white, Lexie. You're in the best position to find who set the fire and gather the evidence. It's our job to find the perpetrators and bring them to justice. It's not our job to decide if they were right or wrong."

Lexie sighed. "You're right. I'm being weird."

"You have to kick it into high gear now," Kate said. "All eyes are on you. The fire ratcheted up this investigation, so Adam is going to be under a severe amount of pressure to produce results. We can't keep the bureaucrats at bay forever."

Lexie rested her head against the car window.

"What else is bothering you?" Kate asked.

Lexie wanted to tell Kate that she felt like she was betraying her only friends, but instead said, "I don't know. Maybe I'm just lonely. I underestimated the amount of alone time I would have on this assignment."

"You need to tell me when you're having these feelings. It's normal for an undercover agent to feel isolated and alone. My job is to support you and to help you when you're struggling. You have to trust me."

"I do trust you. And I appreciate everything that you do for me. It hasn't gone unnoticed how much interference you run between me and the front office."

"No worries, girl. That's what I'm here for: to keep you sane in an insane world."

CHAPTER TWENTY

Savannah

Savannah was sitting on her bed watching the morning news when Haley came back from the shower. Savannah had been crying.

"What's wrong?" Haley asked.

"On the news they showed the person killed in the fire. He was a security guard with three small children."

Haley sat down on the bed next to Savannah.

"We killed him," Savannah sobbed.

"Pull yourself together. We didn't kill him. He was a casualty of war. It's regrettable, but sometimes innocent people die in war."

Savannah couldn't believe her ears. "Do you seriously believe that?" she snapped. "He died because of what we did."

Haley took a deep breath and turned toward Savannah. "Listen to me. We did not kill that man. It was an accident. If anyone is to blame, it's the vivisectionists who work in that awful lab hacking up innocent animals in the name of science. We didn't set out to hurt anyone. In fact, we were trying to save as many lives as possible from the lab."

Savannah was still crying when Haley reached over and wrapped her arms around her. "We're going to be fine. You need to quit thinking about it. We have to stay strong together. Remember the motto, 'Nobody talks, and everybody walks.' We're going to take care of one another, and we'll be fine."

The words didn't make Savannah feel any better. Her insides were in knots.

"Are you okay?" Haley asked.

"I will be," Savannah answered. "I guess I need to quit watching the news."

"Things will get easier," Haley promised.

"What about Badger?" Savannah asked.

"What do you mean?" Haley asked.

"I mean what will happen to Badger? He was the one who got us into this mess. He was the psycho who started the fire and almost killed all of you."

"He's underground, where he'll stay until all the heat clears. No one knows where he goes to hide out. Probably in Oregon. How about if I buy you breakfast?" Haley offered.

"Thanks, but I have to be in class in an hour. I can't afford to miss any more classes this semester." Savannah covered her eyes. "My parents are not going to be happy with my grades. I need to get serious about studying and lessen my activist activities."

Savannah got up and gathered her clothes.

"Chin up, girl," Haley called out.

Savannah gave Haley the thumbs-up sign without turning around. She didn't want Haley to see she was crying again. Savannah went into the bathroom and texted Lexie, *Want to have coffee today?*

Savannah was throwing on her clothes when her phone buzzed and showed a text from Lexie. *Sure. When and where? I'm free all day.*

Savannah had already planned to skip her morning classes, so she texted back, *Coffee Bean on Main St. in Santa Monica? I can be there in an hour.* Savannah slapped on a little blush and some lipstick. Her phone buzzed again with the answer, *Perfect, see you then.*

Savannah grabbed her backpack so Haley would think she was going to class. She needed to see a friendly face and knew Lexie would fill the bill. Haley was in the bathroom when Savannah left the dorm, so she hollered goodbye through the door. She didn't wait around for a response. She headed out the door and made a beeline to her car.

After Savannah left the dorm, Haley came out of the bathroom and sent Nick an encrypted message stating, *We need to meet. Alone. We might have a problem with S.*

CHAPTER TWENTY-ONE

Alexis

With shaking hands, Lexie punched in the numbers to call Kate.

"Hey there, girl," Kate answered. "What's new?"

"Holy shit, Kate, I think this might be it!"

"What it?" Kate asked.

"*The* it!" Lexie exclaimed. "Savannah just texted me for coffee. I know she has morning classes today, so something must be up for her to want to skip her classes and meet me. I have a weird feeling she'll want to talk about what happened at the lab."

"That's wonderful, Lexie! You might be right. Take a breath, and let's talk this through for a minute."

"I have a button camera ready to go," Lexie stated.

"Good girl. Where are you meeting her?"

"At the Coffee Bean on Main Street in Santa Monica," Lexie responded.

"Outstanding. I'll be in the area. There are tons of places I can blend in around the Coffee Bean. If she starts to talk, remember to let her. The more she says on tape the better. Is she coming alone?"

"I assume so. She didn't mention anyone else coming."

"Okay, good luck. Text or call me when you're clear," Kate instructed.

"Will do."

"And Lexie," Kate added. "I know you like Savannah, but keep in mind the mission. These activists killed a human being."

"I know. It's weird because part of me doesn't want Savannah to be involved in this mess, but part of me wants to solve the case and bring the culprits to justice. I'm torn."

"It's a tough position to be in, but ultimately you have to do your job."

"I know and I will. I'm an FBI agent first and foremost."

Lexie checked her equipment one last time and left her apartment. When she pulled up to the Coffee Bean, she saw Savannah's car parked down the street. After parking, Lexie activated her body wire while in the car. When she was sure everything was working properly, she walked to the coffee shop.

Savannah was seated at a corner table and had a coffee sitting in front of her. *Perfect*, Lexie thought. *Couldn't have picked a better table myself.* She waved at Savannah and indicated that she was going to get a coffee. Lexie grabbed a large vanilla soy latte and joined Savannah.

"Hey! How are you?" Lexie asked.

Savannah got up and hugged Lexie. "Better than the last time you saw me." Her voice sounded ragged.

"I was worried about you."

"It was just a twenty-four-hour stomach bug. I'm feeling

much better now."

"How's chemistry class? Are you doing any better in it?" Lexie asked.

"That's a giant NO. I seem to have a mental block when it comes to that freaking class. I can't understand the Chinese professor. He sounds like he just got off the boat. I swear I don't think he's even speaking English. I'm majoring in cinematic arts, film, and television production. Why do I even need chemistry?"

Lexie laughed. "I have an instructor from India who I can't understand. Since you and I are both from the South, maybe it's a Southern thing."

Savannah laughed and almost choked on her coffee. "You might be right."

Savannah shifted nervously in her chair and twirled a piece of her hair.

"What did you get?" Savannah asked.

"Oh, you know, my usual."

"Let me guess: a soy latte with a shot of vanilla?"

"Am I that predictable?"

"Yes, you are, but there's nothing wrong with being predictable," Savannah reassured her. "I could use a little predictability these days."

Lexie leaned closer to Savannah and talked softer.

"Can I ask you something?"

"Sure. What's on your mind?"

"You've been stressed out the last couple of days. Is anything wrong? I feel like we've grown close, and I want you to know if you need to talk about anything, I'm here for you. I would never tell anyone anything you told me in confidence."

Savannah teared up, so Lexie decided to strike. "I know since you moved to Los Angeles, you and Nora have drifted apart. I understand what it's like to move away from home and not have anyone in your life you can trust. You can trust me."

Tears were streaming down Savannah's face. Her nose was red and running. Lexie reached into her purse and pulled out a travel pack of tissues and offered them to Savannah.

"Thank you," Savannah uttered as she took a tissue. "I do trust you, Lexie, and I know you would never betray our friendship. I'm so thankful I met you."

A wave of nausea hit Lexie. She was, in fact, planning to betray the poor girl.

"The people in this city can be so plastic," Savannah continued. "I know you're a true friend and a genuine person. I really love you, Lexie, but I'm not ready to talk about it yet. But when I'm ready, I'll tell you."

Lexie smiled at Savannah. "Call me day or night, and I'll always be here for you."

"I know you will," Savannah acknowledged.

Lexie, not wanting to scare Savannah off, decided to move on to another subject matter. "Let's talk about boys," Lexie stated.

Savannah laughed. "Now that's a subject I can totally get into!"

Lexie entertained Savannah with her latest attempt to talk to the totally hot dude who sat next to her in her photography class.

Savannah laughed hysterically at Lexie's story.

"You'll meet the right guy someday," Savannah said.

Lexie started thinking about how nice it would be to have someone to go home to each evening. Her job made dating difficult. She shook herself back to the present.

"Wow, that was some reaction," Savannah stated. "I'm sorry; I didn't mean to make you sad."

"Oh, you didn't. I'm fine."

Savannah reached across the table and took Lexie's hand. "You don't have to hide how you feel from me."

"I can't seem to find a nice guy. I want someone that I can be myself around." *How ironic*, Lexie thought.

"I know how you feel," Savannah said. "Until Nick, I never understood how two people could be so drawn to one another. I'm lost without him and utterly terrified I'll wake up one morning and it'll be over. I have to have him in my life. A couple of days ago, Nick took off with a friend and went on a short trip. I almost died, being away from him."

"Don't you and Nick talk on the phone or text when you're separated?"

"Are you kidding? Nick *hates* talking on the phone. He hates almost all technology. I can't get him to talk or text when he's away from me."

Bingo, Lexie thought. "Really? That's surprising," she said.

Savannah looked around erratically, as if looking to see if anyone was watching.

"What's wrong?" Lexie asked.

Savannah got up and moved around the table so she was sitting on the bench seat with Lexie. "If I tell you something, will you promise never to say anything to anyone?" Savannah asked.

"Of course. What is it?" Lexie took Savannah's hand. She could feel her shaking. "Tell me, Savannah."

"Promise me you won't judge me. I . . . I don't want you to think I'm a bad person."

"I would *never* judge you. You're my best friend. I'm here to support you, not judge you." Lexie remembered Kate telling her to let Savannah talk, not to interrupt. It was difficult for Lexie not to console Savannah with words. She quietly sat at the table with her hand still resting on Savannah's hand. She squeezed her hand to show encouragement but remained silent. After the longest minute of her life, Savannah spoke again.

"I did something bad, Lexie. Really bad, and now I don't know how to fix it."

"What did you do? Whatever it is, we can fix it together. I'll help you."

"I want to tell you, but I can't. I'm not supposed to talk to anyone about what happened."

Lexie's head was spinning. She had to keep Savannah talking. She couldn't lose her now, not after coming this close to the truth. "You can trust me, Savannah. I'll help you through it. It'll make you feel better to have someone to talk to about whatever is bothering you. We'll get though this together."

"I can't. Nick would kill me if he found out I told you this much. I love him, and I can't risk losing him."

"Nick will never know you talked to me. I would never tell him."

The undercover motto, "You build relationships to betray relationships," was banging around in the back of Lexie's brain.

"I know you wouldn't, but I can't lie to him. He knows me too well. He will know something is wrong as soon as he sees me."

Lexie was trying to process everything. Savannah had done something that was bad and Nick was involved. She decided to take another approach. "What about Haley? Have you talked to Haley about this?"

Savannah was staring at the table, apparently trying to formulate her next thought. "I can't talk to her either. She wouldn't understand."

"Tell me. I want to help you. I promise I'll never tell Nick or Haley you talked to me. You will feel so much better to have someone on your side."

Lexie could feel Savannah regressing. *Should I push or let her go and try again later?* She decided to roll the dice. She gripped Savannah's hand, took a deep breath, and asked, "Savannah, does this have anything to do with the fire at the lab?"

Savannah's head jerked up. She glared at Lexie, her eyes blazing. "No! Why would you even ask me that?"

"I don't know. Since the fire, you seem distraught. I thought you might have heard something and feel bad about what you know. I'm not accusing you of anything. It was a crazy thought."

"Jesus, Lexie! Let's just drop it."

"Okay. Whatever you want. I'm trying to be supportive."

Savannah jerked her hand away from Lexie.

"By accusing me of burning down the fucking UCLA lab? That doesn't sound very supportive to me."

"I'm sorry, Savannah. I didn't mean to upset you. I know you didn't burn down the lab. I've been trying to figure out what has you so upset, and I let my imagination run wild. Please don't be mad at me."

Savannah seemed to relax a little.

Lexie took a sip of her latte to give her hands something to do. A moment passed, and she looked at Savannah. "Are we okay? It makes me sick to my stomach to think you're mad at me."

Savannah looked up at her. She had tears welling up in her eyes. "We're good, Lexie. I'm sorry I got so mad. I overreacted."

"Well, I did go out on a limb with that theory."

Savannah chuckled. "Can you imagine me with a black mask and red spray paint?"

Lexie's heart skipped a beat. She faked a laugh. "Yeah, I guess that speculation was pretty out there. Let's lighten the mood. Do you want to do some shopping this weekend? Or perhaps hit a movie?" Lexie pulled two dark chocolate vegan candy bars from her purse and handed one to Savannah. "Chocolate is the cure for any woe," she said.

"You got that right, girlfriend."

They finished their coffee and candy bars and decided to go shopping in the small, overpriced boutiques on Main Street. Lexie caught one quick glimpse of Kate as she darted across the street and ducked into the sunglass shop. She found a cute pair of earrings she couldn't live without.

"Hey, Savannah, I was thinking of either getting my

eyebrow pierced or maybe getting a tattoo. What do you think?"

"Seriously? What kind of tattoo, and where would you get it?"

"What would you think of a palm tree on my foot or ankle?"

"That would be cute. I'll go with you."

"You'll have to. I'll need the moral support. I'm a huge coward when it comes to needles."

Savannah threw her arm around Lexie's shoulders. "I'll be there to hold your hand to keep you from screaming or record it on my phone and post it on Facebook."

Lexie walked Savannah to her car. "Are you sure you're not mad at me?" Lexie asked.

"We're fine, but you better pick out a tattoo, because I'm going to get one with you. We're going together, BFF."

Lexie laughed. "You got it!"

She closed Savannah's car door for her and headed toward her own car. She dashed back into the coffee shop and hit the restroom to turn off her body recorder. While in the Coffee Bean, she decided one more cup of coffee wouldn't hurt. After all, she had a report to write when she got home, so an extra shot of caffeine might help.

Lexie called Kate on her way home. Kate answered on the first ring.

"We got her! Meet me at my apartment as soon as you can."

CHAPTER TWENTY-TWO

Savannah

When Savannah arrived back at her dorm, both Haley and Nick were waiting for her. "Hey, guys. What's up?"

Nick was lounging on Savannah's bed with a beer in his hand. He got up, walked over, and hugged Savannah. "Hey, babe, where have you been?"

"Class."

"You've been at class all day?" Nick inquired.

"Yeah, why?" Savannah bit her lip. She didn't like lying to Nick, but because of his suspicious nature, she didn't want to tell him she was with Lexie.

"I drove over to meet you after your history class this morning, and you weren't there. I wanted to surprise you and take you for coffee. The redheaded girl you usually walk out with told me you weren't in class, so where were you, Savannah?"

"Jesus, Nick! Why the inquisition?"

Nick cleared Savannah's desk with a single sweep. Her books and a coffee mug crashed to the floor. Savannah gasped and jumped out of the way.

"I'm trying to figure out why you lied to me and where the hell you've been all day."

Savannah took a moment to regain her composure. Her knees were weak and shaking. "If you must know, I met Lexie for coffee and shopping. We spent the day relaxing and hanging out."

Nick clenched his teeth. "What did you tell Lexie?" he asked.

"I didn't tell Lexie anything." Savannah's breathing was labored and shallow. "We just hung out and shopped. Why on earth do you think I would tell Lexie anything about what we did?"

"Then why did you fucking lie to me?"

"Maybe I didn't feel the need to justify every minute of my day to you. You certainly don't share your comings and goings with me, and you're way more mysterious than me."

Nick abruptly grabbed Savannah's wrist. "I'm trying to protect you, Savannah, so I'm asking you again: what did you tell Lexie?"

Savannah flinched. "You're hurting me." She jerked her wrist from his grasp. "I didn't tell her a fucking thing, Nick!"

Haley stepped forward. "Let's all calm down. We can sit down and discuss this quietly without all the neighbors hearing our conversation."

Savannah tossed her backpack and purse in the corner and flopped down on the end of her bed.

Haley took a breath. "Savannah, this is very serious."

"I know. Don't you think I know how serious this is? I'm well aware we could all go to jail if I open my mouth to anyone, which is why I have not and I will not ever tell anyone what we did."

"Lower your voice, Savannah," Nick whispered. "We need to discuss this quietly and rationally. We shouldn't be discussing the subject inside."

"You should've thought of that before grabbing me and accusing me of betraying you. I'm just defending myself in my own home. You and Haley ambushed me."

"Maybe we came on a little strong," Nick said in a gravelly voice. "Haley thought you were a little upset this morning when you left for class, so I decided to meet you for coffee. When you didn't come out of your first class, I searched for you. You didn't answer your cell phone, and you always answer that damn phone of yours."

Savannah felt her pockets. She stepped over and lifted her cell phone from her dresser and held it up. "So I forgot my phone. That's not exactly a federal offense."

"No, but torching the lab was a federal offense," Haley added.

"I realize that, Haley!" Savannah was having trouble keeping her voice low. "How many times do I have to tell you two? I did not tell Lexie or anybody else anything. What do I have to do to get you to believe me?"

Haley's eyes glowed with rage. "Then why lie?" she asked through clenched teeth.

"I needed to get away and have a little fun," Savannah said. "I've been stressed out, and I wanted to relax and not think about anything important."

Nick snatched his beer and took another swig. "Savannah, if you tell us you didn't say anything to her, then we have to believe you. But please remember our fate is in your hands. It's not just you who gets in trouble if you tell anyone; it's all of us. We could all go to jail for a very long time. We put our trust in you."

"I know, Nick, but remember I'm just as involved as you two. I put my trust in you as well. In fact, I trusted you, and it was your maniac friend who got all three of us in this fucking mess. If anyone should be pissed off, it should be me."

"You wanted us to include you," Haley sneered. "All we heard from you is that you wanted to take your activism to the next level. Guess what, hotshot? This is the next level." Haley kicked a coffee mug lying on the floor across the room, smashing it into three pieces.

Nick got up and walked across the room. He stared for a moment at a painting of historic Charleston's Rainbow Row. It belonged to Savannah. He turned, and Savannah expected him to be angry, but instead he had a rueful expression on his face. "You're right. I brought Badger into your life. He caused this. But he is one of us, and we have to protect him by staying strong. I'm sorry I involved you in this mess. Hindsight is twenty-twenty. If I could do it over, I would keep you away from the direct action."

Savannah's heart sank. She didn't want Nick to feel bad about including her in the mission. She got up and walked over to face him. "I'm not sorry I was involved. I am sorry it went bad, but I'm glad you trusted me enough to bring me in to help with the action. I wish you trusted me now. I haven't told anyone about what we did, and I never will. I'll take it to my grave."

Nick wrapped his arms around Savannah. She could

smell the lingering scent of the vanilla soap he had bought from the co-op.

"I do trust you, Savannah. This was your first action, and it went about as bad as a mission could possibly go."

"I'm okay. A little shaky still, but I'll be fine. You and Haley don't have to worry about me."

Nick whispered in Savannah's ear, "We'll get through this together. I love you."

Haley stared at Nick. He could read Haley's expression and knew she was thinking that this situation didn't smell right.

CHAPTER TWENTY-THREE

Alexis

Kate arrived at Lexie's door in record time. Lexie opened the door and pulled her into the apartment. She had her yellow legal pad out, where she had been jotting notes about the encounter so she wouldn't forget the details.

"You want a glass of iced tea?" Lexie asked.

Kate laughed. "Always the consummate Southerner, ready with a glass of tea and cookies. Your mother would be proud."

Lexie gave her a sideways smile. "Tea or no tea, smart ass?"

"Tea, please," she answered. Kate continued, "The pressure is mounting at the office, Lexie. I hope you're close to a breakthrough. If not, I'm not sure how long we can fend off the vultures. You need to produce something substantive soon, or else headquarters might pull the plug on our case."

Kate sat down in the living room, and Lexie emerged with a glass of iced tea and a plate of key lime cookies.

Kate took a cookie from the plate. "So tell me what happened."

Lexie took a sip of tea. "It was apparent from the moment I arrived that Savannah was distraught. I took a calculated risk and straight out asked her if her anxiety had anything to do with the UCLA arson."

Kate choked on her tea. "Oh God, Lexie! Are you sure that was a wise move? What did she say?"

"It felt like the right thing to do at the time. Anyway, she went apeshit, but in her fury, she gave away something."

"What?"

"She asked, 'Can you see me running around wearing a black ski mask with red spray paint?'. Didn't you tell me the ski masks and red spray paint facts were not released to the public? I know black ski masks are probably used in all ALF actions, but the fact that the arson inspectors found a black bag with red spray paint was kind of a stretch for her to guess."

Kate sat quietly for a moment.

Lexie's heart pounded erratically, awaiting a response.

With a broad smile, Kate said, "Please tell me you have that conversation recorded."

Lexie realized she had been holding her breath while Kate was contemplating the news. She sucked in a breath and said, "If the body recorder worked properly, I have the entire conversation recorded."

"Let's get the recorder to ELSUR and make sure we have the conversation before we get too excited." ELSUR was the FBI evidence storage center for all electronic evidence. "This is huge, Lexie!" Kate said.

Lexie continued to recount the details of the day to Kate, who sipped her sweet tea and ate key lime cookies.

"You do love sugar," Kate said.

It was true, Lexie treated sugar like a food group. She hit the cotton candy stand on the Boardwalk at least twice a week.

"Well, my sweet tea isn't nearly as sweet as my mother's. She'd be embarrassed to serve this sweet tea."

Kate laughed. She and Lexie had a natural rhythm.

"I'll take the equipment to ELSUR and make sure we have a recording. We probably should do a strategy meeting at some point tomorrow."

"Sure. What time?"

"Let me call Adam and set it up. I'll call you with a time after I hear from him."

* * * * *

The next morning, while driving to the meet location, Lexie popped a Green Day CD into the car stereo and skipped to "Boulevard of Broken Dreams." Lexie had a new appreciation for this song. She woke up in a dismal mood and couldn't shake the feeling. It was her birthday, and she didn't have anyone to share it with. None of her friends or family members had her undercover phone number to call her to wish her a happy birthday. It was the price she paid for being a full time undercover operative.

She contemplated her relationship with Savannah. She liked Savannah, and if the situation were different, she could easily be friends with her. Lexie believed Savannah was a sweet, naive girl who glamorized the activist lifestyle.

She hoped, when the time arrived, Savannah would cooperate with the FBI and save herself. If it came down to it, Lexie didn't feel guilty about jamming up Haley or Nick, because they knew what they were doing, but Savannah was a different story. Lexie tried to shake the nagging knot in her stomach. As much as she wanted to arrest and convict every person responsible for the death of the security guard, she secretly hoped Savannah was not involved. Now it looked like Savannah was in fact involved in the arson.

Lexie arrived at the pier where she was meeting Kate and Adam. She noticed Adam's unoccupied car parked in the corner of the lot. Lexie rounded the corner and heard Adam and Kate engaged in a heated debate. She stopped abruptly and listened.

"I think Lexie is too close to the targets," Adam said. "She's developed a friendship toward the Riley girl."

"She's doing her job, Adam. She has to befriend the targets in order to get close."

"I'm not talking about befriending them. I think she actually sees them as friends."

"That's ridiculous," Kate snapped. "Lexie is a trained undercover agent. She's doing what's necessary to make the case."

"I think you need to reel her in. Either you do it, or I will."

"How about you concentrate on being the case agent," Kate hissed. "Lexie is my responsibility."

"You're right. She *is* your responsibility. And you need to make sure she's not going off the rails on this one."

They both took a moment to calm down.

"Look, Kate, I'm not trying to be a hard-ass on this. It's just, well, HQ is all over me. I need to produce some results soon, or they're going to close us down."

"I understand. But you need to cut Lexie some slack. She's going as fast as she can. If she pushes any harder, Nick and Haley will get hinked up. We have to let this play out naturally."

Adam ran his hand through his hair. "Okay. We'll play it your way."

"Thank you," Kate said.

Lexie knees were shaking. She waited a few moments to regain her composure before popping around the corner.

"Hello, guys," Lexie said, trying to sound natural.

"Hey there, you," Adam responded.

"Hi, Lexie," Kate said. "How are you?"

"I'm good. Did the recording come out?" Lexie asked.

"It certainly did," Kate answered. "You captured the whole conversation. Adam and I listened to it this morning. You did fantastic. I have to admit I was holding my breath when you brought up the fire, but your gamble paid off."

"Let's sit down," Adam said.

The three found a bench in the shade and sat down.

"Hey, I've got good news," Lexie said. "Savannah, Haley, and Nick are coming over to my apartment for dinner next week. We're eating then going to the NWM meeting together."

"That's great, Lexie," Kate said.

Adam abruptly changed the subject. "We've been discussing various strategies this morning. We wanted your input. We're considering putting Savannah in front of the grand jury to see if she would talk."

"I . . . I didn't realize we were at that stage," Lexie stammered. "I'm almost positive that Savannah will plead the fifth."

Adam rubbed his temples. "We could interview Savannah using the information that you've gathered up to this point. If we go that route, you'll more than likely be exposed as an undercover agent."

"What's your opinion, Lexie?" Kate asked.

Lexie's right foot bounced like a jackhammer. "I think we should allow things to continue business as usual. Savannah doesn't know she slipped up, and she desperately wanted to tell me what happened that night. Maybe if nothing happens to her, she'll open up to me. If not, we can always use the information against her down the road."

Kate and Adam nodded, so Lexie continued. "I think we're all pretty confident Haley and Nick are the more culpable targets. If Savannah opens the door so I can get closer to Haley, we'll have a much stronger case. We're relying on the premise that Savannah will flip on the group, but there's no guarantee she'll cooperate. She may tell us to pound sand, and we'll be left with a weak, circumstantial case. I think we all realize Savannah is not sophisticated enough to pull off organizing this type of action. For one thing, she hasn't been involved in the movement long enough to have the kind of connections she'd need for the animal liberation side of the direct action. Savannah definitely has knowledge of the crime, but my guess is she was a worker bee and not an organizer."

"I agree with Lexie's assessment," Kate said. "She's been

around the targets and is in the best position to make the decision."

Adam sighed. "This is a tough call. It could go either way."

"What's the harm in going a little longer?" Kate asked.

"Okay," Adam said. "We'll go with your plan, Lexie. Keep in mind, we're on a time crunch."

Adam's tone irritated Lexie, but she decided to let it go.

Lexie reflected on her life as she drove the scenic stretch of the Pacific Coast Highway on her way home.

Happy birthday to me.

CHAPTER TWENTY-FOUR

Savannah

Nearly a week later, Savannah was still irritated that Nick and Haley had accused her of telling Lexie about the fire. She *had* lied to them about going to class that day, but there was such a double standard when it came to information sharing in her relationships. Neither Nick nor Haley felt the need to tell her about their comings and goings, but the first time that she wasn't forthright about her location, they went ballistic.

Savannah jumped when her phone rang. She grabbed it off the desk and smiled when she saw Nick's name on the screen. "Hi, handsome."

"Hey," Nick said curtly.

"What's new?" Savannah asked.

"Are we still on for dinner at Lexie's and then the meeting?"

"Yep, that's the plan."

"I'll pick you and Haley up about five."

"Sounds good. I'll text Haley and let her know the plan."

Savannah had a surge of energy after talking to Nick.

She showered and walked to class. On her way, she called Lexie. "Are we still on for dinner at your place tonight?"

"Absolutely. Come over anytime."

CHAPTER TWENTY-FIVE

Alexis

Lexie planned to make soy tacos for dinner, so she spent the morning grocery shopping. She decided to keep it simple, since she wasn't much of a cook. She bought a vegan dark chocolate cake for dessert. Her phone rang.

"Hey, Kate."

"Hey, Lexie. How are you?"

"Good. Just getting everything ready for this evening."

"Need any help?"

"Naw, I got it. I'm keeping it simple. I have to pick up some beer, and then I'm done."

"Did you test the audio/video equipment in your apartment?"

"Yep. I tested it last night. Everything appears to be working fine."

"Since this is the first time any of these people have been in your apartment, do you mind if I swing by to do a quick walk through to make sure that nothing sticks out as weird?"

"I don't mind at all. I'll be home in about a half hour. Swing by anytime."

Lexie finished her shopping and returned to the

apartment. After unloading the car, she chopped up the lettuce, tomatoes, and onion for the tacos.

Lexie performed a cursory examination of her apartment. Everything looked good to her. There was a knock on the door. Lexie checked the peephole and saw Kate standing nonchalantly outside. Kate blended into the neighborhood well with her loose fitting hemp pants, organic cotton T-shirt, and fair-trade purse slung over her shoulder.

"Come in," Lexie said.

"Thanks. Wow, you cleaned the place up."

"A little bit."

"Do you mind if I walk through?" Kate asked.

"Be my guest."

Kate opened drawers and cabinets, checking for anything out of the ordinary. She looked through Lexie's books on the small bookshelf in the bedroom. While Kate was searching, Lexie fixed them each a glass of iced tea. Kate returned carrying a couple of paperback books.

"You might want to take a black marker to the name in the front of these two books."

Lexie opened the books, and her mother's name was written on the inside cover.

"Fuck! I never thought about checking my books."

"No worries. That's why I always do a walk through. It's good to do periodically, because as time goes by, it's easy to become complacent."

Lexie crossed the name out with a marker and tossed the books in a coffee table drawer.

"These targets are snoops and will take every opportunity to toss your shit when you aren't looking."

"Thanks for checking for me," Lexie said as she handed Kate a tall glass of iced tea with lemon.

"No problem. Are you sure there isn't anything that I can do to help?"

"Everything is done. I just have to heat up the soy crumbles for the tacos. The toppings are all chopped and in bowls in the fridge."

"Leave all the dinner dishes on the table," Kate instructed. "I'll come over later and take custody of a few items to send to the lab for DNA comparisons."

"Great idea."

Lexie and Kate sat at the kitchen table and sipped their teas.

"How's everything going at the office?" Lexie asked.

"People at headquarters are giving Adam grief. The arson put our investigation on their radar. He's been a real grouch lately."

"What's it like working so closely with Adam?"

"It's fine. He's more of a *typical* FBI agent, a little high-strung and anal. Put it this way, I enjoy working with you so much more than him. In fact, I'm going to miss you when this case is over. It's been nice having you around."

The two women leisurely drank their teas and shared a few laughs.

"Well, I better get out of here so you can finish getting ready for tonight." Kate gathered her purse and headed toward the door.

Lexie walked Kate to the door. "I'll call you when I get back from the meeting."

"Sounds good. Good luck."

CHAPTER TWENTY-SIX

Savannah

Savannah and Haley were waiting for Nick to pick them up when Savannah received a text. *Check your e-mail.*

"That's strange."

"What?" Haley asked.

"Nick sent me a text telling me to check my e-mail."

"He must be sending you something encrypted."

Savannah grabbed her laptop and logged into her Rise Up account. Most of the activists used Rise Up because the service refused to cooperate with law enforcement subpoenas. Savannah kept her Hotmail account to use with Nora and her parents, but she used her Rise Up account for everyone else. She used PGP to decrypt the message and read it to Haley. "*S. I can't make it tonight. You and H go and have fun. I'm heading out of town for a few days. The less you know, the better. I found a tracker on my car. I've destroyed it, but I need to lie low. I'll e-mail you when I can. My cell phone is off, so don't call me. I love you. N.*"

Savannah finished reading and looked at Haley. "What's a tracker?"

"It's a device the fucking feds put on your car so they can track everywhere you go. I bet they stuck it on Nick's car after the fire. He checks his car periodically, so it probably hasn't been attached long."

"What did he do with it?"

"He either smashed it to smithereens or threw it in the ocean. Those motherfuckers think they're so sneaky."

"Oh God. Do you think they know Nick had something to do with the fire?"

"No. They're grasping at straws. They probably have trackers on a shitload of animal rights activists' cars right now. Don't panic."

"That's easy for you to say. I'm scared to death."

"We need to go on with business as usual."

"Should we check our cars?" Savannah asked.

Haley laughed. "Do you know what a tracker looks like?"

"Well, no, but I figured you would."

"I have an activist friend who works at a body shop. I'll give him a call and see if he can give our cars a quick once-over."

"What about going to dinner at Lexie's house?"

"Nothing wrong with going to a friend's house for dinner. How close does she live to Jeannette's house?"

"It's within walking distance," Savannah said.

"That's good. After dinner we'll walk to the meeting."

"Speaking of that, we'd better go so we aren't late."

"Just remember, Savannah, business as usual. When Lexie asks about Nick, we'll tell her his band got an out-of-town gig."

"Shouldn't we tell Lexie about the tracker?"

Savannah asked.

Haley pondered the question. "No, I think for now, we keep it to ourselves. I don't think we should say anything at the meeting either."

"Whatever you think. You know better than I do."

They hopped in Savannah's car and drove to Venice. Savannah could tell that Haley was in deep thought.

"I've changed my mind," Haley said. "We should tell Lexie and the others about the tracker so they can have their vehicles examined. If they ask about Nick, we'll tell them he's lying low. No one needs to know he's out of town."

"Whatever you think, Haley. I'll do whatever you say."

Savannah found a parking spot down the street from Lexie's apartment. She and Haley walked up and knocked on the door. Lexie opened the door and greeted each of her guests with a hug. "Where's Nick?"

"He had a change of plans and couldn't make it."

"Too bad. I made a ton of food. Come in. Come in."

Savannah and Haley entered the apartment.

"Make yourselves at home. The bathroom is down the hall if you need it. Can I get anyone a drink?"

"Wow, you're quite the hostess," Haley stated.

"Thanks. My good Southern upbringing, I guess."

"How about some wine?"

"Sounds good to me," Savannah said.

"Me too," said Haley.

"White or red?"

"White," both replied.

"I'm really disappointed that Nick couldn't make it," Lexie said as she poured them each a glass of Chardonnay.

"I was looking forward to getting to know him better."

Lexie handed a glass to both Savannah and Haley.

"This is good," Savannah said after taking a sip of her wine.

"I have a Riesling in the fridge if you prefer something sweeter. I prefer sweeter, but I realize not everyone shares my love of sweet wine."

"I have the same taste in wine as you do," Savannah said.

"Don't be shy. Help yourself."

Haley wandered to the table and filled a plate with carrots, hummus, chips, and salsa. "This looks great, Lexie. Thanks for having us."

"It's my pleasure. I've been meaning to have you guys over. I'm not the best cook, so I hope you like tacos."

"Love them," said Haley.

"Me too," added Savannah.

The three girls took their plates out to Lexie's small patio.

"This is a cute patio," Haley stated.

"Thanks. It's not very big, but I love it. I sit out here all the time."

"I miss having a porch," Savannah said. "Haley, when we look for an apartment, we have to find one with a patio area for entertaining."

"Because we entertain so frequently," Haley said sarcastically.

"Well, we might entertain if we didn't live in a dorm."

"Are you guys looking for an apartment?" Lexie asked.

"We've tossed around the idea of renting an apartment or a house," Haley answered. "We'd like to get a few people and rent something we could use as an activist house."

"That sounds like a great idea."

"Would you want to move in with us if we did rent a house?" Savannah asked.

"I would love to move in with you guys when my lease is up."

"When does your lease expire?" Haley asked.

Crap, Lexie thought. *When does my lease expire? Just say something.*

"Not ah, not until June," Lexie stammered.

"What kind of early termination penalty do you have if you leave before June?" Haley asked.

"I can't remember," Lexie said. "I'll have to check my lease to see."

The women sat on the patio sipping wine and munching on hors d'oeuvres. Lexie decided it was time to warm up the soy crumbles.

"I'd better get our tacos going so we can make our meeting on time," Lexie stated.

"Can I help with anything?" Savannah asked.

"You can get the taco fixings out of the fridge and put them on the table if you want."

"I can do that."

During dinner, Lexie approached the subject of Nick.

"What happened to Nick? Is he coming for the meeting?"

Haley and Savannah exchanged glances.

"We're not going to tell anyone outside of our activist group, but Nick found a tracker on his car," Haley said.

Lexie froze in disbelief. She forced herself to speak. "Really? Wow! Who do you think put it there?"

"Probably the fucking FBI," Haley said.

Lexie's heart raced. *Did Adam install a tracker on the car and choose not to tell me? Act normal,* she told herself. "Why would they put one on Nick's car?" Lexie asked.

"The cops are always fucking with us. Who knows why they do anything."

"Did he take if off?"

"He did, but he thinks he should stay clear of us for a while, since it's obvious someone is watching him. He'll be back when things have cooled off."

"I don't know what a tracker looks like," Lexie stated. "He should take a photo of it, so we know what to look for on our cars."

"That's a good idea, Lexie," Savannah chimed in. "I don't know what one looks like either."

"It's a good thing he found it. Do you know how they put them on cars?" Lexie asked.

"I think the trackers are magnetic, so someone walks by and slaps one on a car when no one is around."

Lexie shook her head and said, "Fucking cops."

Savannah jumped up to grab the dinner dishes.

"Don't worry about the dishes, Savannah. I'll take care of them when I get home," Lexie said.

"Are you sure? I'm happy to help."

"I know you are, but it's almost time for our meeting. Should we take the chocolate cake with us?"

"That would be nice," Haley said. "Do you want to walk over from here?"

"Yes," Savannah said. "I need to walk off all my tacos so I can make room for cake."

"Sounds good to me," Lexie said. "It's not far."

* * * * *

The three women told stories and laughed all the way to the house. The meeting was just getting started when they arrived.

Jeannette greeted them at the door. "Hello, ladies. Phillip and the rest of the gang are in the living room."

Jeannette looked around behind the girls as they entered the house. "Where's Nick?"

Haley answered for the group. "Nick found a tracker on his car. He's laying low for a bit just in case the cops are following him."

"There's no end to what those Gestapo motherfuckers will do," Jeannette declared. "I hope that tracking device is sitting at the bottom of the Pacific Ocean."

Haley laughed.

Lexie handed Jeannette the chocolate cake. "Here's a little contribution for the snack table."

"Thank you, Lexie. It looks good. I love dark chocolate. Go on into the meeting. I'll be along behind you."

The three strolled into the meeting. Lexie plopped into a worn-out purple beanbag chair. Haley and Savannah each grabbed a spot on the threadbare couch.

Savannah overheard Ryan discussing the UCLA incident with one of the other guys in the group. She suddenly felt sick to her stomach. They weren't supposed to discuss past acts. Of course, Ryan wouldn't know that any of them had a part in the UCLA action. She concentrated on slowing down her heart rate and tried her best to appear calm, cool, and collected.

Haley took control of the meeting. Without mentioning that it was Nick's car, she explained that a tracker was found on a vehicle. The floodgate was opened for questions. Haley did her best to answer all the questions, but a couple of the people seemed to be in a panic.

"Does this have anything to do with the UCLA fire?" Ryan asked.

"Police randomly place tracking devices on activist vehicles, so it has nothing to do with that fire," Haley said. "The cops follow us around all the time for no reason at all. Always be aware of your surroundings and check your car for trackers periodically."

"How do we know what to look for?" one of the girls in the back of the room asked.

"I'm sure there has to be a photo on an animal rights website somewhere. I'll find a photo for our next meeting."

The conversation kept shifting back to the UCLA fire. Haley avoided the topic, but everyone was curious.

Lexie finally asked the question that they were all wondering. "Does anyone know how many animals died in the fire?"

"It's funny how the news footage never mentions the loss of nonhuman lives," Ryan added.

"That's because the average person doesn't know the atrocities that go on behind those walls," Jeannette stated. "The general public doesn't understand the hideous experiments that take place in the name of science."

Haley was finally able to steer the meeting away from the UCLA debacle. After the meeting, most of the people left the house. Phillip, Jeannette, Haley, Savannah, and

Lexie had cake and coffee.

"Let us know if Nick needs anything from us," Phillip said. "We'll be happy to help any way we can."

CHAPTER TWENTY-SEVEN

Alexis

Lexie sat down and scribbled notes prior to calling Kate. She was seething when she speed dialed Kate.

"Hello, Lexie. How are you?"

"Who the fuck put a tracker on Nick's car and why didn't I fucking know about it?"

"Whoa, calm down."

"I'm not going to calm down. Nick found a tracking device on his car today, and I'm asking you if you knew about it."

"No, Lexie. Of course not. Are you sure it was a tracker? Tell me what happened."

Lexie took a swig of wine to try to calm down. "Savannah and Haley showed up for dinner without Nick. They said he found a tracker on his car. He removed it, but was lying low in case the cops were watching him."

"Lexie, I promise I will get to the bottom of this. I don't know if it was us or another agency, but I will absolutely find out who's keeping track of him."

"Surely to God our people didn't do this, Kate. That

would be really jacked up if our own people did this without telling us."

"I agree. And I'll find out first thing in the morning. Are you okay?"

"No, I'm not okay, I'm pissed off to high heaven. I don't like the idea of law enforcement doing shit like that and not telling us. I just got in tight with Nick and the rest of the group, and now a tracker shows up on Nick's car. Kind of a big coincidence, don't you think?"

"I completely agree. Do you want me to come over tonight?"

Lexie took another drink of wine. "No, I'm fine. I know that these activists are normally nonviolent, but given the lab incident, we should be careful."

"We'll get this figured out. Did anyone at the meeting ask about Nick?"

"Yes. Haley told Jeannette that it was Nick who found the tracker on his car, but at the meeting she told the group that a member of the activist community found a tracker on a vehicle. She didn't disclose that it was Nick. In fact, I heard her tell a couple people that Nick had an out-of-town gig with his band."

"Lexie, that's a good sign."

"Why do you say that?"

"Haley told you and Jeannette information she withheld from the others. She's starting to trust you."

"I guess I hadn't thought of that. Haley does seem more comfortable with me these days."

"You get some sleep. I'll find out about the tracker and call you as soon as I have some answers."

"Hey, Kate, I'm sorry I flew off the handle at you. I know it wasn't your fault, and I'm sorry I took it out on you."

"No worries, girl. I intend to get to the bottom of this first thing in the morning. I hope it was the police department that did it and not the FBI."

"Knowing my agency, I wouldn't be surprised if it was a bureau fuck up," Lexie said.

"We'll know for sure tomorrow."

* * * * *

The next morning, Lexie went for a relaxing jog on the beach. She stopped at the Venice Beach Skateboard Park to watch the kids skate. She loved watching the youngest riders. She watched one little guy who looked about seven years old fly through the air and land with ease near where she was standing. *He must have started skating shortly after he learned to walk*, she thought.

When Lexie got back to her apartment, she discovered she had missed a call from Kate. *Oh boy*, she thought, *this can't be good*. She grabbed a sports drink and returned the call.

"Hi, Lexie. How's your morning so far?"

"Good. I just got back from my run. What have you found out?"

"Are you sitting down?"

Lexie flopped down on the couch, propping her feet on the coffee table.

"I am now. Go ahead."

"It was a bureau tracking device. The Intel group working Nick Harris decided it would be a grand idea to install a tracker on his vehicle but didn't feel the need to share that information with the criminal side. These people are the biggest fuckups I've ever met."

Lexie took a deep breath. She was so angry that all she could do was laugh.

"Lexie, are you okay?"

"I absolutely can't believe it. I convinced myself it had to be another police department watching Nick. The bureau couldn't be that fucking idiotic. What did they say when you confronted them about it?"

"That's the really messed up part. They couldn't understand why I was so upset. I tried to explain that their stupidity endangered the life of an undercover agent. I felt like I was talking to a wall."

"What did you do?"

"I had a sit-down with Adam and Mike. They were both livid. Mike called up the supervisor on the Intel squad and had some serious words with him. Mike told him that from this point on, they were not to do anything relating to any of the extremist targets without notifying him first."

"Then what happened?"

"As you can imagine, it didn't go over well. It resulted in a shouting match, and both threatened to go to the SAC with the problem. I've never seen Mike that riled up about anything. Believe me, this issue is not over."

"So in other words, the right hand had no idea what the left hand was doing," Lexie said.

"Oh, the right hand knew, but it was too stupid to care."

"Speaking of riled up, you seem pretty irate."

"I am! Lexie, I'm responsible for your safety. The fact that those idiots were out running willy-nilly without any consideration for the safety of an undercover agent in the field makes me furious. I'm not sure how things will shake out, but I know Mike has an appointment with the SAC about the matter."

"I can't believe our own people were running operations on our targets without informing us."

"I'm still reeling from it myself," Kate said. "What are you up to today?"

"I'm going to write up my FD-302 from last night."

"Is it okay if I swing by and pick up the body recorder and the hard drive from the apartment system? I also need to grab some of the dishes from last night to send to the lab. I'll be quick."

"Of course."

CHAPTER TWENTY-EIGHT

Savannah

Savannah hit the speed dial number for Lexie. She heard Lexie's voice on the other end.

"Hi, Lexie. You ready?"

"Sure am. Are you close?"

"Right around the corner. Should be out front in about two minutes."

"Cool. I'll be right out."

Savannah pulled up in front of the apartment building. She and Lexie were spending the day hiking. Lexie tossed her CamelBak in the back seat and jumped in the front.

"Thanks for driving," Lexie said.

"No problem. We might as well take advantage of the hybrid."

"How come Haley didn't come?"

"She's behind in her school work, so she's spending the day studying."

It was a Saturday morning, and traffic was light for LA. They took the 405 freeway to the I-101 and drove toward Calabasas.

"Would you ever consider living this far out of the city?" Lexie asked.

"I haven't spent much time out here, but it sure is pretty. What're you doing after you graduate? Do you plan to stay in LA?"

"That depends on whether or not I get a job and can afford to stay," Lexie said. "I love California, and I don't have anyone waiting for me in Alabama. What about you?"

"I pretty much have to stay in this area if I want to work in the entertainment industry. I'm not sure what will happen with Nick and me, but either way, I plan to stay in LA after I graduate."

"Have you and Nick talked about it?"

"Nick doesn't make plans past lunch, much less for our future together. Besides, he hasn't been around since he found the tracker."

"Jesus, Savannah. I didn't realize he was still gone. Are you okay?"

"Not really, but I don't have a say in anything Nick does."

"Where's Nick staying?" Lexie asked.

"I have no idea. I've only heard from him one time in almost a month. I don't know when or *if* he plans to return to LA. He just took off and left me behind."

"That really sucks. I know how much you care about him. I'm really sorry."

"I'm sure he loves me, but he has a funny way of showing it. Or should I say, *not* showing it."

"Why did he think he had to leave town in the first place?" Lexie asked.

Savannah glanced over at Lexie before answering. "I

don't know. I guess he thought he was protecting us, since the police were looking at him."

"I'm not judging, but that seems a bit extreme, unless there was some other reason he needed to leave town. I know the police watch all of us from time to time, so why take off?"

Savannah shrugged. "I wish I knew."

"Do you think he may have been involved in something serious and didn't want to tell you? Maybe he's trying to protect you from something bad."

"Like what?" Savannah asked.

"What if he did something before he started dating you and it's just now catching up with him?"

"Nick would've told me if that was the case."

"Would he? You said he hasn't told you much about his past."

"That's true. But he knows I'd never tell."

"I'm sure you're right."

Savannah took the exit, which led to the hiking area. She drove a few miles to the trailhead and parked the Prius. "We're here. Let's see if we can do this without getting lost."

Lexie laughed as she rolled out of the car and grabbed her CamelBak from the backseat.

A light breeze kept the girls cool as they hiked. Admiring the view from the top of a majestic ridge, Savannah asked Lexie, "Have you ever been to an Animal Rights Conference?"

"I've been to one. What about you?"

"I haven't been to one yet, but I would like to go. How was the one that you attended?"

"It was okay. Mostly stuff I already knew, but it was fun to socialize and meet people. I would definitely recommend going if you've never been to one."

Savannah was nervous about asking the next question, but she did. "Would you consider going overseas to train?"

Lexie turned and looked at her. "What do you mean, to train? Like a conference, or more like a training camp?"

Savannah swallowed hard before answering. "Haley told me about the International Animal Rights Conference that's held every year in Europe. It's called The Gathering, and people from all over the world attend to learn tactics to battle animal abusers. Would you consider going?"

Lexie sat down on a rock and Savannah sat down beside her.

"I'd go if I had someone to go with. I wouldn't want to go by myself. Why? Are you planning to go?"

"I'm thinking about going. Haley and Nick are going. They go whenever they have the money. Nick won't go to the Animal Rights conferences in the United States, because he says they're only a bunch of welfarists who sit on their asses and wish away animal abuse. He says most of the US activists like to get together to argue with one another over who's the more righteous, but none of them have ever done the first thing to actually save an animal."

Lexie shifted around so she could see Savannah better. "If you guys go, I'd like to go with you."

"Oh, thank God. I was afraid you were going to think I was too radical."

"Savannah, I would never think you're too radical. I want to save animals as much as you do. I'm just not sure how to do the most damage to the animal abusers, and everyone is afraid to talk about direct action. It's hard to find people who feel the same way about direct action."

Savannah relaxed a little. "I'm glad that you feel that way. I definitely think you should come with us to The Gathering."

"Where is it and when?" Lexie asked.

"The next one will be held in the Netherlands in July. I'll let you know when I get more details. It's not like in the United States where everyone stays in a nice hotel. Haley said we'd sleep in tents in an anarchist camp. Does that bother you?"

"Naw, I love camping. We used to camp when I was a kid. Sleeping in a tent doesn't bother me one bit."

"I wish I could say the same," Savannah said. "We never camped when I was a kid. My mom's idea of roughing it was not having a spa on-site."

Lexie laughed. "Count me in. I'd love to go. It sounds like an adventure."

"We will; that is, if I ever hear from Nick again. All this planning might be moot if he's gone for good."

"Oh Savannah, don't worry. He'll be back."

"I don't know. The longer he's gone, the more I wonder if he'll ever come back. Haley tells me not to worry. She said he does this all the time."

"And you don't have any communication with him at all?"

"Nope. Just one encrypted e-mail."

"That sucks."

"It sure does."

"If Nick doesn't come back, will you and Haley still go to the Netherlands?"

"I don't know. Maybe."

"Well, if you do, I'll go with you."

"Cool! Let's plan on it."

They got up and resumed their hike.

At one point in the hike, they stopped to admire another particularly beautiful vista.

"Do you miss South Carolina?" Lexie asked.

"Sure. Don't you miss Alabama?"

"I guess. Sometimes. What do you miss most?"

Savannah thought for a moment. "My family and the beach," she responded. "There's a stretch of beach on Pawley's Island where a person can walk out and stand with the ocean on one side of you and the salt marsh on the other. It's where I went when I needed to clear my head. I think it's the most beautiful place in the world."

"Sounds nice. I'd like to see it someday."

"You can come home with me sometime, and I'll take you to see it."

"That would be nice. I'd like that."

"Do you ever think about moving back home?"

Lexie tilted her head for a moment before saying, "Can you ever really go home?"

"What do you mean?"

"Once you leave home, can you ever go back again . . . and truly belong? I'm a much different person now than I was when I lived in Alabama. I've seen so much and changed so much. I'm not sure I would fit in anymore. Do you know what I mean?"

"I think I do," Savannah answered.

They stared at the California horizon in silence, both deep in thought.

"Let's finish this hike. I'm hungry," Lexie said.

CHAPTER TWENTY-NINE

Alexis

Lexie's phone rang early the next morning. She fumbled around and grabbed it from her nightstand. "Hello," she grumbled into the phone.

"Morning, sunshine," she heard Adam say.

"Ugh, why are you so chipper?"

"Well, I've been at work for over an hour. Some of us have to work for a living," Adam joked.

"Some of us need our beauty sleep to keep up with much younger targets," Lexie quipped.

"Are you available to meet with Kate and me today?"

"Yeah, sure. Where and when?"

"Let's meet for lunch. I want to get you away from that area so we can talk. Drive up the coast, and we'll meet you at Gladstone's in Malibu."

"That works for me. You buying?"

"Don't I always?"

Lexie laughed. "No."

"Well, I probably won't this time either."

Jimmy Buffet blasted from Lexie's car stereo as she drove

up the Pacific Coast Highway to Malibu. Her windows were down; she breathed in the fresh ocean air. Arriving before Adam and Kate, Lexie requested an outside table. Eyes closed with the sun warming her face, she heard the sound of a familiar voice.

"How's it going, stranger?" Adam asked.

Lexie blinked a couple of times and focused on Adam and Kate.

"Hi y'all. Have a seat."

As they waited for their food to arrive, Adam shifted in his chair.

"What's up, Adam?" Lexie asked. "You seem antsy."

Adam cut his eyes toward Kate. "Lexie, I've been talking to HQ about the case. They're pushing for results. They interjected themselves into the case after the arson. I've done my best to keep them at bay, but it's getting harder to do. The HQ unit chief called our SAC last week and wanted a status update. They're champing at the bit for us to make an arrest."

"Have you told them the targets are extremely paranoid and we're finally making some progress?"

"Of course I have, but they don't care. It's all about numbers to them, the amount of money we're spending versus the number of arrests we've made."

Lexie clenched her teeth.

"I don't know what else I can do, Adam. I'm going as fast as I can."

"I understand, but most of these HQ suits have never worked an undercover operation, so they have no concept of how long it takes to build trust."

Lexie gave a slight smile. "Well, something happened yesterday that might help our cause."

Kate pulled her chair closer. "What happened?"

"Savannah invited me to go overseas with her, Haley, and Nick for some kind of international animal rights conference. It's called The Gathering, and from her description, it sounds more like a terrorist training camp than a conference."

"I've heard of The Gathering. That's outstanding," Adam said.

"You've made so much progress in such as short period of time," Kate added. "Don't let these headquarter assholes get to you. This isn't about you or your work quality. It's strictly about their little stat game. We'll figure it out."

"You don't think HQ would shut the undercover op down, do you?" Lexie asked.

"I don't think so, but we need to start thinking of an exit strategy," Adam suggested. "We need to decide how to proceed, who to press, and when to pull out."

"Well, obviously I'm the closest to Savannah. She and I spend a great deal of time together. Although she hasn't admitted to being at the fire, I think we agree she probably had something to do with it."

"I think we all agree that Savannah is the weakest link," Adam said. "Kate and I will work on an interview strategy for Savannah. When the time comes to scoop her up, we'll be ready. I was hoping that we'd have more time to develop intelligence on this group, but the arson changed our time schedule. We need to change our line of thinking from intelligence gathering to prosecution. Lexie, you have to push Savannah for information. It's full-court press time."

The server brought their food, but Lexie didn't have much of an appetite. She had a sick feeling in her stomach.

"If you don't want those fries, I'm going to eat them," Adam joked.

"Step away from the fries," Lexie warned.

After lunch, Lexie took a stroll down the beach. She kicked off her shoes and felt the sand squish between her toes. *This has to be the best feeling in the world,* she thought as she strolled along the water's edge. The Pacific coast was a sight to behold, and the ocean had a calming effect on her. After a half hour of walking, she consoled herself with the fact that no matter what happened with the investigation, she was going to leave LA knowing she gave it her all.

CHAPTER THIRTY

Savannah

After English class, Savannah came back to her dorm, expecting to find it empty. Instead she found Nick lounging on her bed.

"Nick! Oh my God."

He stood up just in time for Savannah to leap into his arms and knock him back down on the bed. She smothered him with kisses.

"Hey, sweetheart. How's my girl?"

"Better now that you're home. You are home, right? Please tell me that you aren't leaving again."

"I'm home."

"I've missed you so much," Savannah said, tears of joy streaming down her face. "I thought you were never coming home."

"I told you I'd be back. I just needed to get out of here and let things cool down a little. Finding that tracker gave me a bit of a scare. I didn't want to put you and Haley under the microscope. So what did I miss?"

"Nothing much. Haley and I have been going to the NWM meetings, but everyone has kind of chilled after the fire. Even the aboveground activists have been quiet. Have you heard from Badger?"

"Not a word. I think we all need to stay clear of Badger for a while."

"I think Badger is a fucking lunatic, and I hope I never see him again," Savannah huffed.

"I don't know what got into him, Savannah. He's always been a little on the crazy side, but he's not usually reckless."

"He almost got you and Haley killed, and that security guard's death is on him. I hope he never comes back."

Nick tightened his embrace around her. "Everything is going to be fine. I'm home, Badger is gone, and things are back to normal. What have you been up to lately? How are classes?"

"Classes are going okay. I'm not going to win any academic awards this semester, that's for sure, but I'm passing everything. Even chemistry. And Lexie and I have been hiking together almost every weekend. I don't know what I would've done without her. She's been a great distraction while you were gone. Since Nora and I hardly ever talk anymore, it's nice to have a nonjudgmental person to hang out with," Savannah said.

"What about your parents and brother? Are you getting along with them any better?"

"Nope. I talk to my mom a couple of times a month. I haven't spoken to Hunter since Christmas. Anyway, Haley and I have decided that we want Lexie to go with us when we go to the Netherlands for The Gathering."

Nick's voice sounded hesitant. "Wow, that was a quick decision."

Savannah unclasped her arms from around Nick's neck and pushed away.

Nick exhaled. "If you and Haley want Lexie to come with us, then that's fine with me. I'll look forward to getting to know her better."

Savannah relaxed. She grinned at Nick. "I'd like that. She's been an amazing friend to me. I trust her completely."

"You haven't said anything to her about the fire, have you?"

Savannah sprung up from Nick's lap and turned on him. "Of course not! Why are you and Haley always thinking the worst of me? I take the security culture as seriously as you do. I haven't told anyone, and I never will." Savannah was so angry she could barely contain herself. "When are you going to trust me, Nick?"

Nick jumped up from the bed. "Calm down, Savannah. I do trust you. That came out wrong."

"Oh really? How was it supposed to come out? You don't trust me, and I've never given you any reason not to trust me. I haven't told a soul about what happened to us. I think you forget I'm as guilty as you."

"I'm sorry. You're right."

Nick sat down and put his head in his hands.

Savannah paced around the small room a couple of times and then went to the mini refrigerator in the corner. "Do you want something to drink?"

Nick looked up. "Sure."

"Water, juice, or Coke Zero?"

"Juice, please."

Savannah poured them each a glass of cranberry juice.

They drank in silence.

Savannah finally broke the silence. "Can we start over? I don't want to argue."

"Neither do I. I'm sorry."

Nick took another sip. "So you and Lexie have taken up hiking?"

"We have. And we've only been dangerously lost one time," Savannah said nonchalantly.

"As opposed to not-dangerously lost?" Nick asked.

"We weren't entirely at fault. The trail wasn't clearly marked, and we missed our turn. At the end of the day, we ended up on the wrong side of the mountain, miles away from the car."

Nick's eyes shot open. "What did you do?"

"We flagged down a motorist, and she drove us back to our car."

Nick chuckled. "Didn't you have a map?"

"We did, but it didn't help."

"Two women with a map and you still got lost. I need to buy you a compass," he told her.

Savannah put aside her anger, and she and Nick made love all afternoon. They were still snuggled up in the bed when Haley came home. "Look who the cat dragged in," she said as she entered the dorm room.

"How are you doing, girl?" Nick asked.

Haley turned her back so Savannah and Nick could put their clothes on. After the two were sufficiently dressed, Haley hugged Nick. "I'm glad you're home. That girl of yours has been worried sick about you."

"I'm glad to be back. Anything on the underground radar?"

"Nothing that I've heard. The police are still investigating the fire, but so far no persons of interest have been named."

"That's good."

"Any other trackers found?"

"Nope. Bobby, who works at the Jiffy Lube, has been checking all our cars for us. I think we might be in the clear," Haley said.

"I hope so, but you know how the feds are. They'll investigate a dead case forever. Hell, they're still searching for Jimmy Hoffa."

Haley laughed. "You got a point there."

Savannah sat quietly dressed in her rumpled up sweat pants, faded "I love NY" T-shirt, and pink piggy slippers.

"You look glamorous in your pig slippers," Haley joked.

"Nick has returned, so I can let myself go," Savannah jovially replied.

"Don't I have a say in this?" Nick asked.

"Nope, you lost your say so when you took a month-long sabbatical," Savannah responded.

"We'll see about that."

Nick grabbed Savannah and pretended to body slam her. He tickled her until she laughed so hard she snorted.

"Stop! Stop! I give."

Nick tickled her just a little longer and then helped her up from the floor.

"When you two are finished wrestling, do you think we could figure out what we're going to eat for dinner? I'm starving, and I don't feel like cafeteria food."

"If you can talk your roommate into leaving behind the

barnyard animal slippers, I'll take you two to dinner, as long as it doesn't cost me over forty dollars."

"Savannah, get those ridiculous slippers off. Big spender here is taking us to dinner."

CHAPTER THIRTY-ONE

Alexis

Feeling a new sense of urgency, Lexie decided to make another hiking date. Savannah seemed more talkative when they were out on the trails alone. *Hey hiking buddy. How about another hike this weekend?*

She drank a large glass of water and poured herself a bowl of cereal. Her phone beeped, letting her know that she had a text message.

Yes. Definitely.

Lexie remembered her lunch with Adam and decided to push things a little further. *Want to grab some coffee later?*

The phone beeped again. *I only have one class this morning, how about lunch instead?*

Lexie answered. *Even better. Where and when?*

Savannah texted back, *I'll come your way. Seed at noon?*

Cool. Meet you there.

Lexie called Kate but reached her voice mail. She left a quick message saying she was meeting Savannah for lunch in Venice. *That's strange,* she thought. Kate always answered her phone.

Fifteen minutes later, Kate returned the call.

"Sorry about that, Lexie. Adam and I were in a conference call with HQ."

"Oh God. What now?" Lexie asked.

"Same old shit. They want arrests, and they want them yesterday."

"Did you tell them we're going as fast as humanly possible?"

"We tried, but they're fucking hardheaded. They think they have all the answers."

"Well, if they think they can do it better, why don't they drag their happy asses out here and try?"

Lexie could hear Kate laughing.

"You have a way with words, Lexie."

"Did Adam even stand up for us? He seems to fold every time he gets a little pressure from those sons of bitches."

"He tried, but he has to be diplomatic about it."

"Diplomacy is over, as far as I'm concerned. Adam needs to find his balls and fight for this undercover operation. We have too much invested for HQ to shut us down now."

"I agree, but Adam has to play the game too. You and I have to concentrate on the case and gather the evidence for an indictment on this arson."

"I'm having lunch with Savannah today, and we're hiking again this weekend."

"Good. The more time you spend with her and the others, the better. Try not to think about all this administrative bullshit. It'll work itself out."

"Okay, I'll try. I'll call you when I get home from lunch."

"Where are you eating?"

"We're meeting at Seed at noon," Lexie answered.

"Is that the little place in Venice just off the Boardwalk, next door to the surf shop?"

"Yep, that's it."

"Okay. Good luck. I'll talk to you later."

* * * * *

Lexie activated her body recorder. It was a short walk to the restaurant from her apartment. Savannah was almost always on time, so Lexie didn't worry about running out of recording time on the device. As she neared the restaurant, she saw Savannah perched at an outside table with Nick sitting beside her. *The prodigal son has returned home,* Lexie thought.

Savannah spotted Lexie and sprang up from her chair. "Hey, Lexie. How are you?"

"I'm great!" Lexie turned to Nick. "Hi, Nick. Welcome back."

"Thanks. It's good to be back."

Everyone stood for an awkward moment.

Lexie broke the tension. "Have you guys ordered yet?"

"No, we were waiting for you," Savannah answered.

"I don't know about you two, but I'm starving."

"You're always starving," Savannah joked.

"Lexie and I love watching people in Venice," Savannah told Nick.

"It sounds like you two have become avid hikers as well," he added.

Lexie was excited to have something neutral to discuss. "We have, and we've been lost only one time."

Savannah giggled.

"What do you expect when you turn two women loose with a compass and a map?" Nick joked.

"Compass? We didn't have no stinking compass," Lexie said. "But for the record, I did buy one at REI after we got lost. So Nick, are you willing to brave a hiking trip with two women this weekend?"

Savannah's face lit up.

"Well, that depends," he said.

"On what?" Lexie asked.

"On whether or not I get to carry the compass."

"Well, I guess I could relinquish control of the compass to you."

"Then count me in."

The rest of the lunch was comfortable. The hiking stories seemed to put Nick at ease—that and the fact that Lexie didn't interrogate him about where he had been the past month. They made final plans for their weekend hiking excursion and went their separate ways after lunch.

* * * * *

Savannah and Nick were two minutes away, so Lexie activated her body wire, did a cursory inspection of the apartment, and walked outside. She was saving the recorder on the CamelBak for the hike. When Lexie saw Nick's car make the corner, she saw that Haley was in the back seat.

Yes, she thought, *this is my chance to hit the jackpot.*

"Hey, girl, long time no see," Haley said as Lexie crawled into the backseat.

"You ready to hike your ass off?" Nick asked.

"You bet!" Lexie said. "I'm glad that you came, Haley. We've missed you lately."

"School has been kicking my ass. I've been stuck studying every weekend."

"That sucks."

"Yes, it does, but I think I'm finally caught up. I need to balance school and my activist projects better."

"I can relate to that," Savannah said.

"Where are we heading?" Lexie asked.

"Have you ever hiked Malibu Creek?" Nick asked.

"No."

"It's an amazing hike," Nick continued. "I think you'll enjoy it. It's a half-day hike. Several movies and TV shows were filmed there."

"Really? That's cool. Which ones?"

"The TV show *M*A*S*H*. They filmed the movies *Butch Cassidy and the Sundance Kid* and *The Planet of the Apes* there, too."

"This is going to be fun," Lexie said. "I can't wait."

"I packed lunch for all of us," Savannah said. "We might have to take turns carrying the cooler unless we leave it behind and eat after our hike."

"Since you took the time to pack our lunch, the least we can do is help you haul it around," Nick laughed.

The mood was light for the rest of car ride. Once they arrived at the trailhead and unpacked their gear, Lexie activated the recording device hidden in her CamelBak. She felt guilty doing so, secretly hoping that these three weren't involved in the arson. The majority of the people she worked with in the FBI were total jackasses. It was refreshing to spend time with people who cared about something besides themselves or their careers.

After hiking all morning, the four took a much-needed lunch break.

"So, are you guys still thinking about attending The Gathering?" Lexie asked. She held her breath waiting for a response. Surprisingly, it was Nick who responded.

"I plan to go if I can scrape up enough money. What about you, Lexie? Have you given the trip some thought?"

"I have, and it sounds like an awesome opportunity. I'd be too nervous to travel overseas by myself, but if you all are going, I'd love to go."

"I think that all four of us should go," Savannah said. "It would be a blast."

"Since you've been before, Nick, what's it like? I mean, is it like a conference where you sit in a classroom, or is it more hands-on stuff?" Lexie asked.

"It's different from the animal rights conferences that we have in the United States. The people conducting the blocks of instruction are all hard-core animal rights activists from all over the world. The emphasis is on underground direct action. At the conferences in the United States, people are afraid they are going to be arrested, so nobody wants to talk about direct action campaigns. Overseas, most of the conference is dedicated to direct action."

"Sounds like it's more what I'm looking for," Lexie

commented. "That's the stuff we should be teaching in the US, not this fucking welfarist bullshit."

All three looked at Lexie with shocked expressions.

"What? You guys know I'm right. We're too soft in the US. Most of the US activists are too afraid to go to jail or that daddy will take their car away if they get in trouble. Am I wrong?"

"You're not wrong," Nick answered. "I just didn't realize that you felt so strongly about direct action."

Lexie continued. "I used to think that the answer was harsher laws for animal abusers, but somewhere along the line, I realized that politicians don't give a shit about animals. There's no money in saving animals, so the greedy bastards won't listen when you try to convince them to write stricter animal cruelty laws. Most animal cruelty statutes are a fucking joke. The only way to get attention is to do something drastic. People sit up and take notice when something blows up."

"The only way to hurt animal abusers is to hit them in the wallet," Nick said. "Money is the only thing that's important to them."

"We make it so difficult for new activists to learn the art of direct action," Lexie said. "There are books and guides out there, but I think the best way to learn a skill is to be able to do some hands-on training and to discuss options in open forums. We're so afraid of each other that we won't help each other learn new tactics."

Nick ran his hands through his hair. Lexie wondered if it was a sign of apprehension, but to her surprise he continued with the discussion.

"You definitely need to go with us to The Gathering. It could be the opportunity that you've been looking for. But let's be careful; I know we're all friends here, but talking about direct action is dangerous."

"I know it is," Lexie said. "That's why I'm discussing it out here in the middle of nowhere. There isn't anyone around who can overhear us, and I trust you three. I really want to go to The Gathering. I'll find a way to scrape together the money."

"I'm glad that you want to go," Nick said. "We need more people like you in the movement, people who aren't afraid to dig in and get their hands dirty."

"I'll start putting some money aside for the trip," Lexie stated. "By the way, this lunch is fantastic, Savannah. Thanks for making it."

"It's very good. Thank you, sweetie," Nick agreed.

"Yeah, thanks, Savannah," Haley added.

"It was no trouble," Savannah said. "This is nice. Friends hiking and socializing. I feel comfortable when I'm with you guys."

"I feel the same way," Lexie added. "I think you three are the first *real* friends that I've made in a long time."

Sadly, there was more truth in that comment than Lexie cared to admit.

* * * * *

Lexie's day had started off badly. After a night of tossing and turning, her cell phone rang at the crack of dawn.

An emergency meeting had been called, and her presence was needed at the office. In her efforts to hustle, she had dripped coffee down her new shirt. *Damnit. I should never buy anything white.* She dabbed at the coffee stain as she walked to the door, only making it worse.

Kate was there to greet her. "Sorry that I had to wake you up this morning," she said.

"No worries. How bad is it?"

"Bad."

"Shit!"

Lexie and Kate sat down near Adam. The conference room was a frantic mess. People were scurrying around in all directions.

"The forensic report came back," Adam said. "We have a positive DNA match on the gloves that were recovered in the dumpster in the alley."

"That's fantastic," Lexie exclaimed. "Who did it match?"

"It's a positive match for Savannah Riley."

Lexie's heart raced, and her palms were sweating. She made an effort to try to look calm and unfazed.

"Are you okay, Lexie?" Kate whispered.

"Fine . . . I'm fine."

Adam continued with an explanation of the results. "The fire destroyed most of the evidence in the laboratory. The accelerant used to start the fire was gasoline. Nothing specific, just regular eighty-seven-percent-grade gasoline. No fingerprints were found anywhere in the lab. We recovered pieces of a two-way radio that was discarded in the alley with the gloves. There were no fingerprints on it, but our lab is still working on trying to reassemble the radio and pull any GPS data from it."

"What's the plan?" Lexie asked.

"As you can guess, HQ is pushing us to arrest Savannah and try to make her flip on her coconspirators. We want your input into her mindset. Do you think that she'll give it up?"

Lexie felt lightheaded. She needed an excuse to get up and move around. "Do you mind if I get a cup of coffee?"

"Of course not. Help yourself."

"I'll be right back."

Lexie walked out of the conference room but stopped just outside the door to catch her breath. She overheard Adam and Kate talking.

"What's up with her?" Adam asked.

"She'll be fine. I think it's just a bit of a shock."

"Isn't this what she wanted? This is good news."

"I know, but we can't forget that she's spent almost every day with these people since she arrived here."

"Are you saying she's friends with them?"

"That's not what I'm saying, but we have to give her a little time to process the information. We can't bombard her with this information and expect her not to be emotional. She'll be fine, but she needs a little time."

Lexie knew she shouldn't be listening, but she wasn't about to leave.

"Unfortunately HQ isn't going to allow us time to *process emotions*," Adam said in a patronizing tone.

"Don't be a jackass, Adam. You really have drunk the management Kool-Aid."

He looked down at the stack of files sitting in front of

him. "I'm sorry, Kate. You're right. I let myself get sucked up in the HQ frenzy."

"I'm sorry I called you a jackass."

"No problem. I was pretty much acting like one."

Lexie took that as her cue to leave and go to the break room, where she poured herself a cup of coffee. She didn't want it, but she needed a minute to collect herself. Lexie took a sip and returned to the conference room. When she sat down, both Kate and Adam looked uncomfortable.

"What? Who died? You two look highly stressed."

"We're good," Adam said. "How are you? We hit you with this information pretty hard. Are you all right?"

"I'm fine. This is great news. We've achieved what we set out to do. Let's talk strategy."

Lexie could hear her own voice as she spoke, but she didn't completely comprehend what was happening around her.

"How fragile is Savannah? Do you think she'll give up the others if we snatch her up and bring her in for an interview?" Adam asked.

"Nick's return is bad timing," Lexie stated. "Savannah was much more susceptible when she was out of contact with him. Now that he's back, she has a renewed sense of purpose. But she's young and has never been in trouble, so we have that going for us."

"What else do you know about her background that might help or hurt us?"

Lexie mulled over the question. "Well, her father is an attorney. I'm not sure if that helps or hurts. Her brother attends The Citadel. They're a very old-South, conservative family. She's estranged from her family and friends back in South Carolina because of her animal rights activism. Her family might be useful to us." Lexie slumped in her chair.

"What are you thinking, Lexie?" Kate asked.

"This doesn't make sense. Savannah isn't sophisticated enough to be able to pull off that lab fiasco. She's still learning the ropes. I know the DNA evidence puts her at the crime scene, but I don't think she was the leader. It had to be Nick. That has to be why he left town so quickly."

"Why do you think he returned?" Adam inquired.

"Maybe he felt safe since no arrests have been made, or perhaps he really loves Savannah. I don't know."

"What about Savannah's roommate?" Adam asked. "What do you know about her?"

"Haley is definitely devoted enough to the cause to be involved. She's more security-conscious than Savannah, too. It makes sense that if someone was going to make a mistake, it would be Savannah. She tossed those gloves without checking for security cameras and discarded the radio in the same alley as the gloves. She wasn't thinking clearly when she ran from the crime scene. How do you suppose she got separated from the rest of the perpetrators?"

Kate looked up from the lab report she was studying. "She was the lookout!" she exclaimed. "That's why she wasn't with the others."

"Yes!" Lexie jumped in. "And when sugar turned to shit, she got the hell out of there. That explains why she was alone and on foot when the rest of the group took off in a vehicle. It totally makes sense."

"I like the theory, ladies," Adam said, "but it's still a

theory. We need to get Savannah's cooperation so we can indict the whole group. Which brings us back to the question of how to proceed with the investigation. With the DNA evidence, we should have enough probable cause for an arrest warrant for Savannah."

"I think we have a couple of options," Lexie said. "One, you arrest her and hit her with all the information and try to get her to cooperate without giving up the undercover operation. I'll remain in an undercover capacity and try to get her to talk to me after her arrest, but it might take more time than HQ is willing to give us.

"HQ is going to push for a quick arrest and prosecution," Adam said. "There was too much publicity surrounding the incident."

Lexie shifted in her chair. "The second option is we quietly arrest Savannah and tell her about the undercover operation and see if she'll work with me to get more substantial evidence on the others."

Kate jumped in. "Whoa, that's risky, Lexie. She could change her mind and expose you as an FBI agent."

"Well, that wouldn't be optimal," Lexie said, "but I don't think she'd do that to me. If she confesses, she'll be a broken mess. We need to persuade her to cooperate and record conversations with her coconspirators. If Savannah was merely a lookout for the group, she could cooperate in exchange for immunity."

Mike, who had remained quiet, spoke up. "You're kidding yourself, Lexie. No judge in his right mind is going to offer immunity to someone involved in an action that resulted in a death. And another thing: the US Attorney's

Office will want more than just Savannah's statement. She'll need to wear a wire to gather evidence to corroborate her testimony."

"Let's worry about getting her arrested and see what happens," Adam said.

"When you bring her in for the interview, can I watch?" Lexie asked.

"That's a good idea," Adam stated. "Kate and I will do the interview, and one of us will consult with you periodically for input. We'll expose the undercover operation only if it's an absolute necessity. I'd better get working on the affidavit for the complaint."

Lexie pulled a USB thumb drive out of the front pocket of her backpack and gave it to Kate. "Here are my latest reports."

"Let's go over to my desk and download them onto my computer. Did you bring the recorders with you?" Kate asked.

"Yep, they're in here too," she said, motioning to her backpack.

"I have a fresh recorder for you on my desk." Kate got up from the conference table and gathered her files.

Lexie spent most of the day with Adam and Kate helping with the affidavit. It was easier to sit with them and have the reports readily available. At the end of the day, the affidavit was finished and ready for review by the assistant United States attorney, whom Adam had an appointment with the first thing the next morning.

On the way home, Lexie played out all the possible outcomes for the case in her head. Deep down, she knew that no matter how she sliced the pie, Savannah would hate her. Like any good undercover agent, she had built the friendship to betray the friendship.

CHAPTER THIRTY-TWO

Savannah

Savannah, halfway dressed for class, leaned over and kissed Nick, who was still naked in her bed. He grabbed her and pulled her back into the bed.

"Don't go, babe. We're still making up for lost time," Nick teased.

"And whose fault is that?" Savannah teased right back.

"Ouch, touché."

"I would love to stay in bed with you, but I have a chemistry test this morning. Some of us have to be responsible."

"I'll show you responsible." Nick jumped on top of Savannah and started kissing her neck despite his scruffy, four-day beard. Savannah burst out laughing.

"We'll finish this later," Savannah promised as she jumped up and finished dressing. "Haley should be home any minute, so you might want to put some pants on."

"Bye, baby," Nick yelled as Savannah was halfway out the door. "See you tonight."

Savannah turned and blew Nick a kiss. "Later, Nicholas."

"It's sexy when you use my full name. Come back

to bed."

"Can't. Later, love."

Savannah threw her backpack over one shoulder and rushed out of the dorm, making a beeline to the chemistry building. She walked her usual route, which took her down an alley shortcut. Before she reached the end of the alley, a dark, American-made sedan pulled in and cut her off. She moved to get out of the way, but two large men wearing bulletproof vests with "FBI" written in large gold letters on the front exited the vehicle and grabbed her by the arms.

"FBI. Savannah Riley, you're under arrest," the larger of the two agents said. He wrenched her arms behind her back and slapped handcuffs on her.

A third agent, who had been driving the car, pointed a gun at her chest.

Savannah was in shock. *Could this really be happening?* "I'm what? For what?" Savannah stammered.

"Everything will be explained to you when we get to the FBI office. I'm going to search you. Do you have anything on you that can hurt me?"

"Hurt you? No. Nothing."

"Do you have any weapons on you or in your backpack?"

"Weapons? No. Of course not."

The agent patted her down and searched her backpack. He quickly stuffed her into the backseat of the sedan and took off. The whole encounter took less than two minutes, and there were no witnesses to the arrest.

* * * * *

Savannah shivered in the frigid interrogation room of the Los Angeles FBI Field Office. Across from her sat Agents Harper and Summers. They had just informed her of her options.

Agent Harper continued, "You are charged with conspiracy to violate the Animal Enterprise Terrorism Act, conspiracy to commit arson, and felony murder."

Savannah's mind was racing. *The fire. I knew that this could happen. What should I do? Nick would tell me to remain silent. Ask for a lawyer. What would my dad tell me to do? Think. Think. What should I do? This isn't some speeding ticket. It's the fucking FBI, and they're talking about me spending the rest of my life in a federal prison.*

"I don't think I should talk to you, sir," Savannah whimpered.

"That's certainly your right," Agent Harper said. "Do you know what the Animal Enterprise Terrorism Act is?"

Savannah could barely speak. "No, not really. I'm ... I'm not sure."

"It's a federal statute that prohibits any person from engaging in any conduct for the purpose of damaging or interfering with the operations of an animal enterprise. The statute includes academic and commercial enterprises that use animals. It carries a steep prison term. You don't want to be labeled a terrorist."

"Terrorist? Oh God, I'm not a terrorist. What are you talking about?" Savannah's voice was thin and scratchy.

Kate pulled her chair closer to Savannah. "What Agent Harper is referring to is domestic terrorism. Any person who violates the Animal Enterprise Terrorism Act is considered a domestic terrorist."

"You mean like Timothy McVeigh?"

"Yes," Kate answered. "You need to talk to us, Savannah. We can help you."

Savannah's stomach seized, and tears flowed down her cheeks. *Oh my God . . . oh my God. What am I supposed to do? My parents are going to disown me. I'm not a terrorist. I can't go to prison. I should ask for a lawyer.*

The male agent's voice broke the silence. "Savannah, before you make your decision, there is something I want you to see."

Agent Harper turned on the television that was sitting on a table in the corner. He hit Play on the DVD player. Savannah's heart sank as she watched a grainy video from the alley on the night of the fire. She thought she might throw up as she watched herself break the two-way radio and throw the pieces in the dumpster. She watched herself remove the gloves and toss them in the dumpster.

"Before you say that the person on this video isn't you, let me assure you that we know it is you." He pulled out another piece of paper from his file folder. "This is a DNA report that confirms the gloves found in that dumpster are a positive match to you, so knowing that we have your DNA on the gloves and a video of you fleeing the crime scene, will you now consent to this interview?"

Without realizing what she was doing, Savannah nodded.

"Savannah, I need you to sign this form stating that we read you your rights and that you are willing to waive your rights and talk to us."

Her hand shaking, Savannah took the form and the pen from Adam. "If I change my mind, I can stop, right?"

"Yes. You can stop at any time."

Savannah signed the Waiver of Rights Form with her free hand. She looked up and felt tears running down both her cheeks.

Adam handed her a box of Kleenex that was sitting near him on the table.

"I'll tell you what I did, but I can't tell you about anyone else," Savannah said.

"That's not how this works," Agent Harper said. "If you want to help yourself, then you have to tell us the whole truth."

"I didn't know any of the other persons involved. I met them the day of the action and everyone was wearing masks."

Savannah told the agents a made-up account of what happened. She claimed to have met everyone involved over the Internet and did not know anyone's real name. Adam put down his pen and crossed his arms.

"I wasn't born yesterday," Adam said. "That story was ludicrous. Lying to a federal agent is a chargeable offense. By lying to us, you're making things worse."

Adam pulled out a family photo of the victim with his smiling wife and beautiful children. He placed the photo on the table in front of Savannah. He then placed a crime scene photo of a charred body next to the family photo. Savannah gasped and averted her eyes.

"Look at the photos, Savannah," Adam said in a raspy voice.

"I . . . I can't look at them," Savannah said.

"Look at the photos! You and your friends did this. Those three children no longer have a father because of you."

Savannah sobbed and shook violently.

"I'm going to give you one more chance," Adam said. "I can rip up my interview notes, and we can start over, or I can book you in the jail. It's your choice, but I'm not going to waste any more of my time listening to this garbage you're trying to feed us."

Kate reached over and touched Savannah's arm.

"I know this is difficult, Savannah, but it's imperative that you tell us the truth. It's the only way to save yourself."

"Listen to me," Adam said. "We've checked your recent travel activity. Are your parents aware of your activities? Are they financially supporting this terrorist cell of yours? I don't think you want us digging into your parents' finances."

Savannah stared at the wall. Neither Adam nor Kate interrupted the silence.

"Okay," Savannah said. "I'll tell you the truth."

Adam ripped the top few pages from the yellow legal pad and tore them up.

"Let's start fresh," he told her.

Once Savannah started talking, everything came pouring out of her. She confessed to it all. Adam pushed her until she broke and told them about Nick and Haley. She told them about how Badger started the fire and that Nick and Haley didn't have any knowledge of his intentions.

"If you were the lookout, how do you know Badger started the fire?" Kate asked.

"Because Haley told me he did."

Kate continued, "Did Haley see Badger set the fire?"

"Yes. Wait, I mean no. Haley wasn't with him when he set the fire. Nick was the only person in the room with Badger."

"In other words, Haley doesn't know for sure who set the fire," Adam added.

"Nick told Haley that Badger set the fire."

"Do you know Badger's real name?" Kate asked.

"No. I don't know much about him. He's extremely intelligent and up until the night of the fire, he seemed like an even-tempered guy. You know . . . the kind of person who thinks things through. Very analytical."

Throughout the interview, Savannah had emotional outbursts. She cried until she was out of tears.

"You're making the right decision," Adam said.

Savannah nodded. The agents took a break, and Kate brought Savannah a bag of potato chips and a Coke. She wrapped an FBI raid jacket around Savannah's trembling shoulders.

Savannah looked down at the blue raid jacket with FBI written in large gold lettering. "When I was in high school, I wanted to be an FBI agent. This isn't how I pictured wearing the jacket," she said.

"So you thought about becoming a special agent?" Kate asked.

"I was a big fan of the TV show *Criminal Minds*," Savannah replied. "Plus the men on TV who play FBI agents are usually hot."

Kate laughed. "Well, it's not like TV."

Adam jumped in. "Hey, I'm sitting right here."

Kate chuckled. "I meant the *Criminal Minds* stuff, not

the hot agents."

Savannah laid her head down on the table. "I can't believe I'm in the middle of this mess. Please help me. My parents are going to kill me. I'll do anything you ask of me, but I can't go to prison."

Kate received a text message. She read the message and showed it to Adam. "Savannah, we're going to step outside for a moment. Do you need anything?"

"No. I'm okay."

CHAPTER THIRTY-THREE

Alexis

Lexie watched through a two-way mirror as Kate and Adam interviewed Savannah. She texted Kate asking to consult with her and Adam on strategy. The door opened, and Lexie bombarded them before they could sit down. "This is our golden ticket. Savannah can get recordings of all the other targets. If she can give us the main targets, then we need to call the AUSA and get her a deal."

Adam sat down and crossed his arms.

Lexie continued. "For Christ's sake, Adam, she was just a lookout. Don't we want Badger and rest of the major hitters? I could work with her and wire her up for meetings. It would look natural, since we spend so much time together."

"Lexie, you're talking about revealing yourself to her as an FBI agent," Adam stated. "What if she changes her mind and double crosses you? Nick Harris has a violent criminal history, and we won't be able to protect you."

"She won't do that. I know her. Besides, once her defense attorney gets the discovery package, I'm burned anyway. Savannah will know from the FBI reports that the undercover agent was me, so if I can work with her to catch the bigger fish, we should do it."

Adam took a breath and ran his hands through his thinning hair. "What do you think, Kate?" he asked.

"Normally I would say absolutely not, but in this situation, Lexie may be right. Savannah came clean almost immediately, and she needs to find a way to get out from under this case."

Kate put her hand on Lexie's shoulder. "You do realize she's going to go ballistic. She's going to be hurt and angry with you. Are you prepared for that?"

"I know, and I am, but if I can talk to her and get her to understand that this is her only way out of this mess, she'll cooperate."

"Careful, Lexie," Adam warned. "You can't promise her anything. We don't know what the AUSA will be willing to do as far as making a deal. Ms. Griffin is a pit bull with these cases."

"I won't promise her anything, but Ms. Griffin is one of the finest assistant United States attorneys in the country. She'll do what's right. She'll be thrilled if we can give her recordings of the coconspirators talking about the crime."

"Don't get ahead of yourself, Sherlock," Adam said. "You know how these extremists operate. Savannah may not be able to get them to talk about the fire."

"You don't know Savannah. She's a Southerner. If anyone can get them to talk, it's her."

Adam shifted in his seat, his body rigid and his expression subdued. "Don't you think that we should slow down and think this through, Lexie?"

"We don't have time. We need to move before she changes her mind."

"This makes me extremely uncomfortable," Adam confided.

"I'm not crazy about it either," Kate added, "but Lexie is right. We need to hit her while she's the most vulnerable."

Adam stood and paced the floor. "Are you absolutely sure that you want to do this?"

"Yes. I think in the long run it's the best plan. I know that Savannah is going to freak at first, but she'll calm down, and we can reason with her."

"Okay. Kate and I will go brief the supervisor. You stay in here until we get the final approval from Mike."

Lexie's right knee bounced as she waited for Adam and Kate to return to the interview room. She returned to the two-way mirror when she heard Kate's voice in the room next door.

Kate and Adam took their previous seats, and Kate continued with the interview. "Savannah, there is something else we need to discuss with you."

"I'm listening," Savannah said.

"You mentioned earlier that you needed to find a way out of this mess. We might have a way to lessen your liability."

Savannah sat up straight. "Really? How? I'll do anything."

"While we were outside, Agent Harper spoke with the assistant United States attorney who is prosecuting this case. Her name is Ms. Griffin, and she is willing to consider cutting you a deal in exchange for substantial cooperation."

"What does that mean?" Savannah asked.

Kate pulled her chair closer to Savannah and continued, "This is a gift, Savannah. AUSA Griffin is not inclined to cut many deals. We explained to her that you were the lookout and not in the lab when the fire was started. She's willing to help you with the charges if you give her something in exchange."

"Like what?"

"You have to be willing to tell us everything you know about the fire and all the people involved. Everything you tell us has to be truthful. And, if necessary, you have to be willing to testify at trial."

Savannah sobbed.

Kate reached out and touched her shoulder. "The more you do to help yourself now, the better the deal in the end."

"I'm gonna have to testify against everyone? Even Haley and Nick?"

"Yes. If they go to trial."

"You people need to go after Badger. He's the one who caused the fire. He's the one who should go to jail. Can't I just testify against him?"

"It doesn't work that way," Kate said. "You have to give complete cooperation to get a deal from the government. We may have a way to help you, though."

"How?"

Lexie continued to watch the interview unfold through the two-way glass. *Please take the deal,* she thought.

Adam took the lead. "Savannah, the lab arson is only one of many crimes that this underground group has committed. The FBI has been investigating this terrorist cell for a long time. We even have undercover agents who have infiltrated the group. Would you be willing to work with one of our undercover agents to gather evidence? Before you answer, let me tell you that this level of cooperation would go a long way in helping make this case go away for you."

Savannah stared at Adam. "You mean if I work with this undercover agent, I won't have to go to prison?"

"I can't promise you anything. Having said that, I have seen cooperators in similar situations walk away without doing any jail time."

"What would I have to do?" Savannah asked.

"You would go back to your normal life. You couldn't tell anyone that you were arrested. At some point, you would be given a recording device to record conversations with various members of your organization."

"You make it sound like we're al-Qaeda. We're just a group of activists. We never meant to hurt anyone."

"Well you did hurt someone," Adam stated. "In fact you killed someone. His children will grow up without their father because of your actions."

Savannah hung her head. "I know. I think about that every day."

"Then help us, Savannah," Adam said. "By helping us, you help yourself. You shouldn't go to jail for the actions of others. You need to protect yourself. Are you willing to work with us?"

Savannah fidgeted in her chair. The handcuff clanked against the metal bar. "Yes," she whispered.

"Was that a yes?" Adam asked.

"Yes," Savannah said louder. "I'll do whatever you need

me to do. Please just get me out of this mess."

Kate once again touched Savannah's shoulder. "You're doing the right thing," she said.

Adam walked over and removed the handcuff from the bar. He freed Savannah's hand from the cuff.

Tears streamed down her face, leaving tracks in her makeup. She rotated her wrist. "Thank you."

"Savannah, what do you know about the backgrounds of Haley, Nick, and Badger?" Kate asked.

"Not very much. I don't even know Badger's real name."

"Did you know that both Haley and Nick have criminal records?"

Savannah's eyes widened.

"Has Nick ever hurt you?" Adam asked.

"No. Never. He would never hurt me."

"Nick was involved in a violent encounter last year," Adam said. "He was convicted of assault and battery."

"I don't believe you."

"We have no reason to lie to you," Kate said. "We need you to understand that there's an element of danger involved in working with us."

Savannah shifted uneasily in her seat. She raked her slim fingers through her mop of blond hair.

"There's something else that we need to discuss," Kate said.

"Oh God. What else?"

"This is going to be difficult for you to hear, but in the end it might just save your life."

Savannah took a deep breath and exhaled. "I'm listening."

Lexie's heart was thumping. She sat down and waited for her cue to enter the interview room. *Please don't let her hate me forever*, she thought.

"We told you earlier that the FBI has been investigating your group of extremists for quite a while," Kate said. "During this time, an FBI undercover agent infiltrated the group. You and this agent will work together to gather evidence against the persons responsible for the fire."

"What kind of evidence?" Savannah asked.

"You'll record conversations with members of the group and get them to talk about the fire."

"Are you crazy? I can't just go strolling in with some FBI agent and start asking people about the fire. They'll never talk to me."

"We're not asking you to do that, Savannah," Adam said. "The undercover agent will help you with the equipment. Chances are she won't be around when you have the conversations."

"She? So the undercover agent is a girl?"

"Yes, and it's someone you know."

The door opened, and Lexie walked in. Savannah's mouth dropped open.

"Savannah, let me explain," Lexie said.

"You! No, it can't be you! You're my best friend. You've been lying to me this whole time?"

"No, of course not. It's true that I'm an FBI agent, but I'm your friend too."

"You aren't my friend! You're a liar."

Savannah's face was bright red, and she was shaking from anger. "I can't believe you're a fucking FBI agent.

All this time I thought we were friends, but you were just using me."

Adam stood up and gave his seat to Lexie.

"I know you're upset," Lexie said. "I would be upset too, if it happened to me, but you need to calm down and think about how this can help you."

Adam intervened. "Savannah, it was Lexie's idea to call the US attorney's office."

"So it was your idea to turn me into a dirty, rotten snitch? Thanks for that! Fuck you, Lexie. Or is Lexie even your name?"

"I'm sorry, Savannah," Lexie said. "I'm sorry you feel betrayed. I was just doing my job."

"Is that supposed to make me feel better?"

"No, I guess not. I like you. When the DNA report came back a positive match for you, I was crushed. Of all the people in the group, I didn't want it to be you."

Savannah squeezed the sides of her head with both hands as if to keep it from exploding.

Lexie continued. "I know you're angry. Like it or not, I'm the person who can help you the most. Together we can gather the necessary evidence to make the US attorney's office happy, and in turn get you the best deal possible. You have to trust me."

"Trust you? After you betrayed me? That's easier said than done."

"I know, but I have to know that you're on board with this plan and aren't going to run back and spill the beans to Haley or Nick."

"Savannah, do you understand that if you disclose

Lexie's identity to anyone, you will negate any deal you have with the US attorney's office?" Kate asked.

Savannah looked over at Kate. "I understand."

"Let's work on a game plan," Adam suggested. "We need to get Savannah home as soon as possible. What time would you normally get home, Savannah?"

"I usually get home from class around four o'clock."

"That's good. It buys us a little time to plan."

CHAPTER THIRTY-FOUR

Savannah

Three days had passed since Savannah's encounter with the FBI. She waited for Lexie at the coffee shop on Venice Beach. She watched Lexie round the corner and head her way.

"You want a coffee?" Lexie asked. "My treat."

"If you're buying, I'll have a vanilla latte."

Lexie grinned. "Sure thing. Be right back."

A few minutes later, Lexie returned carrying two lattes. "Here you go."

"Thanks."

"How are you doing?" Lexie asked.

"As good as can be expected, I guess. I'm still a little in shock."

"That's understandable. Are you ready for tonight?"

Savannah took a sip of her latte. "Ready as I'll ever be. I'm scared, Lexie."

"I know. You'll do fine. Just be yourself. How are you going to bring up the topic?"

"Haley and I are riding to the NWM meeting with Nick.

I'll bring it up in the car on the way home."

"Sounds good. Do you need a refresher course on the equipment?" Lexie asked.

"No. It seems easy enough. I'll turn it on in the bathroom before we leave the house. Are you going to the meeting?"

"Yeah. I'll walk over from my apartment."

Savannah looked lost in thought. She repositioned herself, crossing her legs Indian style. "I'm dreading the day I have to tell my family about all of this."

"If you want, I can go with you."

"You would do that?"

"Of course. I know you're still upset with me, but I do care about you. All the time we spent together hiking and hanging out wasn't completely for work. I enjoyed our time together. It made me sick to lie to you."

"How many cases have you worked like this one?" Savannah asked.

"You mean where I was an undercover agent?"

Savannah nodded.

"This was my first."

"Really? Wow."

They sat in silence sipping their lattes.

After a few minutes, Savannah continued. "You're really good at it . . . the undercover stuff."

"Thanks," Lexie murmured.

"I'm still mad at you, but I understand you were just doing your job."

"Do you think you'll ever be able to forgive me?" Lexie asked.

Savannah thought about it for a moment before

answering, "I already have."

Lexie looked up from her latte. "In training they told us that undercover agents build relationships to betray relationships. I never understood the gravity of that statement until three days ago."

They sat in silence finishing their lattes.

* * * * *

Savannah, Nick, and Haley arrived a few minutes before the start of the NWM meeting. Both Savannah and Haley hugged Jeannette as they entered the house.

"Hi, beautiful," Nick said as he kissed Jeannette on the cheek.

"Such a sweet-talker," Jeannette joked. "Everyone's in the living room."

Savannah saw Lexie in the corner talking to Phillip.

The meeting was uneventful. Toward the end, Lexie asked if anyone had any updates on the animals in the UCLA fire. To Savannah's relief, it sparked a discussion about the lab action. Prior to leaving the meeting, Savannah made a trip to the bathroom and activated the recording device that was installed in the lining of her jacket. Savannah, Haley, and Nick said goodbye to Phillip and Jeannette and strolled to the car. Haley jumped in the backseat. They were halfway back to the dorm when Savannah turned sideways so she could see both Haley and Nick.

"Guys, I'm still wigged out about the fire."

Haley and Nick looked at her at the same time.

"What are you talking about, Savannah?" Nick asked.

"You know what I'm talking about. Every time someone brings up the lab fire, it makes me want to throw up. I know you said never to discuss it, but it's just the three of us, and I need to talk."

"There's nothing to discuss," Nick said angrily.

"A man died, Nick. You and Haley act like it's no big deal, but it is a big deal. Badger killed that poor guy, and he went off on his merry way, leaving us to deal with the mess."

The tires screeched as Nick violently pulled the car into a parking lot. He turned so he could face Savannah. "There is no mess. The police aren't looking at us, and Badger is gone," he said.

"What happens when he comes back?" Savannah asked.

"He's not coming back. He's up north, and he plans to stay there. Killing the security guard was an accident. He was at the wrong place at the wrong time."

"He was a casualty of war," Haley added. "Sometimes, bad shit happens."

"I can't accept that, Haley," Savannah spat out.

Nick reached over and grabbed Savannah's chin. "Fucking accept it, Savannah!" he said. "It happened. We can't change that fact. We have to move on and continue fighting for the animals."

Savannah jerked her chin out of Nick's hand.

"You have to stop obsessing over this," Haley added. "It's in the past, and you have to quit bringing it up."

Nick took a breath and spoke more calmly. "Remember when we first discussed the security culture?"

"I remember."

"What was the first rule?" he asked.

"That we never discuss past actions."

"And what are you doing right now?"

"Don't act so condescending, Nick. I know the fucking rules. It's just the three of us here, and we can't be overheard. What's the harm in talking about it right now?"

Nick became hostile. "We do not talk about past acts!" he screamed. "I'm sorry that you're upset, but you have to fucking let it go. If you snap, you take us all down with you. Do you want to do that, Savannah? Do you want to go to jail?"

"Of course not. I'm sorry that I'm not coldhearted like you and Haley. Killing the security guard bothers me, and I was just the lookout. Not to mention that when the fire was raging, I thought you both were dead. I was terrified I would never see either one of you again. You could be a little more understanding and help me through this ordeal instead of shutting me out. Maybe I'm not cut out for this shit after all."

"Just chill, Savannah," Haley said. "As long as you stay cool, nothing's going to happen to any of us. We need to stick together. Badger is gone. He's not coming back to LA. The other people involved have all scattered. You're the only person who can fuck this up."

"How am I going to fuck it up, Haley?"

"By running your mouth."

"I'm not talking to anyone. Just you two."

"Are you sure that you haven't said anything to Lexie?" Haley asked.

"Of course not. Why would you even ask me that?"

"You two seem awful chummy these days."

"She's my best friend." The words almost choked Savannah to say.

"That's why I'm asking."

"I haven't told Lexie anything. I wouldn't want to involve her in this fucked-up mess."

"Let's keep it that way," Nick sneered.

The conversation was going worse than Savannah imagined. She needed to rehabilitate herself, in order to get more information. It was time to turn on the waterworks. "I'm sorry," she said through sobs.

They sat silently for a few moments.

Nick broke the silence. "Savannah, it's not that we're trying to be cruel, but you can't bring this up again. The fire was an awful thing, and I'm sorry that it happened on your first action. It was an accident. You have to understand that Haley and I had no idea that Badger was going to start a fire. He was crazy that night."

"Nick's right," Haley added. "Badger didn't let us in on his little plan to burn the place down. We feel bad that the guard died, but he was working for the enemy. You have to stop thinking about the fire. It's over and done. We have to learn from the experience and move on."

Savannah looked back at Haley. "What about the other people who were involved that night? What happened to them? Will they talk?"

"They scattered to the wind after the fire," Nick said. "They knew the risk they were taking. Trust me, they'll never talk about that night."

"And you must never bring it up again," Haley said.

"This has to be the last time we ever discuss it."

"I understand," Savannah acknowledged. "I'll never bring it up again."

Nick reached out and touched Savannah's face. "When the fire started, all I could think about was you. I escaped the fire to get back to you. I love you, Savannah."

Savannah thought she would die. Her heart was breaking into a million pieces. "I love you too."

CHAPTER THIRTY-FIVE

Alexis

Lexie walked back to her apartment checking her cell phone every couple of minutes. Savannah was supposed to text when she made it home. Lexie was worried about her, so she called Kate to pass the time.

"Hello," Kate said. "How was the meeting?"

"Pretty typical. Nothing noteworthy."

"Has Savannah checked in yet?"

"No, not yet. I'm a little worried about her."

"She'll be fine," Kate said.

"I hope so. I started a discussion about the fire near the end of the meeting."

"Good thinking. Should make it easier for Savannah to initiate the conversation."

"That's what I'm hoping."

Lexie's phone beeped to indicate a text message.

"Hold on, Kate. I just got a text."

The text was from Savannah. *All good. See you tomorrow for coffee.*

Lexie texted back, *See you tomorrow.*

Lexie returned to her conversation with Kate.

"That was Savannah. She's home."

"Great. Are you meeting with her tomorrow?"

"Yes. At the coffee shop at ten o'clock."

"Call me when you finish your meeting. I'll plan to swing by your apartment tomorrow afternoon to pick up the equipment."

* * * * *

Lexie saw Savannah sitting at an outside table at the coffee shop with two cups sitting on the table.

"My treat today," Savannah said, motioning toward the cup.

Lexie smiled. "Thank you." She sat down next to Savannah and took a sip. "Yum. Vanilla latte."

"Yep."

Lexie noticed Savannah's jacket draped over her chair.

"Leave the jacket on your chair when you leave. I'll stay a few extra minutes and grab it. It'll look like you forgot it."

"Okay."

Lexie looked around to make sure no one could overhear their conversation. "How did it go?"

"They were really pissed that I brought up the subject, but I made them talk about it. I hope I got enough, because that was a one-shot deal. I've never seen Nick that mad."

"How was Haley?"

"As pissed off as Nick, but she'll get over it. I didn't see her this morning."

"I'll have your jacket back to you tomorrow afternoon with a fresh recorder."

Lexie pushed a key fob across the table to Savannah.

"What's that for?"

"It's a recorder. I want you to put it on your key ring and keep it with you. If you need to record anything, push the red button."

Savannah put the recorder in her purse.

"I'm not comfortable recording my conversations with Haley and Nick. I don't want to do it anymore."

"Too fucking bad you don't want to. It's essential that we gather as much evidence as possible against all of the subjects. You can't pick and choose who you record. This is the only way you can earn credit for substantial cooperation."

Savannah wouldn't make eye contact with Lexie.

"I'm sorry, Savannah. I wish that I could make things easier for you. But I can't."

Lexie's throat felt like sandpaper. "How are you going to handle things with Nick?"

"What do you mean?"

"Your physical relationship. Are you comfortable being around him right now?"

"I'm still trying to figure that out. I told him I'm busy with school."

"How's school going?"

"My chemistry teacher allowed me to make up the test I missed."

"That's good."

"Honestly, I'm finding it a little hard to concentrate. Betraying my boyfriend and my best friend tends to take away from my study time. I'm not sure I'm going to get the grades I need for this semester. Mom and Dad aren't going to be happy. Of course, when they find out about all of this, grades will be the least of my worries."

"Guess that's one way to look at it," Lexie said.

"Lexie, do you think I'm going to be okay?"

"What you do you mean?"

"With the court case. Do you think I'll go to jail? I'm scared."

"I don't know for sure, but I think all this work you're doing is going to help you out considerably. AUSA Griffin will tell the judge everything that you've done for the government. Between that and the fact that you've never been in trouble, you should be okay."

"I hope so. I would hate to think I was doing all this for nothing."

"That's not the case. You're saving yourself. I know you don't want to hear it, but Haley and Nick are not the people you think they are. Both have been involved in actions all over the Pacific Northwest before coming to LA. It wasn't fair of them to drag you into this lifestyle without telling you the consequences."

"They told me; I just wasn't listening. I thought it would never happen to me. In my mind we were simply saving animals. I never considered what would happen if we hurt someone." Tears filled Savannah's eyes. "I'm sorry. I get emotional at weird times."

"Don't be sorry. I totally understand." Lexie reached over and took Savannah's hand. "I'm here for you. I know our relationship has changed, but I'm here to support you."

Savannah looked up and gave Lexie a half smile. "Thank you."

Lexie picked up the jacket Savannah left behind, walked home, and waited for Kate to arrive. The doorbell rang. Assuming it was Kate, Lexie ran to the door and flung it open to find Haley. Trying to cover up her shock, she smiled. "Hi, Haley. What a surprise."

"Can we talk?"

"Sure. Come in."

Savannah's jacket was lying on the end table. If Haley recognized Savannah's jacket, Lexie knew she was fucked. She tried to be as nonchalant as possible.

"Have a seat. Can I get you something to drink? I have tea, Coke Zero, or lemonade."

"No, I'm fine."

All Lexie could think about was that damn jacket lying in plain sight and the fact that Kate could walk in at any moment. She needed to get to the switch in the bedroom to turn on the recorder for the apartment.

"Hold on a sec, I have to pee. You sure you don't want anything to drink?"

"No."

"Be right back."

Lexie went back to the bedroom, hit the switch on the recorder, and pretended to go to the bathroom. She quickly sent Kate a text telling her not to come. She dashed back into the living room. Haley was flipping through a *Vegetarian Times* magazine.

"Sorry, too much coffee today."

"Not a problem. Look, sorry to just drop in on you, but I

wanted to talk to you about Savannah."

"Sure. Is she all right?"

"That's what I want to know. Has she said anything to you?"

"About what?" Lexie asked.

"About anything. She seems preoccupied all the time. Nick and I are worried about her. We were wondering if she might have said something to you."

"No, nothing. She's been struggling with school. I think things at home are still a little rough too."

Lexie was getting a weird vibe from Haley. She seemed suspicious. "You know Savannah. She's so sensitive," Lexie added. "Someone probably said something that hurt her feelings, and she won't let it go."

"You're probably right."

Lexie tried changing the subject. "Any news on the international trip? You guys still planning to go?"

"As long as we can raise the money, we're going. What about you?"

"Definitely. I'm looking forward to it."

"You'll benefit from going. It's a good time too."

Lexie needed to lighten the conversation. "Hey, you guys want to come over this weekend for dinner? Nick missed out on my cooking the last time. We could have some food and drinks and watch a movie."

"Sounds like fun. I'll ask them. Well, I'd better go," Haley said. "Sorry to drop by. I was in the neighborhood and took a chance you'd be home."

"No worries. Swing by anytime you like."

"Do me a favor and don't tell Savannah I came by. I

don't want her to think I'm checking up on her."

"I won't. Between her parents being assholes and school not going well, I think she's a little stressed. She'll be fine once this semester is behind her."

"I hope you're right."

Lexie was walking Haley to the door when Haley turned and held up a handwritten note with one hand and put her index finger across her lips to indicate silence.

Lexie silently read the note: *Go to the end of the Santa Monica Pier tomorrow night at nine. Someone will contact you there.*

Lexie looked up after reading the note. Haley was looking for some kind of response.

Lexie bobbed her head up and down. Haley smiled and left the apartment.

CHAPTER THIRTY-SIX

Alexis

Lexie's heart was racing. She turned off the recorder and sat down to call Kate, who answered on the first ring.

"What's going on? You all right?" Kate asked.

"Yes, but you won't believe who just stopped by *uninvited.*"

"Who?"

"Haley."

"What did she want?"

"I'm fucking freaking, Kate. You won't believe what happened." Her heart pounded in her chest as she told Kate everything."Can you believe that shit? I'm fucking in! They're going to ask me to do something illegal. We got them, Kate."

"My God, Lexie. That's incredible. Did she say anything?"

"Nope, she just held her finger up to her lips for me to be quiet."

"Then what?"

"I nodded yes to her. She smiled and left."

"Wow. This is huge."

"I know. I'm still in shock. I'm shaking like a leaf."

"Do you think the camera picked up her showing you the note?"

"The camera captures the door, so it should be on there."

"This is interesting. I wonder if they're having doubts about Savannah, so they decided to recruit you for the underground movement?"

"She did ask me not to tell Savannah about her visit."

"That gives even more credibility to the theory. If they're going to move Savannah away from the direct action campaigns, they'll need a replacement."

"Guess we won't know until I show up tomorrow."

Lexie could hear Kate shuffling papers and assumed she was writing notes.

"At least it's a public spot. We can get a few people on the pier early for surveillance," Kate said. "We have a lot to do. Do you think it's safe for me to come over to your place? I don't want to come over if they're watching your apartment."

"Good question." Lexie thought for a second. "Come over and bring carryout Thai food. You're a friend coming for dinner."

"Is that your way of getting me to buy you dinner?"

"Busted."

"Thai actually sounds good. What do you want?"

"Pad thai with tofu."

"You got it. I'll be over in a couple of hours after I brief Adam."

Four hours later, Kate arrived with a bag of Thai food.

Lexie opened the door to greet her.

"A girl could starve to death waiting for you," Lexie said.

"I've been in administrative hell since our last conversation."

"Come in. How about a beer?"

"Yes, please."

Lexie walked into the kitchen and returned with two plates, some utensils, and two cold beers balanced on top. They sat down at the tiny two-person table.

"Spill it," Lexie said.

"I told Adam the good news about Haley's visit. He had to tell Mike, who had to run to the SAC, who had to tell the chief legal counsel. I was bombarded with the most asinine questions. What is it with bureau lawyers? They have no common sense, and on top of that they're sanctimonious assholes." Kate took a sip from her bottle of beer. "They asked me if you could postpone the meeting to give them more time to prepare. Can you believe that bullshit? This is the moment we've been waiting for, and they want us to put the meet on hold."

"Kate, please tell me you told them no."

"Of course I did, but that didn't stop the ridiculous questions from coming. How the fuck does the FBI ever get anything accomplished?"

"I have no idea. We get things done despite ourselves."

"It took me two hours to talk some sense into them. They were one step away from having SWAT on standby."

Lexie laughed.

"I'm serious, Lexie. I'm not exaggerating. This level of incompetence infuriates me." Kate took another swig of her beer.

"I hate to ask, but how did you leave it? I don't have to do anything weird tomorrow night, do I?" Lexie asked.

"No. I finally got through to Mike, and he was able to calm down the fools in the legal division. The knuckle-heads were feeding off one another."

Lexie exhaled. She took a sip of her beer and loaded the plates with food.

"We'll have a surveillance team keep eyes on you. Depending on who shows up for the meet, we may not want you to leave with them."

"I can live with that. Please make sure the surveillance team keeps its distance. I can handle myself, and it's a public place."

"I'll do my best. Do you have all the recording equip-ment ready for me to take to the office?"

"Yep. It's in a canvas bag in my bedroom. After Haley's unexpected visit, I decided to keep that stuff out of sight."

"Probably a wise move."

Kate dug into her plate of food. "I went with your sug-gestion and ordered pad thai too. Glad I did, because this is good."

"Thanks for picking up the food."

"No problem. Let's talk about the meet tomorrow," Kate said. "What do you need as far as equipment?"

"I think I'll wear a jacket with the recorder in the lining. I don't want to spook them by carrying a purse or a backpack."

"Sounds like a good plan."

"Kate, you have to make sure the surveillance team stays

back. I fully expect the targets to do counter surveillance."

"I'll do my best. Are you nervous?"

Lexie thought about it a few seconds. "More excited than nervous."

"This could be a game changer," Kate said.

*   *   *   *   *

Lexie parked her VW bug a few blocks from the pier and wandered over to meet her contact. Kate and Adam were waiting in a Starbucks a few blocks from the pier. Kate assured Lexie the surveillance team was properly briefed and would be discreet. Two agents were already staged at a window in the restaurant on the pier, giving them a birds-eye view of the meeting location. It was eight forty-five, so she grabbed a soy latte from the Coffee Bean. It served two purposes: she loved coffee, and having the cup to hold would keep her from making any nervous movements.

She walked to the end of the pier and waited for her contact to arrive. After the longest ten minutes of her life, a white male who looked about thirty years old approached her.

"It's a lovely view from the end of this pier," he said.

Lexie turned and looked at him. She didn't recognize him. "It is. I love coming out here."

"I'm Tim," he said as he extended a hand to Lexie.

Lexie reached out and shook his hand. "Lexie."

"Yes, I know."

Tim had a short, military-style haircut and was covered with tattoos. He had *Vegan* tattooed on the side of his neck. His right eyebrow and lower lip were both pierced.

"Did it hurt when you pierced your lip?" Lexie asked.

Tim laughed. "A little."

"Oh."

Lexie was trying to think of something to say to Tim when she noticed *XXX* tattooed on his wrists. "Are you straight edge?" she asked, gesturing toward the tattoos.

"Yep. Straight edge for life."

"Is it true that straight edge people don't drink caffeine?"

"Depends. I don't ingest any substance that alters my perception on life, including alcohol, nicotine, drugs, and caffeine. Some still drink coffee, but not me."

"Wow. That's awesome. How long have you been straight edge?"

"Since I was seventeen. I joined a punk band in high school, and our lead singer was straight edge. He taught us all about the lifestyle."

"Very cool," Lexie responded.

"What about you? How did you get involved in animal rights?"

"I had a friend who was an activist. She gave me some leaflets and a vegetarian starter kit. I was vegetarian for a couple of years and then made the final jump to vegan."

"How did you become an activist?" Tim asked.

"It seemed like the next step. I started out leafleting and going to meetings. Nothing ever seemed to change. I've become more and more angry over the years. I'm ready to make more of an impact in the movement."

Tim turned around and looked behind them at the pier. Lexie turned around as well.

"Hypothetically, if you could become more involved, what would you be willing to do in furtherance of saving animals?"

Lexie thought about it, turned, looked Tim in the eyes, and said, "Anything. I'm willing to do anything to save innocent animals from torture and abuse."

Tim looked at Lexie with a skeptical expression. "Many people have said those same words to me. Why should I believe you, Lexie? What have you done that would make me believe you?"

"I haven't done anything. That's the problem. Since moving to LA, I've met other like-minded individuals who are dedicated and unselfish. I want to be more like them. I need to do something with my life to help animals. I know that sounds cheesy."

"It doesn't sound cheesy, but you have to understand my reservations."

"I do. And if I were standing in your shoes, I'd be asking me the same questions. I can't tell you that I've participated in any large-scale underground actions. What I can tell you is that I am dedicated to the cause. I'm trustworthy and discreet. I understand the security culture, and I would never violate the rules."

Tim nodded. "My friends and I are careful who we allow into our inner circle. There are many wannabes out there who like to talk the talk, but when it comes down to action, they're limp dicks."

"If you give me a chance, I promise I won't let you down."

Tim turned back around and faced the ocean. He pulled a cellphone from his jeans pocket and punched in a security code.

"I need your phone number and date of birth."

"Sure. Why do you need my date of birth?"

"I do a little homework on every person before they're allowed to meet the rest of my friends. Do you have a problem with that?"

"Nope. I've got nothing to hide." Lexie provided Tim with her contact number and undercover date of birth.

The pair stood on the pier a few more minutes and discussed the straight edge subculture. Tim seemed happy to discuss his beliefs with Lexie.

"It was nice meeting you, Lexie," Tim said as he turned to leave.

"Nice meeting you too, Tim. I hope to hear from you."

"I think you will," he said as he walked off.

Lexie smiled as she walked back to her car. After she pulled away from the area, she turned off the recorder and called Kate. She was afraid that she might be followed and didn't want to be seen debriefing after the meeting.

"We saw you leave. How'd it go?"

"Good. I think. He asked me for my phone number and my date of birth. Guess he plans on having someone check my backstory."

"That's a good sign. Did he give you his name?"

"He said his name was Tim. I didn't recognize him from any of my meetings. White male, late twenties or early thirties, about five eight, close-cropped blond hair, thin build, with numerous tattoos and piercings. He had straight edge tattoos on his wrists and the tops of his hands. He also had *Vegan* tattooed on his neck."

"That's great. I'll see what I can come up with in our database."

Lexie told Kate word for word what she could remember from the meeting. They made a game plan to meet for lunch the next day in Malibu. Lexie returned home and typed her lengthy FD-302. She had trouble falling asleep, so she watched several episodes of *Grey's Anatomy*.

CHAPTER THIRTY-SEVEN

Alexis

Lexie's phone rang the next morning earlier than she expected. She reached over and grabbed it off the nightstand.

"Hello," she said in a not-so-chipper tone.

"Lexie, it's Adam. Can you meet us at the office this morning?"

"Does that mean lunch in Malibu is canceled?"

"Yes. It would be better if you came to the office. Bring your equipment for download, and make sure you're not followed."

"Okay. What time?"

"As soon as you can get here. Watch your rearview mirror. We don't want one of the targets following you to the office."

"Is everything all right?"

"Just get here."

Adam hung up without saying goodbye. *That was rude,* Lexie thought.

Lexie rolled out of bed, threw on clean clothes, grabbed

a travel mug full of coffee, and called Kate en route.

"Did you get any sleep last night?" Kate asked.

"Not much. I was pretty wired. Ended up watching TV till all hours of the night. By the way, who pissed in Adam's Wheaties this morning?"

"What do you mean?"

"He called and was kind of rude. Very un–Adam-like."

Kate chuckled. "You have a unique way of putting things, Lexie."

"He abruptly changed our meeting. Pretty much ordered me to the JTTF."

A long silence followed. "Kate, what's up?"

"Adam is getting headaches from HQ again. That and we have some bad news."

"Oh no, what happened?"

"We'll discuss it when you get here."

"You can't leave me hanging like this. What happened?"

Lexie heard Kate exhale. "Savannah's recorder didn't work."

Lexie's throat closed up. She couldn't breathe.

"Are you all right?" Kate asked.

"No! That conversation was critical."

"I know. We'll find a way to recover."

"Will we? I'm not sure we will. Savannah is extremely fragile. How are we . . . how am *I* supposed to tell her that we failed her?"

"We didn't fail her, Lexie. The equipment failed. It happens."

"Are you sure that the conversation can't be recovered?"

"The tech tried everything. It appears that the recorder

was activated, and then almost immediately turned off. He sent the recorder to HQ to have another expert examine it, but he's ninety-nine percent sure there's nothing on it. I need to prepare you for one more thing. I don't want you to get blindsided."

"What else could there possibly be?"

"I want you to be ready for questions regarding Savannah's loyalty."

"What? Does Adam think that Savannah deliberately turned off the recorder?"

"He has to consider all options. I didn't want you to be surprised."

"Thanks. I appreciate the heads up. Traffic isn't terrible, I should be there in about thirty minutes."

The office was in chaos when Lexie arrived. Analysts were running all over, pulling files. Adam was on the warpath over something.

"What's up?" Lexie asked Kate.

"HQ is asking for status reports. They're trying to shut down the case. Adam has been on the phone all morning trying to appease them."

"Why?"

"Our case is no longer the flavor of the month. Plus, they're getting pressure from the director to make an arrest for the lab arson."

"The director? Why does he even know about this case?"

"When the security guard was killed, it escalated our case value. HQ wanted daily status reports. Adam didn't want to tell you because he didn't want to put any undue pressure on you."

"Wow, that's terrible! No wonder he's been in such a foul mood."

"He's been dealing with something different almost every day."

"Do they know about the meeting I had last night?"

"He briefed them on it this morning. They can't see the forest for the trees."

About that time, Adam came rushing through with a giant stack of files.

"Hello, Lexie. Sorry to change plans on you."

Adam had dark rings under his eyes. His normally snug-fitting dress shirt hung loose and baggy. Lexie felt guilty for thinking he was a dick.

"No problem. How can I help?"

"Let's sit down in the conference room. I'm not sure if Kate told you, but we have two problems. HQ is trying to shut us down, and the conversation between Savannah and the other subjects wasn't recorded."

"I heard."

The three sat down at one end of the sizable conference table.

"I'm going to cut to the chase, Lexie, do you think Savannah purposely turned off her recorder?"

Lexie concentrated on staying calm. "No, I don't. Savannah was a nervous wreck. She knew she only had one shot at getting the conversation, so she would never jeopardize her cooperation agreement."

"It wouldn't be the first time a cooperator played both sides," Adam said.

"I know. But I also know Savannah, and she wouldn't

do it. She's trying her best to get out from under this case."

"Maybe she's scared of one of them," Adam offered.

"I think she's more scared of Nick than she wants to admit, but that's all the more reason for her to get this over with. I'm telling you, Adam, she didn't turn off the recorder. She must have bumped up against something and turned it off. Or maybe the batteries were bad."

"The batteries were new when you gave her the equipment."

"That doesn't mean anything; they still could be bad. I've had equipment fail on me in the past."

"How do you think she's going to take the news?" Kate asked.

"Not well. I can promise you that."

"If you want, Adam and I can meet with her to explain the situation."

"No. I think she'll take the news better coming from me."

The conference room looked like a war room. There were stacks of files everywhere. Surveillance photos were hung on the wall next to a chart showing the relationships of all the targets.

"Wow, what an operation!" Lexie exclaimed.

"Our team has been working around the clock the past few days trying to fend off the vultures," Adam stated.

Lexie wandered around the room examining the photos and charts.

"Between keeping HQ happy and trying to prepare the evidence for indictment, we've been busy," Kate said.

"This is impressive."

"AUSA Griffin is coming over in a couple of hours to

meet with you and look at the evidence," Adam told Lexie.

"Great. I've heard so much about her."

"She's fantastic," Adam said. "We're lucky to have her prosecuting this case."

Lexie spent the rest of the morning pouring through reports. Denise Griffin arrived, and Adam escorted her to the conference room. Her personality was much larger than her five-foot, two-inch frame.

"Ms. Griffin," Adam said, "this is Alexis Montgomery, our undercover agent."

Lexie extended her hand to the attorney.

"Hello, Alexis. I've heard good things about you from Adam and Kate."

Lexie grinned as she shook Denise's hand. "I can say the same thing about you, Ms. Griffin."

"Please, call me Denise. How about we sit down and you tell me what happened at the meeting last night?"

Lexie sat across from Denise and laid out the previous night's events. They discussed the case at length and after a couple of hours, Denise left carrying a sizable file folder filled with FD-302s and other reports.

Adam had one of the analysts pick up sandwiches so they could work through lunch. Late in the afternoon, Adam's Blackberry rang. He walked off to answer it. He returned a few minutes later. "Good news, ladies."

"What?" Lexie asked.

"We got notified that a private investigator in town just ran Lexie's alias and date of birth."

"That's a good sign, right?" Lexie asked.

"Definitely," Kate said. "It appears the group is vetting

you for participation in criminal acts."

"I hope they contact me before HQ closes us down."

"I can use the hit on your alias as leverage," Adam said. "Tim didn't waste any time getting your information to their PI."

"Thank goodness," Lexie said.

She looked at her watch; it was nearly eight o'clock. No wonder she was hungry.

Adam must have noticed that his team was running out of steam, because he said, "Okay guys, wrap it up for the day."

Everyone gathered their belongings and left.

"Thanks for coming in and helping out, Lexie."

"Sure, Adam, anytime. It was nice to meet Ms. Griffin."

"These guys aren't going to know what hit them when she gets ahold of them," Adam said with a smirk.

"Is there anything else that you need from me?" Lexie asked.

"No, go home and get some rest. When are you going to meet with Savannah?"

"Tomorrow. I want to get it over with."

"Let me know how that conversation goes. I'll keep fighting to keep our case going. I'm not sure how long I can keep us afloat; so don't pass up any opportunity to gather information. And be careful. You're playing in a whole different league now."

Kate walked Lexie out to her car, which was hidden in the garage.

"Adam looks beat," Lexie said.

"He's tired. I'm not sure how much more pressure that

guy can handle. He seems to be near the breaking point every day. He's bombarded by headquarters from morning to night."

* * * * *

Early the next morning, Lexie waited for Savannah. *I could get used to this view*, Lexie thought as she watched the sun peek over the horizon, casting a pink hue on the deserted beach. She heard a car door slam.

"So, what's so important that you dragged me out of bed at this hour?" Savannah asked.

Savannah's sloppy sweatshirt looked like she pulled it out of the dirty clothes hamper. Her uncombed hair stuck out wildly from under a Pawley's Island baseball cap.

"Good morning to you too."

"Sorry. I'm not a morning person."

"Me neither."

"It must be something bad if it couldn't wait until after my morning class."

"It is." Lexie took a deep breath. "Savannah, the equipment we gave you failed and the conversation from the other night wasn't recorded."

Savannah's eyes shot open wide. She plopped down on the beach and sat with her face in her hands. Lexie sat down beside her.

"There must be a mistake. I did exactly what you told me to do."

"You didn't do anything wrong. Our equipment isn't

perfect. I've had it happen to me before."

"I can't do that again. Nick and Haley were furious when I brought up the subject. I can't bring it up again."

"We'll figure out something," Lexie said.

"I think I'm going to be sick."

Lexie put her arm around Savannah's shoulders. "Take a deep breath."

Savannah shook violently. Tears rolled down her cheeks.

"What now? I trusted you people, and look where it's got me."

"Nothing's changed. We still have time. We need to figure out how to get Nick and Haley to discuss the fire again."

"*We*? There's no we; there's only me. And I can't do it again. I almost had a nervous breakdown the first time."

"Savannah, you're stronger than you realize. You can do this."

"No, I'm not. I'm not strong. You have no idea how much working with the FBI has affected my life. I'm sick all the time. I can't concentrate on my classes. Forget it, I'm done with you people." Savannah shoved Lexie's arm away.

Lexie stared at the sunrise, allowing Savannah time to compose herself. She repositioned herself on her knees in front of Savannah. "Look at me. You can't quit on me now. I've put myself on the line for you. You have to do this to save yourself."

"I can't. I don't know how."

"You and I will figure it out together. The opportunity will present itself, and you have to be ready."

"I'm scared. Nick was so angry. I'm afraid he might hurt

me if I bring it up again."

"Then you don't bring it up to him. Keep the key fob recorder with you and if the opportunity presents itself, you'll get it."

"What if that never happens?"

Lexie grabbed Savannah and hugged her.

"It will. Trust me."

CHAPTER THIRTY-EIGHT

Savannah

Savannah returned from class, tossed her backpack on the bed, and flopped next to it. Across the room she noticed her dresser drawer wasn't completely closed. *That's weird,* she thought. Savannah was slightly compulsive when it came to drawers. She never left a drawer open. She got up from her bed and looked around the room. Some of the stuff on her dresser had been moved around. Savannah opened the drawer that was left askew and noticed some of her clothes had been moved around in the drawer. Someone had gone through her stuff. She checked her closet. She was fairly sure someone had searched her closet as well. She didn't know if she should confront Haley or pretend she hadn't noticed. She wanted this whole ordeal to be over. She decided to text Lexie. *Someone's gone through my stuff. Should I ask Haley about it?*

As soon as Savannah hit send she realized something horrible. She sent the text to Haley instead of Lexie.

Fuck! What have I done? Oh God . . . oh God, what do I do now? She dialed Lexie.

"Hey Savannah, what's up?"

"I fucked up! I fucked up bad. I sent a text to Haley that was meant for you. I don't know what to do."

"What did the text say?" Lexie asked.

"I came home and someone had gone through my stuff, so I texted you to tell you and then I asked if I should ask Haley about it."

"Are you sure someone tossed your stuff?"

"Yes. I'm a little neurotic about closing drawers. One of them was left open. Stuff was moved around on my dresser too."

Savannah's phone beeped. She read her text message from Haley. *What are you talking about and who was that message supposed to be sent to?*

Savannah read the message to Lexie.

"Lexie, I have to get out of here. I can't believe that I sent that message to Haley. What do I tell her? I think I'm going to throw up."

"Take a breath, Savannah. I'll think of something. Do you have a recorder?"

"Yes, I have the one on my key ring that you gave me."

"I think you should confront Haley. Make sure you record it. You might get her to admit to something."

"I'm nervous. How do I explain the text?"

"Stand your ground and tell her you were trying to send the message to Nick."

"Okay, I'll do it."

"Remember to erase this phone call from your call log when you get off the phone."

"I will."

"You'll do fine. Text me when you can. Do you want me to come over?"

"No. If it goes bad, I'll leave and call you."

"Sounds good. Are you okay?"

"No, not really. Living this lie is killing me. I'm sick all the time. I don't know how you do it, Lexie."

"Remember why you're doing it. It will save you in the long run," Lexie said.

"That doesn't help."

* * * * *

Savannah waited for Haley to return from class, becoming more nervous with each passing minute.

Haley barged through the door and threw her backpack on her bed.

Savannah activated the recorder and quietly placed the keychain on her dresser.

"What the fuck was up with that text message?" Haley demanded.

Remember what Lexie said. Stand your ground.

"Why don't you tell me, Haley?"

Haley gave a Lexie a quizzical look. "What do you mean?"

"How about you tell me why you tossed my room?"

"What are you talking about?"

"Someone went through my drawers and my closet. Are you telling me it wasn't you?"

"Oh course it wasn't me," Haley said. "Why would I

do that?"

"I don't know. That's why I'm fucking asking."

"You're losing your mind. I didn't go through your stuff. I have no reason to do that."

Haley stood up to leave. Savannah jumped between Haley and the door and stood eye to eye with her.

"No, you don't have a reason. You also have no right to rummage through my stuff. I thought we were friends. I thought we trusted one another."

"Speaking of trust," Haley said. "Who was that text message intended for?"

Savannah picked at her cuticle. "I was trying to send it to Nick and accidentally sent it to you. I wanted his advice, but then I decided it was better to keep things between us. So, I'll ask you again, why did you go through my stuff?"

"Savannah, for the last time, I didn't go through your shit. If someone went through your stuff, it wasn't me. How do you even know someone went through your stuff?"

"Never mind how I know. I just know."

"Maybe I'd better check my closet," Haley said.

Haley walked over to her closet, which was a mess.

Savannah sat down on Haley's bed and sobbed. "Why did you do it? Why did you go through my stuff? I'm not hiding anything from you."

Haley sat down on the bed next to Savannah. "Why do you think it was me?"

"Who else could it be? No one else has access to our place. Just tell me why you did it."

Haley stared at the floor as if studying something on the carpet.

"Why!" Savannah screamed.

Haley jumped at the sound. She stared at Savannah like she was trying to see through to her soul. "Because you're acting weird, Savannah. Ever since the fire, you've been freaked out. Nick and I are worried about you."

"Did Nick know about this?"

"No. I did it on my own."

"What were you looking for, anyway?"

"I don't know. I was worried you might be working for the cops. I went through your drawers looking for answers."

"And what did you find?"

Haley was quiet.

"What?" Savannah screamed again.

"Nothing, Savannah. I didn't find anything."

"Fuck you, Haley. After all we've been through together. Fuck you!"

"I'm sorry. I didn't mean to hurt you, but I'd do it again."

"Don't you think if I was going to go to the cops, I would have already done it? I'm loyal to you and Nick. I told you that I would never tell anyone about the fire, and I haven't. Why don't you trust me?"

"You've been so wigged out lately. I'm worried about you."

"I explained my feelings to you in the car after our meeting. A man died. All four of us have his death on our hands. We can't change that. I'm learning to live with it. It's taken me longer than it took you and Nick. I'm not as strong as you."

Haley put her arm around Savannah, who had started to sob again. "You are strong. You're just more sensitive than the rest of us. That's what makes you special, but it can also cause you to break."

"That's why I needed to talk about it. After our talk the other night, I was much better. I still get furious when I think about Badger, but I'm getting better."

"Fuck Badger. He's an idiot."

Savannah looked at Haley and laughed. "He *is* an idiot. He almost killed you and Nick. I will never forgive him. He was the cause of all this mess."

Haley hesitated. "What mess?"

Savannah's heart skipped. "You know. This . . . you and me fighting. Me freaking out every other day. You not trusting me. If it makes you feel better, Haley, you can go through all my stuff right now. I don't care. I want to go back to being friends and trusting one another."

Haley gave Savannah's shoulder a little squeeze. "You're a neat freak, Savannah."

"You're a pig, Haley."

They laughed.

"Does Nick think I'm working for the cops?"

Haley shook her head and didn't speak for a moment. "No, but he *is* worried about you. He regrets getting you involved. We both do."

"I wanted to help. You didn't twist my arm."

"I know, but we should've been more upfront with you about what could happen."

"Neither one of you knew that Badger was a pyromaniac. You couldn't predict he was going to lose his fucking mind and try to burn down the whole lab."

"That's true. But we should have talked to you more

about legal consequences. We allowed you to jump in too quickly."

"Have you ever been involved in anything else that went this bad?"

Haley removed her arm from around Savannah. She clasped her hands together in her lap. "Once. A few years ago, but no one died."

Savannah didn't expect Haley to reveal that information. "What happened? Did anyone go to jail?"

"We set a small fire inside a store to make a statement. The building was old and the fire spread out of control. We ended up burning down an apartment building next door to the store. No one was killed, but people who had nothing to do with the animal torture lost their homes."

"Oh. Wow."

"Since that action, I've been careful. I never wanted to end up in a situation where innocent people were hurt."

"So all that talk of casualties of war was just talk?"

"Of course. I'm not a coldhearted bitch. I said all that to make you feel better."

"This talk made me feel better, Haley. Just knowing that you've been in this kind of situation in the past and everything turned out okay makes me feel better."

Haley looked up at Savannah and smiled. "Let's make a deal. I won't go through your stuff anymore, as long as you promise to talk to me anytime you get freaked."

"That's a deal."

Savannah hugged Haley, her heart breaking. She knew she had just sealed the deal on the government's case against Haley.

CHAPTER THIRTY-NINE

Alexis

Lexie was sitting in front of the TV eating a microwaved vegan meal. Her phone beeped, alerting her to a text message. She snatched the phone from the coffee table.

I'm okay. Let's meet tomorrow.

Where and when? Lexie texted back.

Ten at Coffee Bean, SM. Savannah responded.

Lexie called Kate. "I just received a text from Savannah. We're meeting tomorrow at ten o'clock."

"Where?"

"The Coffee Bean in Santa Monica."

"Great. I'll be in the area. Did she tell you anything?"

"Nope. Just that she's okay and we need to meet."

"I wonder if she was able to get Haley to talk," Kate said. "Guess we'll know tomorrow."

"Guess so."

"I'll talk to you tomorrow, Lexie."

* * * * *

Lexie was waiting at an outside table at the Coffee Bean when Savannah arrived. Two cups were sitting in front of her.

"Bought you a latte," Lexie said.

"Got anything stronger than coffee?" Savannah asked.

"Not at ten in the morning."

"It's five o'clock somewhere," Savannah said.

"Sit down. Tell me what happened."

"It was horrible, Lexie. I confronted Haley about going through my stuff."

"Did she deny it?"

"She did at first. I kept pushing her, and she finally admitted she searched my room."

"Did she say why?"

"She said she was worried about me and worried that I might be working for the cops."

"Oh God, what did you say?"

"I screamed at her and told her that I wasn't."

"Did she say anything about the text message?" Lexie asked.

"I told her that it was intended for Nick because I wanted his advice. Then I told her that I wanted to keep it between us. I think she bought it, but sometimes it's hard to tell with Haley. She's so damn suspicious."

Savannah dug through her backpack and pulled out the key chain recorder. She gave the recorder to Lexie. "It's all recorded. At least I hope it is."

"Did she talk about the fire?" Lexie asked.

"She did more than that. She told me about another fire she was involved in a few years back."

"Are you kidding me?" Lexie asked, leaning in closer to Savannah.

"Nope. She thought it would help me manage my feelings. She told me she set a small fire to make a statement, but it got out of control. Apparently it burned down some apartment complex. I didn't want to ask too many questions and make her suspicious. If that thing worked, it's all recorded," Savannah said, motioning toward the key chain recorder. Her eyes were shiny as tears formed.

Lexie reached over and took Savannah's hand. "Are you all right?"

Savannah jerked her hand away from Lexie. "No, I'm not all right. In the past two weeks, I found out my best friend is an undercover FBI agent who betrayed me. Then I turned around and betrayed my boyfriend and my roommate. So no, Lexie . . . I'm not all right. I'm far from all right." Trying to fight back tears, Savannah took a sip of her latte.

She continued, "I shouldn't have cooperated. I threw the people I love under the bus to save myself. I'm a terrible person." She started weeping.

"You're not a terrible person," Lexie said in a soft voice.

"How can you say that after what I've done? I'm a coward."

"You're not a coward. Far from it. What you're doing takes a great deal of courage."

"They trusted me. Nick and Haley trusted me, and I'm sealing their fates. They're going to go to prison because of me."

"You're in this position because of them, Savannah. They were the ones who dragged you into this lifestyle.

You should be having a normal freshmen year, going to frat parties and eating junk food, but because of them, you ended up in FBI custody. Now you're doing what you have to do to get yourself out of the mess."

"I know, but I feel like shit."

Lexie shifted in her seat. She picked up her latte and swirled it around. "I understand that emotion."

Savannah looked up at her and managed a smile. "I've been so mad at you that I haven't taken the time to tell you thank you."

"For what?"

"For talking to the US attorney for me. I know that if it weren't for you, I would have ended up in prison. I do appreciate it."

"You're welcome."

"Now if you'll explain everything to my parents, we'll be square for you betraying me."

Lexie looked at Savannah to see if she was joking.

Savannah laughed.

"I'm only kidding."

"I'll talk to your parents for you when you're ready."

"I'm going to take you up on that offer. If you're with me, they can't kill me."

"Not until I leave, anyway," Lexie joked.

Savannah looked terrified as she discussed her parents. Lexie wanted to make her feel better but didn't know how. "Hey, you wanna go to the movies?" she asked.

Savannah thought about it a moment.

"I'd love to, but I have a two o'clock class. I'm barely going to pass this semester. I can't afford to miss any more classes. Rain check?"

"Sure."

Savannah finished her latte and gathered her things to leave. "Thanks for the talk."

"Anytime. Why don't we go hiking this weekend? Might take your mind off things for a few hours."

"That's a good idea. Should I invite Haley and Nick?"

"I'll leave that up to you. You can, but if you need to get away from them, it can just be us."

Savannah's strained expression smoothed a bit. "That sounds better. Just the two of us."

"It's a date. Now go to class, young lady."

Lexie waited until Savannah was gone before she called Kate. "Let's meet. Our girl did good. Let's just hope the recorder worked."

"Great!" said Kate. "You may have just justified keeping this case open."

"I hope so. I'm not ready to go back to New Orleans yet."

"I told you that you'd fall in love with California," Kate said.

CHAPTER FORTY

Alexis

Lexie was stretched out on the couch, watching TV, when her phone alerted her to a text message. She picked it up and checked the message from an unknown number.

Half hour at the end of the Venice Beach Pier. I know you're home, so don't be late.

Lexie checked her watch; it was nine at night.

She texted back *Okay,* grabbed her hoodie with the recorder in it, and called Kate. "Please go to voice mail . . . please go to voice mail," she muttered to herself. Kate answered. *Shit*, Lexie thought.

"Hello."

"Hi, Kate. Don't panic, but I just got a text message to meet someone at the end of the Venice Beach Pier in half an hour. I'm going. I have a recorder. I'll call you when I'm done. Whoever sent it knows I'm home. Please, Kate, don't make a big deal of this. I'll be safe. I won't go tripping with anyone that I don't know."

"Damn it, Lexie. Are you sure you can't put them off?"

"Not if I'm going to get them to trust me. I have to do

this. The case is at stake."

"I don't give two shits about the case. I care about your safety, and you know that I can't get to Venice Beach in thirty minutes."

"Get here when you can, and please don't alert Adam. He'll want a surveillance team in place, and there isn't time."

"You're putting me in a horrible position. Adam is going to shit himself if I let you do this."

"Then I didn't tell you. I just did it. I'll take the hit, but I have to go."

Lexie could hear the discomfort in Kate's voice and the shuffling of equipment being gathered on the other end of the phone. "Be careful. Don't do anything stupid. Call or text me as soon as you can. I'm on my way to you."

"Thanks, Kate."

"Don't thank me until this is over and you're safe."

Lexie tested her recorder and headed out the door. As she walked to the pier, she had the feeling someone was following her. She arrived at the pier five minutes ahead of schedule. Tim was waiting for her.

"What's with all the cloak-and-dagger shit?" Lexie asked as she approached Tim.

"Had to be sure you didn't have time to gather forces if you were a cop."

"A cop? Please." She waited a beat. "Did you have someone follow me from my apartment? Because I noticed them on my walk over, and I'm hoping it was one of your people and not some crazed psychopath."

Tim grinned. "It's one of my guys."

"Why follow me?"

"Don't you know?"

She didn't say anything.

"I like you, Lexie. You're honest."

She met his gaze but stayed silent, though the irony of his statement made her want to smile.

"Guess you're wondering why I called you?"

"I'm hoping it's to help with something."

Tim laughed, showing real mirth for the first time. "Geez, you really are honest. How do you feel about doing something important and perhaps a little dangerous?"

"I would feel good about it."

"Even though you don't know anything about it yet?"

"You'll tell me what I need to know when I need to know it, right?"

He eyed her closely as he spoke. "Have you ever done any direct action before, Lexie?"

"I wouldn't tell you if I had."

He grinned again. "Touché."

* * * * *

Lexie called Kate from her apartment.

"I'm home."

"Thank God. What happened?"

"Tim was waiting for me. He told me he needed help with a small mission. Someone will call me, give me fifteen minutes preparation time, and then pick me up at my apartment."

"When?"

"He didn't say. He just said that I wouldn't have any

notice. He told me to think of it as a tryout. If I was willing to put myself out there for a small mission, then down the road he might have something more interesting for me."

"What else did he say?"

"He said to have clothes ready. Told me to wear all black with no identifiers on anything. He said all other tools would be provided."

"Holy cow, Lexie."

"I know! How are we going to sell this to Adam? He's going to have a coronary."

"You're right about that. I'm going to call him on my way home. I'll think of some way to smooth it over."

"Kate, I don't feel comfortable coming to the office anymore. If they're watching my apartment, I don't want to be tailed to the JTTF office."

"I agree. I'm going to avoid meeting you at your apartment as well. We can meet at different places around town and exchange equipment in the bathrooms. I think we have to go on the assumption that someone is always watching you."

"Speaking of that, I need to change out recorders with you."

"I have an idea," Kate said. "How about if you go to the Coffee Bean on the Santa Monica Promenade? After you finish your coffee, go to the public restroom behind the coffee shop. I'll meet you in there at ten in the morning."

"Good plan," Lexie said.

"And Lexie?"

"Yeah?"

"Don't be late. I don't want to hang out in a public toilet all morning."

CHAPTER FORTY-ONE

Alexis

Lexie sat on the couch picking at a salad on a TV tray. She knew it was only a matter of time before she would have to talk to Adam. Her stomach was in knots. She had exchanged the equipment with Kate and was waiting for an update on the quality of the recording. The phone rang, and Adam's name popped up on the screen. *Here goes nothing,* she thought.

"Hello," Lexie said.

"Good morning, Lexie. I hear you had an interesting evening."

"Don't be mad, Adam. I did what I had to do."

Adam sighed. "You didn't have to do any such thing. It was reckless and stupid. What if something had happened to you? Kate should have stopped you."

"Don't blame Kate. I didn't give her any choice."

"Don't ever do that again! You could've been killed. Who knows what these people are capable of?"

Lexie took a deep breath and responded, "I know these people better than any of you. I've been living with them for almost a year. My gut told me to go, and I relied on my instincts."

"Your instincts could have gotten you killed, Lexie. We have a team of people in place to support and protect you. You can't go running off doing your own thing any time you get the notion."

"I'm sorry, but look how well things turned out. We need to concentrate on the next phase. They could call as early as tonight. What's our game plan?"

"You are exasperating, but what you accomplished was just short of amazing." Adam continued, "I met with the tech agents this morning, and they gave me some equipment for you."

"What kind of equipment?"

"A GPS tracker to put in your shoe so we can track your whereabouts. Kate is on her way back to Venice with it. Starting tonight, we'll have a surveillance team in your area every evening. Team members will keep their distance, but we want them near when you activate the tracker. The tech agents are on their way out to install a pole camera so we can monitor your apartment and the street in front of your apartment building,"

"I can live with that."

"That's the point, Lexie. We want to make the case, but more importantly, we want to keep you alive."

"Adam, I'm not scared of these people. They have good intentions but just go a little too far."

"You should be scared of them. You don't know who you'll be getting in the car with. Don't underestimate the danger factor."

"I know. I just don't think they'll hurt me."

"There's a catch, Lexie."

"Oh God. What?"

"If you find out they're going to harm anyone or put anyone's life in jeopardy, you have to contact us immediately. The tech agents installed an emergency extraction device in a belt buckle. If you think you're in danger, or if the group is going to harm an individual or do significant property damage, you have to engage the device. It calls in the cavalry. We'll immediately take down the operation. Do you understand?"

"What constitutes significant property damage?"

"That's going to be a judgment call. If it's just vandalism, follow through with the action, however if they're planting incendiary devices, hit that button. We can't take the chance on another arson."

"Got it. So, gluing locks or spray painting a building is fine?"

"Yes. We have approval from HQ for property damage as long as it's not significant. Just don't go burning down any SUV dealerships."

"Okay. Got it," Lexie said, snickering. "Don't worry, I'll be careful."

"You'd better."

CHAPTER FORTY-TWO

Alexis

Lexie waited, but two nights passed with no call or text from Tim. She was getting discouraged. She put on her pajamas, washed her face, brushed her teeth, and climbed into bed. Her phone beeped. Exhilarated, she read the screen.

Walk out front in fifteen minutes.

Lexie put on her black clothes as instructed, activated the GPS device in her shoe, and put on the belt with the emergency device embedded in the buckle. At the fourteen-minute mark, she walked out front. A few seconds later, a white panel van pulled up, stopped, and the door slid open.

"Get in," a male voice said.

It took Lexie a few moments to realize that the voice belonged to Nick. She jumped into the back with him. A quick glance revealed Tim was driving and Haley was in the front passenger seat. The back of the van was piled high with crates.

"You didn't bring a phone, did you?" Nick asked.

"Nope. I followed the instructions Tim gave me. No cell,

no identification, just some money in my pocket."

"Good girl," Nick said.

Haley turned around and smiled at Lexie. "Hi, Lexie."

"Hi, Haley. Great to see you."

Tim merged onto the freeway traveling away from the city.

"Where are we going?" Lexie asked.

"To free some beagles," Tim answered over his shoulder. "Is that okay with you?"

"I love beagles. Let's free them all."

"This place breeds beagles for use in laboratory experiments. We're going to rescue as many as we can," Nick told her.

"That's awesome. Where do we take them once we rescue them?"

"Our contact will meet us and take the dogs. She has a network of people working for her. The dogs will be examined by a vet and then placed in foster homes until permanent placements can be found for them."

"Does this place have a security system?" Lexie asked.

Tim answered, "Not that we could see. We've done recon missions off and on for the past month to figure out the schedule. Our most recent visit was four nights ago, and we didn't see any cameras. The last employee leaves at about ten at night, and the person who opens doesn't arrive until seven o'clock."

"That leaves us plenty of time," Haley added.

They rode in silence for nearly an hour. Lexie wondered if her shoe GPS was working. She couldn't see out the back of the van, but noticed Tim periodically checking his side mirror. They left the freeway and took a series of small streets. Lexie had no idea where they were but figured they must be getting close, because Nick was grabbing bags.

He handed a black duffle bag to Lexie. "Can you carry this?"

"Sure. Whatever you need."

Lexie draped the strap over her shoulder and across her chest.

"We didn't bring radios, because we shouldn't be more that a few feet from each other. Let's work in pairs to carry the crates. Lexie, you and I will work together."

"Okay," Lexie replied.

"Once we get in, let's move quickly."

Tim turned off the paved road onto a gravel road.

Lexie's heart was pounding, and her hands were shaking.

"Nervous?" Nick asked.

"Excited," Lexie responded.

"You're a natural," he said and smiled.

"We're going in without lights from this point," Tim announced. He slowed the van down, and they bounced the last hundred yards or so in the dark. He spun the van around and backed up. "We're here."

Nick nodded at Lexie to open the door. She slid the side door open and jumped out, hoping her eyes would soon adjust to the dark. Nick placed a flashlight in her hand.

"Thanks."

The group quickly moved to the back of the van. Lexie could hear the dogs barking inside. Tim opened the rear doors on the van so he, Nick, Haley, and Lexie could reach the crates.

"Let's go inside and see how many crates we're gonna need," Tim ordered.

They crept up and tried the door. It was locked. Nick reached into the bag that he was carrying and pulled out a crowbar. "Step back."

The three moved out of the way, and Nick pried open the door to the Quonset hut–style building. The dogs were going nuts inside.

"I wish they would stop barking," Lexie whispered to Haley.

"They always go crazy. Wait until you see them. They're always so happy to escape these places."

The door slung open and the group entered the building. Nick and Tim shined their flashlights around the large building. The noise from the barking was deafening. Lexie was shocked by the living conditions of the dogs. They were stuffed in metal cages and walking around in their own excrement. Tears filled her eyes. She was trying to shake off the shock when she heard Tim say, "There are more than we expected."

"Let's get started," Nick ordered.

The activists ran back to the van and carried in two empty crates. Nick and Lexie worked together grabbing beagle puppies and loading them into their crate.

"They're so cute," Lexie said.

"I know. I don't know how those fucking monsters can experiment on these cute little guys," Nick said.

"Looks like our crate is full," Lexie said.

"Ready to lift?" Nick asked.

"Yep."

"On three. One . . . two . . . three."

They lifted the heavy crate and hauled it to the van. The beagles were barking and trying to lick Lexie through the bars on the cages.

As Nick and Lexie were on their way back inside with an empty crate, Tim and Haley were coming out with their full one.

"Are we going to have enough crates?" Haley asked Nick.

"I hope so. They might be a little jammed in tonight, but it's a small price to pay for freedom."

They loaded more than fifty beagles into the van. Once the group was finished with the dogs, Nick reached into his bag and pulled out cans of red spray paint. He tossed a can to Lexie. "Go crazy, girl."

Lexie caught the can in midair. "You got it," she said.

She ran over to a blank wall and in large block letters wrote, FUCK YOU AND YOUR EXPERIMENTS. WE'RE FREE. —THE ANIMALS!

Nick found another blank wall and wrote, ALF WAS HERE! IF YOU CONTINUE, WE WILL RETURN!

While Nick and Lexie spray-painted, Tim and Haley trashed the cages that had imprisoned the beagles.

"At least they'll have to buy new cages," Haley said.

Lexie was surprised that the dogs were quiet once they were moved into the van. It was as if they knew they were being rescued.

"Can I take one home with me?" Lexie asked Nick.

"You want to adopt one?"

"Yes. They're adorable."

"I'm sure that can be arranged. Let the vet examine them, and then you can pick one out."

The four conspirators were about to jump into the van to leave when the unimaginable happened. The place lit up like a Christmas tree. Lexie was blinded when a light shined in her eyes.

"FBI. Get your hands up."

No, this can't be happening, Lexie thought. *I didn't hit the emergency signal. This wasn't the plan. We need to save these dogs.*

Lexie thought about running, but someone grabbed her and slammed her to the ground. The side of her face was ground into the dirt. She was lying on her stomach next to Nick, who was being handcuffed.

Nick looked at Lexie with shock and disbelief. "You fucking snitch!"

CHAPTER FORTY-THREE

Alexis

Lexie, Nick, Haley, and Tim were handcuffed, separated, and put in vehicles for transport to the FBI office. Lexie was thrown into the backseat of a black SUV where Kate was waiting. Lexie was so angry she could barely process what had just happened. "What the fuck, Kate?"

"Calm down, Lexie. I'll explain everything."

"Explain what? How you guys just fucked me over royally? We were on our way to meet a second cell. We'll never get that information now."

Lexie was on the verge of hyperventilating. After she was able to catch her breath, she continued in a more controlled manner. "Why? Why now? I didn't hit the emergency signal. Everything was under control. We were taking the dogs to a second activist group. What will happen to those poor dogs? Did you see the conditions they were living in?"

"The owner of the kennel was notified. He and his manager are on their way out to help with the dogs," Kate stated.

"So those poor animals are going to be returned to the assholes who abused them? We can't allow that to happen.

The owner is a monster."

"Lexie, listen to what you're saying. You sound like the targets."

"Fuck you, Kate. I'm just making an observation. The dogs were being abused. Rescuing them would have been the best thing for them. Sometimes these activists perform illegal acts for the right reason. This is one of those times."

Kate rubbed her temples.

"What? Did I give you a headache, Kate?"

"You need to calm down and listen to me. You can't let Adam or anyone else in the FBI hear you talking like this. I understand where you're coming from, but they won't be quite so understanding. You can vent to me, but only me. Trust me, if you want to stay in the undercover program, then you'll shut up and listen to me."

Lexie slammed her head on the back of the seat and closed her eyes. She was seething.

After a few minutes, Kate asked, "Want me to take those handcuffs off?

Lexie opened her eyes and slid around in the seat so Kate could reach the cuffs. "Please. These things hurt."

"As we tell the bad guys, they're not built for comfort," Kate joked.

Lexie rubbed her wrists to try to get the circulation restored.

"Thanks."

"Are you all right? You weren't hurt in the takedown, were you?"

"No. I'm fine. Ate a little dirt, but that won't kill me."

"Adam told the person arresting you to make it

look real."

"From the amount of dirt in my mouth, he did."

The driver of the SUV, a short, bald man, opened the front door and looked in the backseat.

"Are you two okay?" he asked.

"We're fine," Kate answered.

"We should be wrapping things up here in another fifteen minutes or so," the bald guy said. "Do you need anything?"

Lexie gritted her teeth and stared straight ahead.

"No, but thanks, Craig," Kate answered.

The agent shut the door to the SUV leaving Kate and Lexie alone.

"This is what happened, Lexie. I called Adam to let him know that you were on your way to the action, and then he called out the troops. The surveillance followed the GPS tracker, careful to stay out of sight. Adam contacted the unit chief at HQ to let him know what was happening."

"Whoa, why did he do that?" Lexie asked. "Why not wait until after the action was done before calling those idiot HQ fucks?"

"I don't know why he chose to do that but—"

"I know why," Lexie interrupted. "He wanted to look like a big shot. The all-important case agent who's looking for his next promotion."

"Maybe. I don't know why he called them. He was told by HQ to take down the action and arrest all subjects involved."

"Did he even try to explain that we had security measures in place?"

"I'm not sure. I was in my car traveling toward the surveillance units when he informed me he was taking it down and making arrests."

"Did you try to stop him?"

Kate looked uncomfortable, as if trying to figure out how much information to disclose. "We rendezvoused in a parking lot a few miles from here to coordinate. That's when I realized he had the Operational Plan in hand. He wrote the Ops Plan right after Tim told you that someone would call and pick you up."

"Are you telling me Adam knew the whole time he was going to arrest them the first time out, even without any kind of significant property damage or risk of life?"

"I don't know, Lexie. It was at least a possibility, because he wrote and had the Ops Plan approved two days ago."

Lexie's face reddened. "That son of a bitch!"

"I'm not telling you this to upset you. I wanted to tell when we were alone. I knew you would be upset and—"

"You think?" Lexie interrupted again.

"I wanted to make sure you had time to calm down before you were around any bureau personnel. I'm trying to protect you."

Lexie sighed and buried her face in her hands.

"I'm sorry. I shouldn't take this out on you. I know you didn't have any say in what happened."

Kate sighed. "In the end, it was The HQ and Adam Show. They made the decision without my input. I pled your case to Mike, but he ultimately allowed Adam the final say."

Lexie sat for a couple minutes processing the

information.

"Thank you, Kate. It's finally dawning on me that you saved my undercover career. If Adam or any other agent would have heard me siding with the targets, my undercover career would have been over. You're a true friend."

Kate smiled. "There are more important things in life than career advancement. Adam hasn't figured that out yet. Do you think you can be around people without committing career suicide?"

"I'll try."

"Try hard. You have a lot of years left, and you're a damn good undercover agent. I hope we can work together again."

Lexie closed her eyes and hung her head.

"What's wrong?" Kate asked.

"I just realized that the case is essentially over. I guess I'll be leaving soon and returning to New Orleans. I'm going to miss working with you."

By the time Lexie reached the FBI office, she had her emotions under control. The game plan was to put her within proximity of each of the prisoners to see if any of the three would make any damaging statements. Kate put the handcuffs back on Lexie and escorted her to the prisoner processing room. Nick was sitting handcuffed to a bar in the corner.

"What's the snitch doing in here?" Nick yelled.

"No one talks, everyone walks," Lexie yelled back.

"Shut your mouths," a crotchety old agent operating the fingerprint system told them both.

The door opened again, and a female agent with a handcuffed Tim in tow entered the room. "Full house," the female agent commented.

"Yep," the old agent responded. "Can you take him to the interview room until I'm ready for him?"

Before the agent could haul Tim out of the room, Lexie decided to roll the dice. "What the fuck did you get me into?" she screamed at Tim.

"Me? I didn't get you into anything. They must have been watching you."

"I wasn't on anyone's radar until I started talking to you. This is your fault!"

"Fuck you, Lexie," Tim yelled as he was pulled out of the room. He was still yelling at Lexie when the door closed.

Nick looked over at Lexie. "Nice try, but I know you're the fucking snitch. I've had a bad feeling about you ever since Savannah dragged you home with her. I should have taken care of you a long time ago."

The comment made a shiver go up Lexie's spine.

"If you had such a bad feeling, why did you invite me along to this shindig?"

"I didn't. Tim did. I voted no."

"You two stop your jawing," the cranky agent shouted. He went over and uncuffed Nick. "You're first, Romeo."

"That's not my name."

"You seem to have a way with the ladies. I figured you were a Romeo."

"Fuck you, dude."

"You have a prodigious vocabulary, young man. Do you know what that word means?"

"Fuck you, old man."

The older agent chuckled as he rolled Nick's fingerprints

on the computerized system. He finished and called another agent to take Nick away. A few minutes later, Haley was brought to the room. Lexie decided to try a different strategy with Haley. Lexie sat handcuffed in the corner crying. A handcuffed Haley was plopped down in the chair next to Lexie.

"Are you okay?" Haley whispered.

"Not really. You?"

"I'm fine. Stay strong, Lexie. Remember: nobody talks and everybody walks."

"What are you two muttering about over there?" the old, cranky agent asked.

"None of your fucking business," Lexie yelled.

"Just for that, I'm going to leave you handcuffed to that bar," he said to Lexie. "Teach you to be such a smart-ass."

He turned to Haley and said, "Your lucky day, girl. You just moved to the head of the line for processing."

"Oh, like that's going to hurt me?" Lexie grumbled under her breath. She whispered to Haley, "Nick thinks I'm a snitch. I didn't have anything to do with this. Hell, I didn't even know where we were going."

"Don't say anything to anybody, Lexie."

Haley was fingerprinted, photographed, and removed from the room.

The older agent came over and uncuffed Lexie. "Hope those weren't too tight."

"As someone told me earlier, they aren't built for comfort."

CHAPTER FORTY-FOUR

Savannah

Savannah's phone woke her up from a deep sleep. She picked it up and saw an unknown Los Angeles number.

"Hello," she answered sleepily.

"Savannah?"

"Yes."

"It's Lexie. Sorry to wake you up."

"Oh. Hello. I didn't recognize the number." Savannah sat up in bed trying to clear her head.

"I'm calling from Kate Summers's cell phone," Lexie said. "I need to talk to you about something."

"Sure. Should I come meet you?"

"There isn't time. Listen closely. You may get a phone call in the next few hours from either Nick or Haley. This is the situation."

Savannah was shocked to learn that Haley and Nick had asked Lexie to work with them.

"You can't let them know I talked to you," Lexie said. "I wanted to give you a heads up so you weren't blindsided, but you need to act shocked and confused if one of them calls you. They may need you to bail them out of jail."

"What should I do?" Savannah asked.

"Tell them you don't have the money. See if they send you someplace to pick up money. If you hear from them, call Kate immediately. Did this number show up on your phone?"

"Yes."

"Good. This is Kate's undercover phone. Save the number and call her if you hear anything. Remember to act surprised over the arrests."

"This is crazy. How come you didn't tell me?" Savannah asked.

"I didn't want you to have to keep more secrets. We know how hard all of this has been for you. This is almost over, Savannah."

"I'll be so glad when it's over. I want my life back."

Savannah laid her head back on the pillow. She was filled with fear and dread, but also hope.

CHAPTER FORTY-FIVE

Alexis

Adam stumbled upon Lexie in the break room drinking a cup of coffee. "Guess you're pretty angry with me."

"Yep," Lexie replied not looking at him.

"Can I explain?"

Lexie turned to face Adam. "I don't know. Can you?"

Adam sat down at the table. "It wasn't my call, Lexie."

Lexie let out a short laugh. "You're the case agent, Adam. Of course it was your call. You wanted to kiss someone's ass at HQ. Are you vying for a promotion?"

"That's not fair. You don't understand the pressure I was getting from HQ. They want this case wrapped up and federal indictments on the lab arson."

"At what cost? We were on our way to meet more people. Perhaps a whole second cell, but we'll never know now. Oh, and I particularly liked the fact that you provided me with a GPS and an emergency extraction device *supposedly* for my safety. When, in fact, it was so you could track me."

"That equipment was solely for your safety, Lexie."

"You couldn't give a rat's ass about my safety. The GPS

was so you could track me, make the arrests, and report back to HQ that you single handily apprehended the suspects."

Adam ran his hands through his hair and interlocked his fingers behind his head. He blew out a deep breath and continued, "I took a risk, and I'd do it again."

"I hope it works out for you," Lexie said as she angrily pushed back her chair and snatched her coffee cup.

"Wait. Hear me out."

She reluctantly sat back down. "I'm listening."

"You did an outstanding job. This case would never have reached this level without you. We're all proud of you."

Lexie sat in silence.

"There will always be things that we second-guess ourselves on. Did I take the case down too soon? Should I have tried a different strategy? In the long run, you have to rely on your gut. Lexie, my gut told me it was time to end it. I know you want to believe I had some secret agenda by ending it like I did, but it came down to a gut call. I didn't want you to get hurt, and I knew we could take the operation down safely."

Lexie uncrossed her legs and leaned forward, resting her crossed arms on the table.

Adam continued, "We still have a ton of work to do on this case. I'm going to need your help. I don't want tension between us. We have to keep Savannah stable throughout the prosecution stage, and you're the best person for the job. She trusts you, and you can relate to her. Are you onboard?"

Lexie dropped her head down on her crossed arms, sat

a few seconds, and then lifted her head so she was eye to eye with Adam. "Of course I'm onboard. I'm your undercover agent. I'm here to support your operation in whatever way you need."

Adam looked a little surprised.

"Just because I'm mad at you doesn't mean that I don't respect you or your decisions. Adam, you and Kate have taken care of me since day one. This has been an amazing opportunity. I'll be here for you until the last defendant goes to jail."

Adam smiled but looked exhausted.

"What's next?" Lexie asked.

"I'm scheduled to present the arson case to the federal grand jury next week. I'm sure that AUSA Griffin will add the events from last night to the indictment. The intelligence analyst was able to identify the previous arson that Haley was involved in, so we'll charge her with that one as well."

"So it's finally happening," Lexie said. "The subjects are going to be arrested for the arson and the murder."

"Oh, I forgot to tell you the good news," Adam said. "We got word from the Portland Division. They've located Gregory Bennett, a.k.a. Badger. They're waiting for us to send them the arrest warrant, and they'll pick him up."

"That's good. How did they find him?"

"They have a well-placed source."

"I hope that piece of shit rots in prison," Lexie declared.

Adam laughed. "There's my Lexie. Since it's almost morning, we're going to keep the subjects here then transport them to the US Marshals Service as soon as they open."

"What do you want me to do?"

"Well, you might as well get transported with them. You never know what they might discuss in lockup over there. We'll inform the Marshals Service that you're an undercover and that you won't be going to jail. We're waiting to see if either one of them calls Savannah for help."

"That poor girl," Lexie said.

"You have to keep her from going off the rails, Lexie."

"I can do that." Lexie stifled a yawn.

"I'm going to find you a couch for a nap," Adam said.

"That would be great. I could use a couple of hours of sleep."

"It's six thirty, so you have about ninety minutes to nap."

"Ugh. No wonder I'm exhausted."

* * * * *

Lexie, Haley, Nick, and Tim were transported to the federal courthouse and taken to the US Marshals Service lockup. There were four cells in the lockup, so each person had a private cell. They were able to see and talk to one another if they desired.

The four were quiet on the trip over to the courthouse. Once in the holding cell, Lexie could hear Nick and Tim whispering to one another, but she couldn't hear what they were saying. Haley had dark circles under her bloodshot eyes.

"You look awful," Lexie said.

"You don't look like you're ready for the red carpet

yourself."

"I'm exhausted," Lexie admitted.

"Me too. This should be over soon."

"What's going to happen to us?" Lexie asked.

"We'll see the judge, who'll make a determination on bail."

"Bail? How much bail? I don't have any money."

"You'll have to put up a percentage. Since this is vandalism, it probably won't be much," Haley explained. "Just remember to keep your mouth shut. You didn't tell those fucking feds anything last night, did you?"

"No, of course not. I pretended to be asleep."

"That's good. They'll try to scare you, but don't listen to them."

"I won't."

Nick yelled from his cell, "Don't talk to the snitch, Haley."

"Told you he thinks I'm a snitch," Lexie said.

"Don't be so paranoid," Haley yelled back.

"It had to be her. She's a fucking snitch."

"Seems like Tim's plan got us into this. Maybe he's the snitch," Haley yelled.

"It's your funeral, Haley," Nick responded.

CHAPTER FORTY-SIX
Savannah

Savannah's cell phone rang. Unknown number. She was exhausted and wanted to let the call go to voice mail, but she remembered her earlier conversation with Lexie.

"Hello?"

"Savannah, it's Nick."

Savannah's eye twitched. *No matter how scared I am, I have to do this*, Savannah thought.

"Nick. Hi. I didn't recognize the number."

"Listen closely. Haley and I have been arrested."

"What? Arrested for what?"

"Don't worry about that right now. I need you to do something for me."

Breathe. Breathe. Calm down. You can do this.

"Okay. I'm listening."

"We need you to go to Jeannette's house. Haley already called her. She'll have some money waiting for you. Take the money and go to Jeremy's Bail Bond Service on Temple Street. You can look up the exact address online."

"Okay, I'm writing this down," Savannah said. "Jeremy's

Bail Bond Service. Got it."

"Give the bondsman our names and the money. He'll post our bonds so we can get out today. We go in front of the judge at ten o'clock, and with any luck, we'll be out of here by noon. Can you pick us up?"

"Yes. Sure. Where?"

"Downtown at the federal courthouse."

"Federal! Oh God, Nick, what did they arrest you for?"

"I'll explain later. Just get that money over to the bail bondsman so we can get out of here."

"I'll leave right now. I love you, Nick."

Nick hung up without saying anything.

Savannah felt like her heart had been ripped out. She followed Nick's instructions and picked up five thousand dollars from Jeannette and took it to the bondsman. She drove to the federal courthouse and waited for her friends' release. Her stomach churned, and her eye continued to twitch.

After waiting several hours for paperwork to be processed, Nick and Haley finally emerged from the holding area. Both had dark circles under their eyes, and their clothing was dirty and disheveled. Savannah rushed over and threw her arms around Nick, who did not appear overly excited to see her.

"Are you guys all right?" Savannah asked.

"Fine. Let's get out of here," Nick said tersely as he shoved Savannah away.

Savannah's feelings were hurt, but she wasn't going to let Nick see how much he hurt her. "Nick, don't be like that. I'm only trying to help," she said.

"Let's get out of this place," he said as he barreled out the door.

Savannah looked over at Haley, who shrugged her shoulders.

"My car is parked in the side parking lot," Savannah said.

"Thanks for picking us up," Haley said.

"No problem. What happened?"

They piled in Savannah's car, Nick electing to ride in the backseat. "You can drop me at my apartment," he stated.

"Okay. Are either of you going to tell me what happened?"

"Why don't you ask your fucking best friend?" Nick said with a snarl.

"What are you talking about, Nick?"

"Lexie is the reason we ended up in jail," Nick stated.

"You don't know that," Haley said. "The cops may have been watching Tim. We don't know anything for sure."

"Oh come on, Haley! You're smarter than that. Lexie is a snitch. That's the only explanation. All our problems started when she showed up. First the tracker and now getting arrested. Don't be an idiot. She's either a cop or a snitch."

"It can't be Lexie," Savannah said. "She's my friend."

"Oh, I forgot—she's your friend so she can't be a snitch!" Nick exploded. "You don't have a fucking clue, Savannah, so shut up."

"Screw you, Nick!" Savannah yelled. "I've spent the whole day trying to help you post bond, not to mention sitting at that damn courthouse all day, and then you treat me like this."

"Calm down, both of you," Haley said.

"You two can do whatever you want, but I don't intend to have any dealings with Lexie ever again," Nick said. "I don't want to be around her or see her. If either one of you choose to remain friends with her, then write me out of your life, because we are done." He stared out the side window and didn't utter another word. Savannah pulled up to his apartment. He leaped out and didn't say goodbye. She thought that he might turn to wave goodbye, but he didn't.

Savannah felt like she was watching the scene from outside of her body. *Who is this person that I've become?* she asked herself.

"He'll come around," Haley said.

"I don't think so," Savannah murmured as she pulled out and drove to the dorm.

On the ride home, Haley told Savannah the whole story. She told her about Tim and how he recruited Lexie.

"Do you think Lexie really is a snitch?" Savannah asked.

"Honestly, I don't know. I think we need to avoid her until we know for sure."

"How did she get out of jail?" Savannah asked. "She didn't call me."

"I don't know. After our initial appearances, we were all separated."

"What were you guys charged with?"

"It's such bullshit. They charged us with a violation of the Animal Enterprise Terrorism Act, but they can't prove it. It'll probably get dropped down to vandalism or breaking and entering. The FBI tries to use scare tactics, charging terrorism, but it never holds up in court."

"I hope you're right."

"I am. Trust me. This isn't the first time I've tangled with the FBI."

"Can I ask you something, Haley?"

"Sure. What?"

"Why didn't you ask me to help?"

Haley took a deep breath and put her hand on Savannah's shoulder. "Savannah, don't take this wrong, but you aren't cut out for the underground stuff. You're better off sticking to the aboveground protests and such. It takes a different kind of person to do the illegal shit, and you just don't have it in you."

"It's because of the fire, isn't it? Because I fell apart after the fire?"

"Partly. But mostly you're just too nice to do illegal stuff. There are roles for everyone to play in our movement, and you need to find yours. The underground stuff isn't your forte. That doesn't make you any less important to the movement."

Savannah thought about it for a few seconds and nodded. "I think you're absolutely right."

"Wow, I didn't expect you to agree with me."

"Why not? I can accept the fact that I'm not perfect," she said laughing.

"You're practically perfect, Savannah."

"Far from it, my friend. Far from it."

CHAPTER FORTY-SEVEN

Savannah

As Savannah and Haley slept soundly in their dorm room, Kate, along with two of her squad mates and two USC campus police officers, approached the dormitory. Simultaneously, a group of agents led by Adam approached the apartment Nick shared with three other guys. The arrests were planned to coincide with Badger's arrest in Portland to prevent anyone in the Portland flophouse from calling the Los Angeles people and warning them.

It was only a matter of time before Haley and Nick would know Savannah had cooperated and that Lexie was an undercover FBI agent. Based on Savannah's cooperation, AUSA Griffin had dropped the charges against her and given her immunity with the understanding that she would be required to testify against all the subjects at trial.

Campus security had keys to the dormitory housing, so they quietly opened the front door to allow Kate and the rest of the agents to make entry. Haley and Savannah were asleep in their beds when the arrest team burst through

318

her door.

"FBI! Get your hands up," Kate yelled.

"What? What's going on?" a startled Haley cried out. She looked over at Savannah.

Savannah trembled so hard her muscles cramped.

"Haley Crosby, you're under arrest," Kate said as she grabbed Haley by the arm and yanked her out of the bed.

Another agent placed his hands on Savannah's shoulders, forcing her to remain seated on the bed.

Kate patted down Haley and searched the surrounding area for weapons.

"What's going on?" Haley asked again, still groggy from sleep.

"You're under arrest. You'll be transported to the FBI office for processing."

"Can I get some clothes on first?"

"Yes. Where are your clothes? You stand still; one of the agents will get them for you."

Haley, still battling sleep and in shock, told the agent where to find her jeans, a shirt, and undergarments.

"All this because we tried to save a few beagles? Doesn't the FBI have anything better to do?" Haley spat out.

"This has nothing to do with the great beagle caper," Kate said with a sneer.

Haley froze, one leg in her jeans and one leg out. She looked up at Kate.

"Then what . . . what are the charges?" she stuttered.

"Conspiracy to violate the Animal Enterprise Terrorism Act, two counts of arson, and felony murder."

Half dressed, Haley sank down on the bed.

Kate leaned down and whispered in Haley's ear, "It's over, Haley. We know about both fires."

Fighting back tears, Haley gathered her composure, looked Kate in the eye, and with as much confidence as she could muster, said, "Fuck you! You've got nothing on me."

Kate stepped back and chuckled. "That's how you're gonna play it?"

* * * * *

Lexie watched through the two-way mirror as Adam interviewed Nick.

"Nicholas Harris, I'm Special Agent Adam Harper with the FBI. Before you say anything, we need to share a few things with you about our investigation. First, you have been charged with conspiracy to violate the Animal Enterprise Terrorism Act, arson, and felony murder, all relating to an arson at the UCLA laboratory where a security guard was killed. Second, you are not the only person who was arrested this morning. We have several of your coconspirators in custody, both here and in Portland."

Nick sat completely still, shoulders squared, showing no emotion.

Adam continued, "Gregory Bennett, I believe you know him as Badger, was most cooperative when he found out that you were trying to pin the fire on him. You told Haley Crosby and Savannah Riley that Badger set the fire, when it was *you* who set the fire. Mr. Bennett tried to stop you, but you wanted to make a statement."

Nick continued to stare straight ahead.

"You know, it would be a shame for someone who had nothing to do with the planning of this action to go to jail, someone who may have been just a lookout person," Adam said.

Nick stared at Adam.

"Nick, do you really want Savannah to go to jail for something that you, Haley, and Badger did? You could assume responsibility for what you did and save the girl you love the anguish of prison. You know as well as I do, she isn't strong enough to survive prison."

Lexie held her breath, waiting to see which direction the interview would go.

Nick went back to staring straight ahead.

Adam pulled out an Advice of Rights Form and read Nick his Miranda rights.

"Nick, think about Savannah before answering this next question. Think about her future and the love you have for her." Adam put down the form and continued, "Nick Harris, do you understand your rights as they have been read to you, and are you willing to answer questions without an attorney being present?"

Nick chewed his bottom lip for a second, turned to look Adam in the eye, and responded, "Fuck Savannah and fuck you. I want a lawyer."

CHAPTER FORTY-EIGHT

Alexis

LOS ANGELES, CALIFORNIA,
TWO WEEKS AFTER THE ARRESTS

It was Lexie's last evening in LA, which had her feeling quite melancholy. She met Kate for their final dinner together.

Lexie picked at her food. "What's new with the case?" she asked.

"We ironed out the plea deal for Badger," Kate said. "He's agreed to testify against Nick in exchange for a ten-year prison sentence."

"I still can't believe that Nick set the fire. This whole time we thought Badger was the psycho, and it turned out to be Nick," Lexie said.

"We didn't believe him at first, but when we followed the evidence it turned out Badger was telling the truth. Don't get me wrong, Badger isn't a boy scout by any means, but Nick's a complete sociopath."

"It's revolting to think how Nick used Savannah," Lexie stated. "He didn't care who got hurt in the process."

"Badger told us that Nick had no remorse for killing that

security guard. According to Nick, the guard was collateral damage in the war against animal cruelty."

Lexie shuddered. "That's harsh. Does Savannah know it was Nick who set the fire?"

"Not unless her attorney told her."

"She should hear it from me. I'll call her tomorrow and tell her."

"Is she back in South Carolina?" Kate asked.

"Yeah. Her parents took her home a few days ago."

Lexie toyed with her chopsticks, picking at the rough wood on one of them. "I'm going to miss you."

"I'm going to miss you too," Kate said. "It's not going to be the same around here after you leave."

Lexie dipped a piece of her California roll in soy sauce and stuffed it into her mouth.

"Are you ready to go home?" Kate asked.

Lexie forced a smile.

"Ready as I'll ever be," she replied in a low, shaky voice.

"Hey, it's me," Kate said. "What's bothering you?"

"I don't know. I guess I'm worried about going home. After doing undercover work for this long, nothing seems like real life anymore. Does that sound crazy?"

"It doesn't sound crazy. It's going to be an adjustment, but you'll be fine. You're a hell of an undercover agent, and it's only a matter of time before another case will come your way."

"I'm not sure I can do another undercover gig. I'm still reeling over how this affected Savannah."

"Lexie, that girl would be spending ten years in prison if you hadn't helped her. She's lucky that you fought to save her. You should never feel guilty about how things unfolded with her."

Lexie put down her chop sticks, giving her full attention to Kate.

"If you think you can't handle another undercover case, then by all means, walk away from the program. I personally think it would be a huge loss to the bureau if you choose to do so, but that's a decision only you can make."

"I'm sorry," Lexie said. "I'm just tired. I haven't slept well lately."

Lexie looked down. She picked at a rough edge on her fingernail. "Kate, thank you for everything that you've done for me."

Kate cleared her throat. "I was just doing my job."

"You went way beyond your job. You saved my career."

Kate wiped away a lone tear. "It was my pleasure."

The lump in Lexie's throat made it difficult for her to speak. "I want you to know that I will always treasure our friendship. Promise me that you'll come to New Orleans for a visit."

Kate grinned. "I've always wanted to visit New Orleans, and now I have a reason. Put it on your calendar and I'll be there."

"*Laissez les bons temps rouler.*"

"What does that mean?" Kate asked.

"Let the good times roll."

CHAPTER FORTY-NINE

Alexis

MAY 2012 - PAWLEY'S ISLAND, SOUTH CAROLINA,
ONE YEAR LATER

The rental car bounced over the potholes in the oyster shell parking lot. Lexie parked the car near the beach access and took a deep breath. Her hands trembled as she removed her shoes then waded through the deep sand out to the point of beach where the ocean met the sound. In the distance, she could see a young woman sitting alone on a deserted stretch. The slight ocean breeze caressed Lexie's skin as she made her way across the beach.

"May I sit down?" Lexie asked.

Without looking up, the young woman said, "How did you find me?"

"I'm an FBI agent. It's my job," Lexie joked.

Savannah looked up and smiled. "Have a seat."

"How've you been?" Lexie asked as she plopped down beside her.

"As good as can be expected," Savannah replied.

The two sat in silence for a few moments.

"You know, it's only been two years since I graduated from high school," Savannah said. "It seems like a lifetime."

Savannah looked over at Lexie. "You look different. More FBIish."

Lexie watched the waves breaking on the sand. "It's beautiful here."

"This is my favorite spot in the whole world," Savannah responded. "This is where I come to think. I've spent a lot of time here this past year."

A pang of guilt hit Lexie. She watched the tiny shorebirds frantically picking insects out of the wet sand.

The two sat in uncomfortable silence before Savannah continued.

"I thought when I returned home everything would go back to the way it was before, but that didn't happen. I can't explain it, but everything is different now. My parents, my friends, this place . . ."

Lexie nodded.

"You're different, Savannah. What you went through changed you. That's why everything seems different to you. When you left here, you were an innocent eighteen-year-old girl heading out to experience life for the first time. You experienced so much love, loss, and betrayal in a relatively short period of time. You came back a different person."

"I guess you're right. I want to feel normal again. Even after this much time, I still expect to turn around and see Nick."

Lexie stared at the horizon. A small tang of guilt lingered. "Maybe this is the new normal. You aren't the same person anymore. You're older, more mature, and more experienced than when you left here."

Lexie shifted so she could see Savannah better and continued, "Haley and Badger will be in prison for nine more years, and Nick will spend almost twenty years in prison. Those three are no longer a part of your world."

"I still can't believe that Nick set the fire. He looked me in the eye and told me that Badger set the fire. He even had Haley convinced."

"Nick Harris is a narcissistic asshole," Lexie said. "I'm sorry that he sucked you into his deranged world."

The ember-red sun began melting into the ocean.

"What happened to Phillip and Jeannette?" Savannah asked. "Their cases were still pending when I left LA."

"AUSA Griffin dropped the Animal Enterprise Terrorism charges and allowed them to plead guilty to aiding and abetting in exchange for their cooperation. Neither one received any prison time, but the government seized their house. Last I heard, they left LA in an old rickety RV heading to Las Vegas."

"I can see them living in Las Vegas," Savannah said, laughing.

Lexie took the opportunity to keep Savannah talking. "How are things between you and Nora?"

Savannah sighed. "Nora and I have patched things up, but things are still tense between Hunter and me."

She picked up a handful of sand and let it pour through her fingers like a waterfall.

"I went to visit Nick and Haley at the Federal Correctional Facility in Victorville a few weeks ago," she said. "My parents didn't want me to go, but I felt like I had some kind of unfinished business. I needed closure with Nick."

"What happened?"

Savannah started to cry but continued, "Haley refused to see me. I flew all the way to California, and she wouldn't give me five minutes of her time."

"What about Nick?" Lexie asked.

"Oh, he came out. He had plenty to say to me."

"What? What did he say?"

Savannah choked on her words as she continued explaining. "He called me a backstabbing, traitorous bitch. Can you believe that? I gave that guy my heart, my soul, and my body, and he called me a traitorous bitch."

"I'm sorry, Savannah. Did he talk to you at all?"

"He talked plenty, but nothing nice. He told me I was the reason he was in prison. I told him that I loved him, and he told me I didn't know the meaning of love. He told me that he hated me, and one day I would get what was coming to me."

"Did he threaten you?"

"It wasn't like a physical threat. It was more like a karma thing. Anyway, he ended our last conversation by telling me to leave and that he never wanted to see or hear from me ever again. As I was leaving, he stood up and yelled, 'Fuck off and die, bitch.'"

Lexie sat quietly for a moment. "I don't know what to say."

"There's really nothing you can say. I did it to myself, but at least now I know and I can move on with my life. I got closure. It wasn't the closure I was looking for, but it's closure."

"I'm sorry that Nick hurt you, Savannah."

"I loved him and he used me. I was so stupid."

"Nick Harris is a psychopath. There was no way for you to know he was using you."

The women sat in silence breathing in the salt air.

"What happened to Agent Harper?" Savannah asked. "Is he still in LA?"

"He was promoted and—"

"No, wait," Savannah interrupted. "I don't know why I even asked. I don't want to know about him or anyone else for that matter."

The two sat in silence watching the sun be devoured by the ocean. After several minutes, Savannah broke the silence.

"Why did you come here, Lexie? I know it wasn't to give me a case update."

A tear trickled down Lexie's cheek. She cleared her throat before answering.

"I needed to know that you were all right. I know you think that I used you to make my case, but the truth is I really care about you, Savannah. I needed to see for myself that you had moved on and that you were going to be okay."

She listened to the lull of the ocean. A soothing, soft breeze rustled her hair.

"Do you know what that smell is?" Savannah asked, inhaling.

Lexie inhaled and shook her head.

"That smell is marsh puff mud," Savannah said, smiling from ear to ear. "That's the smell of my childhood. Some tourists don't like the earthy smell, but to me it's what happiness smells like. It represents carefree days of shrimping, fishing, and crabbing: a childhood of innocence and happiness."

At that moment, Lexie saw Savannah's true face, not the hardened face of a girl who had endured loss and betrayal, but the innocent face of a girl who was once ready to single-handedly take on the world. In this spot, surrounded by sand and water, the carefree girl returned to the shores of her youth.

Staring out over the ocean, Savannah sighed and continued, "I ran away to California to try to find myself. I realize now that it takes more character and courage to stay and face things that are difficult. Sometimes you have to lose something to truly appreciate it. I've done that; I will never stray from this area again. I'm a low-country girl who needs the smell of puff mud and the sound of surf hitting the sand. You're right about one thing, Lexie. I'm not the same person I was when I left here two years ago, but I am a South Carolina girl, born and raised. I'm going to do my best to take full advantage of the second chance you've given me. I'll strive to be a better person and give back to my community. Remember the day we were hiking and you asked me if I thought a person could ever go home again?"

"I remember," Lexie said.

"The answer to that question is yes. Home is where your heart lives. When I left South Carolina two years ago, my heart stayed on the white sandy shores of Pawley's Island. When I returned home, my heart was waiting for me."

Lexie became overwhelmed with emotions. A tear rolled down her cheek.

"What's the matter?" Savannah asked.

"Nothing. Everything is falling into place. You and I are both at crossroads in life, and it's time we each write the next chapter of our lives. I came here to see you because I needed to know that you were okay. The past two years have changed us both, some for the better and some for the worse."

Savannah reached over and grabbed Lexie's hand. "I'm okay because of you, Lexie. Without your support and guidance, I'd be in prison. You saved me, and I will never be able to repay you for that."

Lexie smiled. "You can repay me by finishing school and making a difference in the world. I expect progress reports, and I better get an invitation to your college graduation."

As the two women sat on the isolated stretch of beach, Lexie's thoughts drifted. She thought about the past and wondered what the future would bring. Like the tides of the boundless ocean, Lexie realized, life itself continues to ebb and flow.

Acknowledgments

Writing a novel may be a solitary experience, but seeing it to publication is not. I owe an enormous debt to the team at Wise Ink Creative Publishing for their excitement and enthusiasm. Huge thanks to Laura Zats for quelling my constant doubts and patiently working with me. Without you, this novel would still be hidden away on my computer. Thank you to my wonderful editors Ally Bishop, Andrew Wetzel, and Jordan Smith, who spent many hours helping me polish and shine *Behind The Mask*. Thanks to Jay Monroe for his expert handling of the cover and book design.

I owe a hearty thank you to my parents, David and Faye Ridenour, my sister, Darla Hill, and my mother-in-law, Ruth Endorf, as well as my extended family for providing me with constant encouragement and love. I am grateful every day to have such an amazing and loving family. You have all helped make my dream become a reality.

Great love to Nora Moloney, who is my BFF and the best cheerleader anyone could hope to have.

A special thank you to my team of beta readers: Bill Endorf, Terry Palmer, Nora Moloney, Jason Lup, Faye Ridenour, Scott Rhodes, and Erin Kuntzelman. Your recommendations helped more than you will ever know.

And finally to my amazing husband, Bill. Thank you for being such an intelligent, insightful first editor, for helping me with storylines, for all the brainstorming sessions, but mainly for your insistence that the book was good, and that I could do it. You are my finest critic, my most rabid fan, and my best friend. I would never have come so far without you by my side.

I lost a dear friend and companion during the writing of this book, my faithful writing dog, Kosmo. I will miss you, Kosmo.